DISCARDED

Books by Michael J. Allen

Scion Novels:
1. SCION OF CONQUERED EARTH
2. STOLEN LIVES
2.5 HIJACKED
3. UNCHAINED

Dumpstermancer:
1. DISCARDED
2. DUPLICITY

Bittergate:
1. MURDER IN WIZARD'S WOOD
2. THE WIZARD'S BANE

Guns of Underhill:
1. FEY WEST

Delirious Scribbles:
- WYRM'S WARNING
- CHRYSALIS

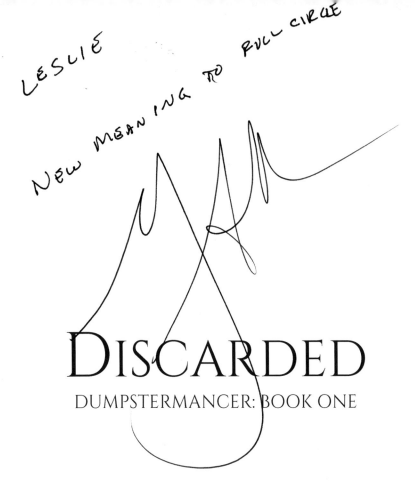

LESLIE

NEW MEANING TO FULL CIRCLE

DISCARDED
DUMPSTERMANCER: BOOK ONE

MICHAEL J. ALLEN

Delirious
Scribbles Ink

Delirious Scribbles Ink

Delirious Scribbles Ink
P. O. Box 161
Fortson, Georgia 31808-0161
www.deliriousscribbles.com

Interior Layout ©2018 Delirious Scribbles Ink
Cover Design ©2018 Delirious Scribbles Ink
Cover Art ©2018 Stefanie Saw

ISBN 978-1-944357-15-3 (intl. tr. pbk.)
ISBN 978-1-944357-16-0 (hc.)
ISBN 978-1-944357-17-7 (epub)

Printed in the United States of America
10 9 8 7 6 5 4 3 2 1
Discarded / Michael J. Allen. — 1st ed.

For Larry who convinced me to get out of my own way and have a little fun.

For B, B & J.

BEAUTY'S BEAST

Darrin paced back and forth in the plush little lobby. Waiting test subjects no longer chatted excitedly on the colorful cushions. Thoth couldn't risk bringing the public close enough to discover its victims or villainy.

He chewed a palm full of antacids and eyed the elevator. A little number climbed steadily toward him, tightening the knots in his gut.

Maybe this test will reveal the problem.

He popped more antacids.

Maybe this subject won't end up—

A bell barely warned him in time to hard swallow the chewables and force a smile. Opening doors revealed Francis' bulky frame and dour expression.

He doesn't look any happier about this than I feel.

The corporate security officer wordlessly gestured a petite brunette out of the elevator. "Nicole, Darrin will escort you from here."

Nicole wore a business suit from the same bargain racks Darrin normally patronized. Her eyes met his for a blink before fleeing to the floor behind a curtain of hair. "Hi."

Francis shook his head behind her.

Darrin took a long, slow breath. "If you'd follow me?"

Darrin led her out of the waiting area into a long clinical corridor disguised with wall screens showing off dazzling, ephemeral beauties. Nicole's eyes flit from image to image, not taking in the frosted glass doors, biometric-runeguard locks or the shadows lurking behind both.

A shadow slammed against a frosted glass and screamed.

Nicole jumped away. She clutched her purse high against her chest, fingers almost atop one of Thoth Corp's eyeSentinel shield charms.

Darrin forced a nervous chuckle. "Sorry about that."

"W-what is that?"

He refused to meet her eye. "You know how people can get when they're bored. Everyone's got to be a practical joker."

"That's it?" Nicole asked. "I'm not in any danger, am I?"

Darrin glanced at a nearby wizard eye monitoring the corridor. He knew what he'd been instructed to say by heart, but repeating the cowardly answer ate at his soul.

As if I have a choice any more.

"Well, you've signed all our waivers," Darrin said. "So, you're aware there's always some danger when working with magic."

She seemed to gather herself, lowering the purse to her side. "Right. It's all worth it."

"May I ask why you volunteered for this...," Darrin frowned. "...quality assurance survey?"

She pushed a lock of hair from her face. "You know. Ugly girls don't have a chance at finding Mister Right these days without a little magic, especially after you guys released this new Glamour spell."

The woman had no future in the modeling circuit, but she had a subtle loveliness Darrin usually sought when he carved out time for an occasional date. "You're hardly ugly, Nicole."

She snorted, covering her reddening face in a rush. "There's a twelve-month backorder on the Glamour spell lease, let alone the components. Volunteering for your survey is the only way I'll be able to bring home a man next Thanksgiving and shut Mom up."

You'll be lucky to go home at all...unless.

Darrin stopped and looked deeply into her eyes. "How about you skip the test, and I take you to dinner?"

Her eyes fled his, sweeping up and down his slacks, dress shirt, and the dark blue lab coat which designated him a spellweaver despite his only marginal gift. "How about I finish the survey first instead. Then we'll go out and celebrate the new me?"

He pushed his spectacles up and rubbed the bridge of his nose. "Yeah, we'll, um, do things your way—a dinner befitting the new you."

She laid a hand on his shoulder. "Are you all right? Are you worried I won't want to go out with you after I'm beautiful?"

He glanced at the wizard eye and shook his head. "No, you'll probably still want dinner with me after."

She squeezed him and offered a bright smile. "Let's make me beautiful so we can go out and celebrate."

Darrin gestured her further down the hall, popping more antacids behind her back. She chattered about how she hoped she'd look after the spells. At long last, they came to a double security door marked "Test Lab 2."

Darrin scanned his eye and fingered the rune unlock spell. The doors parted, revealing a sizeable pentagonal lab ringed with tables and bustling lab techs in white coats. Inlaid concentric metal circles and accompanying rune marks sectioned the otherwise single stone tile. Sour urine and vomit smell from their last test subject lingered just below overpowering waves of artificial lemon.

Above, a glass-fronted mezzanine looked down on them. A half dozen lawyers sat in front row seats, braced by a videographer and Thoth Corp's two top executives.

"Who are they?" Nicole asked.

Before Darrin could answer, a gorgeous woman with radiant deep brown skin offered Nicole a thousand megawatt smile. "Welcome to Thoth Corp, Nicole. I'm Thecia Crospe, Chief Operations Officer and this is Adam Mathias."

An element of awe suffused Nicole's voice. "Thoth's CEO."

She gazed up at Adam as if looking upon a god. Adam's smile sent her eyes scurrying behind hastily rearranged hair.

"Proceed, Mister Silus," Adam said.

Darrin closed his eyes, took a deep breath and nodded. He led Nicole to a table inside the innermost ring just offset from the room's exact geometric center. He showed her placement marks for their new model spell board, stepped to the opposite side of the table and gestured to the components arrayed on its surface.

"Now, Nicole, you're going to go through the spell like any other consumer."

Nicole picked up a thick elm wand. "I don't have anything as nice as this at home."

"Yes, we'll be providing all the implements and materials, but I need you to read and follow the instructions exactly." Darrin took the wand and set it back on the table.

For all the good it'll do.

Nicole picked up the spell lease scroll and flipped from the legalese to the spell directions. The lawyer line shifted closer, scribbling notes. She touched each of the items as she came to it in the instructions.

"What's this chest?" she asked. "I don't see it listed."

Darrin opened his mouth, but Adam spoke first. "Safety equipment, should Mister Silus be forced to...assist you."

Darrin nodded without meeting Nicole's inquisitive gaze. "When you're ready to begin, please walk us through what you are doing, step by step."

"All right. First I need to be sure I and my wand are safely within the power radius of the mananet." She searched the walls, quickly finding the five glowing mananet pylon crystals mounted at its corners wirelessly projecting magical energy throughout the area. "Looks good, now I'm going to insert the rune chips into the wand haft in order."

Nicole picked up the first delicately-inscribed crystal wafer, inserting it into the slot nearest the silver-embossed Eye of Thoth corporate symbol. She fumbled with the second chip, initially trying to insert it upside down. Darrin corrected its orientation, earning blushing thanks.

She double-checked the instructions once more, unfolding a thin interlocking elm mat and arranging it within the marked floor diagram. "This sure is a lot of stuff."

"Transformation spells aren't on-the-fly magic," Thecia said. "It requires a lot more power as well as precise component placement."

"Will I be able to do this spell at home?" Nicole asked. "I live on an Edison block."

Darrin shook his head. "Not unless you have a tier two or higher mananet within range—"

"But," Adam spoke over Darrin. "All Thoth eyeStore locations have spell actuation chambers available for a small fee."

She frowned, collecting the patented, octagonal component cylinders from the table. Each clear, chemically-neutral plastic container holding the components was uniformly two inches in width but varied in height as needed to hold magical ingredients. She consulted the instructions once more before bending to the mat. A push and a twist clicked component nodules into their proper spell locations. Nicole reviewed the directions one last time and looked expectantly at Darrin.

"That look all right?" she asked.

"Mister Silus may not advise you during this test," a lawyer said.

Right. Can't have me confirm she's done everything correctly before testing our spell ruins her life...or worse.

Nicole walked herself through the wand motions three times then took a deep breath. "Transformation means you're changing the real me, right? So this is going to hurt?"

"Spell subjects may feel some discomfort," another lawyer said.

Nicole smiled the shy, expectant smile of a child about to open a Christmas present. "Beauty is pain."

She invoked the spell.

Magic flared in the spherical receiver crystal on the wand's end. Power drawn from the mananet flowed over and around Nicole in a gentle shower of pink sparkles that smelled like spring rain.

Nicole's screams tore out of her throat, the sound of her agony threating to peel paint.

She'd positioned everything perfectly. She'd followed the directions without error. Her wand moved well within allowed deviation, but once again the spell went wrong.

Slightly stained teeth transformed into dark needle-sharp fangs. A dark mint green tinted her skin, pockmarked by oozing brown pustules. Her eyes shrank, pupils turning a glowing, vomit yellow. Gnarled claws replaced her delicate hands. Her screams became snarls. She launched herself at Darrin.

Darrin dove backward. "Second ring, fifth rez, mag one!"

A swirling, milky cylinder sprang up around Darrin, Nicole, and the table. She leapt at him over the table. Her claws shredded his pant leg. Blood welled from deep gouges that hadn't started to hurt yet.

Darrin leapt over her prone form and spun. He bent and grabbed her around her midsection, trying not to grope the writhing woman gurgling blood-curdling obscenities.

"Darrin!" Thecia yelled. "The chest!"

"You think I don't know?" Darrin shoved Nicole into the milky wall.

"Watch your tone, Silus," Adam snapped.

Darrin ignored him, cringing as he slammed Nicole's face into the wall once more. He seized the chest as he rounded the table to the cylinder's center. He dumped rats from the chest atop the spell board as Nicole vaulted the table at him.

"There you go," Darrin shook his head. "Dinner."

The squealing rats fled. Nicole's nose went into overdrive. She abandoned her assault on Darrin. She fell upon the rats with mystifying rage typical to all worst-case Glamour victims. Nicole thrust her first catch into her mouth, ripping open the writhing body and spraying her suit with blood.

Darrin threw himself against the far outer circle. He kicked the nearest rat toward Nicole and the spell board. "Close the first ring!"

Another milky white cylinder swirled to life, pinning him in the safe ring between swirling magical walls. Nicole feasted two-fisted on screaming rodents within the new circle.

Darrin turned away, unwilling to watch her a moment longer. He closed his eyes to hold off tears, breath short and heart hammering. The second ring disappeared from where his forehead pressed against it. He sniffed, wiped his eyes and marched to the monitoring station, looking over the feeds with another technician.

Bury it in work. It'll be there this time. This will all be worth it when we fix the spell.

"Darrin?" Thecia asked.

He slammed a fist, rubbing the stinging hand. "Nothing. None of these problems arose in initial testing, but I can't figure out what's changed. Four dozen victims and—"

"Test subjects," a lawyer corrected.

Darrin shot the man a furious glare. "And even after this *test* turned Nicole into a *victim*, we have nothing. We don't know any more about the cause of this corruption than we did after testing the other *victims.*"

"None?" Adam asked. "Results have varied widely from irreversible disfigurement to this worst scenario. Surely somewhere in all the data we've collected, there's a way to identify and correct this aberration."

"Let's not forget the cases where the spell worked, making the subjects beautiful," Thecia said.

"Except it made them *permanently* beautiful," Adam said. "We can't sell this spell if the temporal thread we added isn't functioning properly."

"Of course we can't," Darrin snarled under his breath.

"Darrin?" Thecia asked.

He balled his fists and looked up into the gallery at the two of them. "Eli's original spell was meant to permanently correct disfigurement of bad burn victims. Maybe if we consulted with him we—"

"That *criminal* has nothing to do with this spell or this company," Adam said. "Not anymore. I'll thank you not to mention him, Mister Silus."

"Maybe Eli could—"

"I pay *you* to figure these things out, Silus," Adam snapped. "Now get Nicole into a cell and fetch our next candidate."

"We need to take the Glamour line off the market," Darrin said. "People are being hurt, attacking their neighbors. If this gets out—"

"Our lawyers assure us that both the disclaimer on the product and the lease damage waiver protect us from litigation," Adam said.

"Maybe Darrin has a point," Thecia said.

"If Mister Silus wants to help our customers, then he should do his job." Adam turned his scowl from Thecia to Darrin. "Spell engineers are supposed to fix spells. They aren't entitled to express opinions that affect this company's bottom line."

∘ 2 ∘

CITY OF MY DEATH

The bus engine coughed a miasma of diesel fumes as it drove into the underground depot, its electric counterpart losing connection with the nearest Edison node. An anguished metal on metal cry pierced my ears as the bus stopped with a stuttered jerk that threw me against the next seat. While I recovered, the other passengers jostled each other to be the first into the aisle and out of the shuddering hybrid.

I let them. The last place I was in a hurry to arrive was Seufert Fells, but I'd had no other answer when asked for a release destination. I certainly couldn't go home, not ever.

The driver gave me a mocha-skinned smile. Sparkling eyes weighed down by industrial-grade eye luggage undressed me. "If you'll give me a minute, honey, I'll finish up the arrival paperwork and get your luggage—a little personal attention."

"Yeah," I frowned. "Don't have any."

"How about dinner then?" She winked. "I'm off tomorrow."

The mention of food made my mouth water and stomach grumble. I hadn't eaten since before departing the Wasteland, but I only had a hundred dollars and no ready options to replenish what I spent. Besides, it seemed pretty clear she wanted a layover lay. I might physically be in my thirties, but my appetite for intimacy had dried out after going without for the first thirty years of incarceration. Seven subsequent decades without giving the

9

prospect much thought, I hardly even remembered the taste of a woman. "Thanks, but I'm just going to go."

I exited the bus and threaded through the milling passengers, keeping my eyes down so as not to catch anyone's gaze. The body-enveloping thrum of the mananet hit me the moment I exited the garage into the station. My heart thumped in my chest, kept inaudible to the other passengers by heavy rain pattering on the station roof. Shudders swept through me as vibrant power tingled against my suddenly sweaty palms.

It's not for me. Not anymore. Not after what it cost me.

I drew in a deep breath as I crossed the bus station threshold, only to break down coughing from an overwhelming aroma of chemical pine.

Despite stubbornly rejecting the power filling the air, my eyes flit unerringly to the nearest of the miniature crystalline pylon hung from the wall. Lesser siren songs drew my eyes to the next nearest pylon and the next. The first mananet pylon drew me over like a recovering junky lured into a den of his addiction.

Closer to the pylon heady magic caressed my dark skin, a long forbidden pleasure turned into aching torture.

Don't give in to it, be stronger, smarter. Push it away. There's no good to be had indulging in magic when you're barred from the means of practicing. You don't need it, not after so long.

Analytical inspection of the node gained me enough distraction for a few detached breaths. Grungy green corrosion scaled the pylon's copper mesh and cast the delicate silver filigree in tarnished emerald.

Poorly maintained. The corrosive layer is jeopardizing operating functionality and increasing the risk of malfunction. At least a pylon failure won't prove as catastrophic as might be the case within the coils of an Edison node. This unit should be cleaned immediately and replaced at the first opportunity.

The node before me only vaguely resembled my last design schematic, but I recognized my protégé's penchant for inefficient but delicate filigree below the Thoth logo. I shook my head

Darrin, Darrin, how many times did I explain to you that a geometrically aligned mesh extends node range?

A thought stiffened my spine.

This is Adam's fault. He probably insisted on the prettier but hampered design to sell more nodes. The delicate filigree probably corrodes faster too.

I forced my eyes away. Pylon designs weren't part of my life anymore. Thoth practices where no longer of my concern.

Adam and Thecia made it abundantly clear that I had no part in that world anymore.

My stiff neck zeroed in on the exit and the pouring rain beyond. A floor to ceiling screen beside the doors drew my attention. Men and women rotated on the digital advertisement, frolicking in the wilderness, tossing long, luminous hair and otherwise epitomizing the ephemeral beauty of elven fairy tales.

A provocative voice whispered out of the speakers. *"Glamour, true beauty is no longer just illusion. Available at a Thoth eyeStore near you. Seek out the Eye that sees your dreams and makes them a reality."*

The blazing orange Eye of Thoth logo filled the screen, and I couldn't help but roll my eyes at the elaborately stylized representation that was just so Adam. The ad repeated, offering me a chance to really listen to Thoth's marketing doublespeak. Their ad promised a powerful illusion straight out of ancient folktales and fantasy novels.

What they're offering is impossible with illusionary cosmetics. Nothing short of fey glamour can do what they're claiming, and the fey went extinct centuries ago. Once a liar always a liar.

I debated braving the rain or staying within earshot of Thoth's bullshit innuendos. The rising heat along my neck shifted the decision. I shoved my itching, bunched hands into my suit pockets and turned toward the exit.

Before I do something that lands me in trouble.

A ghost from my past watched me from the doorway, shaking rain from a London-style raincoat. "Hello, Eli."

On the list of people I never wanted to see again, my protégé fell in the top five. "Go away, Darrin."

His stare mixed disquiet and excitement much as it had in my lab that very first time. Time had filled out the last corners separating him from the boy I knew and the grown man blocking my escape. His spectacles seemed the same, though whether the same pair or a new one of a similar model I wasn't sure. His damp, brown hair was still a little too Beatles for me, but he dressed like he'd found success in my absence.

He rushed forward to embrace me. I dropped back, lowering my eyes. He grabbed me anyway. "Jesus, Eli. You look like a scarecrow."

The sudden emergence of his boyish grin made him look years younger, but the smile faded when I didn't embrace him back. He stepped away, turning two shades ghost and three more green. "Eli, about that. I'm so sorry. You told me to tell them the truth. I never imagined they'd twist it around like that to—"

I folded my arms. "I don't want to talk about it."

"If I'd known—"

The words attacked him in an ursine snarl. "I'm over it. That was a century ago. Leave it alone."

He fiddled with a Thoth Corp security badge on a retractable lanyard connected to his belt. He followed my disapproving glower, flushed and shoved the badge into a pocket. "I had no choice, nowhere else to go."

"You're bright and talented, you could've gone anywhere."

"Adam made it clear defending you in court and claiming to be your friend would kill any chances I might otherwise have had at another company. He claimed Thoth would be the only company willing to overlook our association."

"Adam's full of shit. He bamboozled you."

Darrin looked away. "Yeah, but I didn't realize it at the time. He's made me do things since then he could misconstrue like...well, I can't leave no matter how much I want to quit."

I should've felt bad, should've pitied Darrin for his predicament. I didn't. "Why the hell are you here?"

"I thought, well you're going to need a ride, right?" He wiped his glasses, a nervous tick that usually preceded bad news. "Let me drive you, keep you out of the rain, and we can get you settled into a hotel and, well, unless you have an apartment waiting—"

"No." It came out sharper than intended. The first test of my resolve twisted my insides in painful knots, but I would not let the system win. I'd take no part in that world. I'd not surrender one more inch. "Goodbye, Darrin."

I marched past him toward the exit, lifting my oversized, once tailored jacket over my head.

"Eli, I need your help."

"I'm walking away." I couldn't help the venom in my voice, and I didn't want to try. "You don't want to be associated with me anyway."

"Elias, please."

I turned, pushed aside any desire to help my former protégé and met his gaze despite the urge to drop my eyes. "Leave me alone."

I exited, ducking the waterfall rolling off the awning into pouring rain that had brought icy cold with it on its trip over the Rockies. After a century in an apocalyptic wasteland, the sound and fresh smell of rain almost made me grin.

Except the last thing I want to be is cold and wet.

My feet took me down slick sidewalks, carefully sidestepping under shop fronts and awnings when doing so didn't require a full-on cold shower. I had no idea where they were taking me. Truth be told, I had nowhere to be.

Holographic and illusionary advertisements pounced on me each time I drew too near to a storefront. The streets themselves weren't that different from those I remembered, but storefronts and advertisements emphasized the changes I'd tried to prevent.

And gotten framed for my efforts.

Evidence lined the sidewalks of mass-produced examples of corrupted arcanology. Even hidden by night and darkened storefronts, the changes that had gone on during the long decades and short years of my incarceration made my stomach physically ache.

The reality I'd feared had come to pass.

Society hadn't hesitated in my absence. They'd plunged down the slippery slope of magical solutions for every frivolous want. Everywhere ads offered an endless supply of franchised magical sloth—solutions that undermined craftsmen and made humankind increasingly more dependent on Thoth and corporations like it.

Magic for laziness sake wasted doing what technology already can. My eyes itched, and I blinked away rain dripping from my curls.

Magic should be reserved for solving big problems technology can't touch yet.

My feet took me in and out of mananet and Edison blocks, powering the various city blocks with either magical or wireless electricity. The former seemed far more frequent than I remembered of the world I'd left behind. Pylon crystals glowed atop streetlamp poles, sometimes just above the remains of decapitated Edison coils hung by a last few stubborn wires.

Hospitals had been among the first public institutions targeted with magic as a backup power that an EMP couldn't knock out. The mananet—much like the Edison initiative—had taken the magical power that had always existed and spread it through the air. The design regulated the ebb and flow of the wild power, homogenized it to the benefit of those few of us that could innately feel and manipulate magic. As the mananet spread, more and more people took an interest in arcanology and the things magic could do to help society.

Big money moved in, creating monopolies that capitalized on thin competition bringing miracles to the common man. Adam, Thecia and I witnessed one too many miracles held ransom and started Thoth to change the cycle—or at least I thought that was what we'd all wanted. We were going to change the world, make it a better place. Adam convinced me—as the only one of us that could touch magic—to design basic safety spells: protective barriers for police, fire protection charms for firemen, or rapid heal spells for trauma wards. We undercut the competition and with those moneys funded bigger research projects like the burn treatment spell which seemed the logical basis for their Glamour line.

Greedy rat bastard.

Big tech companies and more established arcanology corporations tried to stop us through lobbying and government regulation. They capitalized on accidents, allergic reactions, whatever they could to slow our growth. Adam proved the slipperier snake, and I supplied him the oil of better spell designs and safeguards to satisfy all the laws and regulations that licensed spell use.

A glowing orange Eye sprang to life, drawing my gaze into a franchise Thoth eyeStore. Illusions blossomed across the storefront beneath the Eye, heartbreaking displays of cosmetic illusions, lost key seeking spells, food enhancers, party decorations and dozens of frivolous, magical conveniences.

I stormed away from the corruption of my life's work. Other stores offered similar products but probably not real competition. *Adam will probably just buy them out if they become big enough to be a threat to his profits.*

When my headlong flight from roiling emotions came to an end, I found myself in the park where I'd spent lunches with Thecia and sound-boarded ideas with intern spell architects like Darrin.

I shouldn't be surprised.

Decorative lighting illuminated flowering bushes arranged in esoteric beds of a hundred varieties. Mananet pylons disguised as rustic streetlights filled the already wondrous garden with literal magic. I stopped at the garden's center, at the foot of a bronze griffon statue and looked up at the meticulous majesty invested in the park's guardian statuary.

"I used to love this place." My eyes drifted over the statue to the glowing orange Eye crowning Thoth Corp tower. *Used to...*

My feet turned me from the griffon, Thoth Corp and its so-called Eye of Thoth logo. The eye was actually an Eye of Horus. Adam had liked the eye and its history, but he hadn't wanted anyone calling our upstart company, "Ho's R Us."

We'd argued about the technical inaccuracy of the corporate name, but Thecia and Adam had insisted that fact was less important than perception. If only I'd understood then what that truism would mean to my future.

The rain worsened in time with my mood. I started to shiver. I could afford a night in a hotel, but only one. My parents had started with nothing. If they could find success despite their circumstances and the color of our skin, then I could too—or so they would've told me if I was willing to talk to them.

Alley by alley, I fled Thoth Corp, yet remained beneath its orange eye. Maybe I braved the alleys in the hope of danger; perhaps fear of freedom made me reckless.

Who am I anymore but an emaciated ghost haunting the streets of my victories and eventual condemnation in a once-tailored suit?

Hot raindrops ran my cheeks with the icy.

I pushed a dumpster from against a brick corner, flipping open its doors to tent the space behind. I huddled beneath the plastic roof and tried not to be washed away with the rest of the trash, one more piece of refuse alongside a stream of floating detritus.

Soaked and dispirited in the future I'd failed to stop, I tried to count my blessings like Dad taught us. Only one occurred to me, thankfulness that whatever the dumpster contained didn't stink.

"Hey, wake up. You can't be here."

I groaned, stiff and cold.

"Seriously, you have to move."

"Leave me alone."

Whoever he was seized my arms. Wasteland instincts woke faster than I did. I grabbed at the white kid's silvery sleeve, but he proved stronger than he looked. He yanked me out from behind the dumpster, grunting as we both slammed into the far alley wall. I pulled a fist back to hit him, but a sudden boom drew my eyes to the dumpster as it slammed into the brick corner.

My assailant's arm slipped my grip. In fact, he wasn't anywhere up or down the alley. The garbage truck driver rolled a window down. "Damn, man, I'm sorry. I couldn't see you."

I blinked up at the driver. "What?"

DISCARDED | 17

"I'm glad you heard me coming and jumped out of the way," the driver said. "I could've killed you."

Would that have been such a bad thing?

"You don't have to sleep here, you know. There's a shelter three blocks up on Tennyson. If nothing else, she has blankets and hot food. Keep you from freezing to death, you know?"

My stomach woke at his mention of food. "Tennyson?"

"Yeah, look, I'm already behind schedule, or I'd show you."

"It's fine. Thanks."

"Yeah, there's not a lot of space along here. I imagine that's why no one lives in this alley. If you've got to live on the streets, make sure you don't hunker down where we might hurt you."

I stepped out of the path of his truck and waved my thanks. The big electric behemoth hardly made a sound trundling past me. The rest of the alley remained empty. Only a small alcove offered a man without any possessions space not easily crushed by garbage trucks. Despite that shortcoming, the mananet barely covered the alley. The barest overlap of outer edges accounted for the thin magical field which suited my aversion to making a crutch out of the alluringly ready magical field.

∘ 3 ∘

DOUBLE JEOPARDY

The garbage truck driver was off by two blocks, but I found a shelter called simply: the Manger. If the name wasn't enough to discourage entry, Christian versions of Thecia's favorite motivational posters covered the walls visible beyond the windows.

Life's detritus filled cafeteria benches in assorted ages and colors with clothes twice as varied. A too-thin, plain-looking Hispanic woman wove through the crowd with a smile too-wide for so early in the morning. She wore an old comfortable blue and white flannel shirt over a black t-shirt, jeans, and hiking boots. Diners cringed into their collars when she neared.

I turned to go. A bell jingled a warning before a grizzled old war veteran exited in a wash of tantalizing aromas: fresh baked bread, eggs, bacon and dark rich coffee.

The scent would've been enough to lure someone who basically hadn't eaten actual food for a century into the establishment, but the veteran gave me a gap-toothed smile. "Had the same reaction myself, but she's got a damn fine cook. Not too bad a singer either."

I took a deep breath.

This is my life now. Survive first, be picky later.

Eyes sought the bell as I pushed open the door. Smirks hid in bowls as the woman set aside her tray and hurried to me. "Good morning. Welcome to the Manger."

"Let me guess," I said dryly. "Where there's always space for God's children."

"Oh, that's good. I'm totally stealing that." Despite all likelihood, she brightened. "My name is Marisol, but everyone calls me Sunny."

I shook my head and tried to step around her toward the food line.

She headed me off, ducking in and out of the kitchen doorway without slowing. "Grace, we've got a first timer."

A deep man's voice answered, "Have it right out."

I expected institutional eggs and overcooked, surplus bacon—the same torture foods they'd given me before putting me under. Instead, they dished me tiny portions on par with brunch at a five-star country club.

The beaming, mole-flecked woman crowded my elbow.

It took two attempts to rouse my little-used voice. "We able to come back for more?"

"Won't need it, slim," an old woman on my opposite side said. "First timers get Sunday breakfast without having to sit through a sermon—mostly."

I eyed Sunny. "You planning to preach while I eat?"

"Maybe," Sunny smiled. "Depends on where our conversation wanders."

"What if I prefer not to talk?" I asked.

Others around the room laughed.

I set my plate down and turned toward the coffee pot, but Sunny had a steaming cup already extended. I took it, inhaling good, medium quality beans both roasted and brewed precisely as long as they should've been.

"Cream and sugar?" she asked.

"Sacrilege."

"Should've known."

I scowled.

Was that a race crack?

She smirked. "You seem like the strong bitter type."

"You don't know anything about me." I shoved a fork of eggs into my mouth and nearly fainted. Light, fluffy and unquestionably fresh from their shells, they were just slightly savory with a delicate hint of something smoky.

"You just got released from prison," she said. "Wasteland?"

It was difficult to eat such excellent food and remain surly, but I did my best. In another time, I probably would've enjoyed funding her little operation, but taking charity sat poorly with me. Handouts were for the incurably lazy or people incapable of caring for themselves, definitely not my father's son. Most of all though, my attitude rooted in the fact that so-called friendship was the very last thing I wanted in the world.

I concentrated on the food, but all too soon my underfilled plate was empty. "Look, Sunny, I don't need friends."

"Everybody needs friends."

"No," I growled. "*I* don't. So why don't you take your nosey questions and petty judgments elsewhere and leave me in peace."

Sunny sniffed. Her brow tightened, and her nose wrinkled, adding unsightly creases to her upper lip.

Dirty looks hit me from around the room. Despite their outward aversion to Sunny, the Manger's clientele were obviously partial to the irritating little sunspot.

A platter of food slapped onto the table in front of me. The guy who delivered it was twice my girth, at least a head taller and considerably darker skinned than I. His expression promised me a slow and painful demise. He put my doom on hold long enough to gather Sunny up into his embrace and usher her into the kitchen.

I ignored the room's increasingly pointed dirty looks. I'd withstood plenty of them before and likely would face more in my future. I dug into a plate of fresh griddle cakes, fried potatoes, eggs, bacon, and sourdough toast. Every glorious bite made me feel a bit smaller.

Sunny ducked into the dining room and rushed out another door. I got only the shortest glimpse. She was an ugly crier.

"Don't touch my food." I rose. "I'll be back for the rest."

I hated leaving such good food behind where it'd be gobbled up by others despite my warning, but Mom raised me well enough that making a woman cry demanded an immediate apology. Truth be told, my stomach had also shrunk far smaller than my eyes.

Reddish blotches covered the parts of her face not hidden behind long ebony locks. She looked up, running a tissue under her nose. "We've got one bed available, now normally—"

I blinked at her. "You're offering me a place to stay?"

"That's why we're here, to help those that need it."

"Even when they're unnecessarily mean to you?"

She shook her head. "It's just been an awful day. I overreacted. I'm sorry."

She's sorry?

"So, I normally interview prospective residents to ensure—"

My voice hardened. "That we're not dangerous?"

"No. That you have a skill or something you can contribute in exchange for your stay, but with the unseasonably cold weather conditions out there, I'll waive that. You look newly-released and probably don't have any practice living on the streets."

"What makes you think you know anything about me?"

She sniffed and blew her nose on the tissue. "That's a court suit, though at one time it was a lot nicer than most I've seen, and that's saying something. You might be a broke stockbroker, but between the ill fit and the gold taps in your forearms, I'm guessing you were jacked into the Wasteland."

I pulled my sleeves down. "Look, Sunny, I came up here to apologize for making you cry."

"Just for making me cry? Not for calling me nosey and petty?" When I didn't answer, she forced a smile. "So, I'll need you to fill out the resident form and agree to help out, then we can—"

"Don't you want to know what I did to end up incarcerated?"

"No. Despite your assumptions about me, I don't judge people by their pasts. God has more than once transformed the worst criminal into a saint. His arms welcome all, and I wouldn't presume to know better. You're welcome until you make yourself otherwise."

"God again?"

She folded her arms. "Look...what's your name?"

I folded my own.

"God provides everything here. You might not believe in Him or His grace yet, but residing here does mean you'll at least pretend to respect that this house and all its blessings come from Him."

"I don't have a lot of respect for a God—"

"That let you down? Abandoned you?" She smiled. "Are you sure everything that happened wasn't part of His plan for your life?"

"God planned to ruin me? Take all I had and...you know what? Thanks for breakfast, but no thanks." I stormed back into the dining room to find all my food where I left it. I snatched up a Styrofoam container, shoved my breakfast inside and left the Manger without utensils or a backward glance.

The bell rang again a few moments after I exited. "Hey, there's a stockpile of large cardboard boxes around back. Dinner and fellowship are at six."

I didn't answer her, and I didn't go around back. Jackson Graham's son could survive anything life threw at him.

It took hours to find a dumpster with fresh cardboard. As choices went, the return on investment wasn't worth the time my stubbornness cost—not that I'd have changed my mind if I'd know that in advance.

I returned to the selfsame alley where I'd nearly been squashed. The Eye glared down at me, but within the urban streets that were now my home, it offered the thinnest mananet coverage I was likely to find. My so-called prize, a thin, waxy television box barely covered my head and shoulders. The opener had cut the tape on both top and bottom. Without one end still taped to use as a center, I was unable to effectively double the available coverage area.

Once upon a time, I'd known a simple adhesion charm that could've fixed it, but Thoth security had confiscated my spell notebooks as a first step in preventing the deranged corporate wizard from hurting the public.

As if I had a single, purely aggressive spell in any of the notebooks.

One of the tenants of my sentence prohibited me from entering any establishment selling spell components and licenses. Some components were common enough they could be bought or grown, but not with my feeble resources.

Even so, magic's constant tickle on my skin was worse than the aching hunger left after breakfast's remains were half a day gone. I'd been physically hungry in the Wasteland, the food tube dribbling only tiny amounts of paste to maintain basic stomach functionality throughout my sentence. After being called back to full duty, my ravenous stomach demanded filling with painful intensity.

The flimsy cardboard held over my head drooped along its edges. Machine gun thumps atop its melting surface sounded differently from those splashing onto alley concrete or ringing off rusting fire escapes.

A plump rat scurried along the alley's far shadows, keeping mostly dry beneath pipes sticking in and out of the old bricks. The hair on my wet arms tried to rise, and I couldn't help initial retreat and revulsion.

They were horrible diseased things responsible for the black plague—as transport at any rate. I know some people claim they're clean, useful pets, but such claims couldn't account for the long lines of urine left in their wake by dragging genitalia. I silently thanked the lack of black lighting and would've wrapped my arms around myself if I hadn't had to hold up my roof.

A rat bit me in one of my family's first houses, and I'd been forced to suffer repeated stomach injections after it escaped capture. They'd been one of the few creatures in the Wasteland I couldn't bring myself to kill and eat. I wasn't five years old and terrified of them anymore, but I didn't want them anywhere near me.

As long as it stays on its side of the alley, it can scurry anywhere it wants.

Once the filthy thing had safely disappeared into a crack in the far building's foundation, I checked my alcove for similar holes then watched the world go by. Business types bustled back and forth. They hurried through day's end with barely a glance away from phone holograms, illusionary equivalents that flickered in the weak mananet or the wet sidewalk. Stray gazes fled the mere sight of me, their watchers taking little unconscious sidesteps toward the road.

A mangy cat's angry snarling yowl stole my attention. A high pitched squeal followed the cat's assault against an almost disintegrated delivery box. An adult rat darted out of nowhere—probably another foundation crack—behind the cat. It batted the stray's tail, whirling the cat around but not fast enough for the cat to stop the brave rodent from scurrying underneath it and into the box barely ahead of a pounce.

Our mouser hadn't stopped me from getting bitten. Since then, I had no use for the little beasts. Rats disgust me, but I have a grudge against cats. "Shut up, cat."

It glared at me, flirted its tail and batted the box with another yowl. A rat inside the box cried out, and other, smaller voices joined the first.

"Hey, leave them alone." I lurched onto my feet, dumping a small, icy lake down myself that didn't extinguish the sudden ball of fury in my empty gut. That I should defend the filthy rodents against a mangy stray emphasized to me just how much that Wasteland had affected me.

My first days inside had proven painful. Dependent on magical defenses and used to winning fights by thinking my way free, I'd been unprepared for the brutal ambushes from my fellow prisoners. Even once I'd learned how better to defend myself, an endless string of small, weak or just unprepared prisoners delighted the many bullies—too many for me to stand up against them all. I'd been forced to stand by and do nothing enough times to last me a lifetime.

I'll admit the cat had as much right to eat as I did, but he wasn't going to devour babies—no matter how repulsive they might be—in front of me. "No one preys on anyone in this alley so long as I'm here."

The cat hissed at me.

I picked up a brick chunk and ricocheted it off the concrete, sending the cat into a hissing leap. I picked up another. There was no way the cat would stay near the box if I marched over, but the moment I retreated, it would return if I didn't convince it to fear me at a distance. In a way, I was bullying the stray, but it was a cat. Its ego could survive the nonlethal dissuasion I had in mind. "I'm warning you, tabby. I'm hungry enough to make you dinner."

The stray batted the box, pretending to pay me no mind.

I bounced another fragment into it. "You really don't want to remind me how much I used to love Korean."

A third rock drove the cat off. I settled back into my alcove, a fourth fragment at hand in case I needed to make a point.

A rat poked his nose out before leading away the younger rodents he'd apparently been hunting. They exited the box and scurried down the alley to the hole the first rat had used. The adult rat stopped just outside the crevice and stared at me several long moments. His head bobbed once. He ducked back inside.

I blinked at its disappearing tail.

"Elias Balthazar Graham."

I turned toward the gravelly voice to find three men approaching with their purpose visible in their body language. The middle man's face seemed familiar, though I couldn't place it after a century away. His dark expression said more about his familiarity with me than the use of my full name. "I've waited years for your release."

I stepped away from the alley wall. Keeping it at my back controlled their angle of approach, but also offered three men the ability to pin me. My hands came up into defensive positions, one still wrapped around the chunk of brick. "What do you want?"

They stalked forward in silence. The middle spoke an instant before he swung a meaty fist. "Justice."

I slid sideways around the blow, but the other two rushed in to surround me. I came up short against the smallest of the three hulking comrades. A body blow from the ugly third slammed into my ribs from behind. The punch stole the wind from my lungs, and my retaliatory blow missed its mark as Tiny stepped backward then forward with a long left.

In the Wasteland, I'd hardened my body through survival, hard work and countless fights for my life. I knew exactly how to move to face three opponents and leave them on the ground.

I ducked the long left too slow. Another flesh hammer pounded my exposed side, and I barely blocked a blow from the furious, familiar face.

I doubled over, barely faking and drove a brick backed fist into Ugly. Pain exploded in a soft, weak hand entirely unlike my Wasteland fists. I staggered to a nearby dumpster, scooping up a plastic net that once held oranges.

Tiny, Ugly and Mister Familiar pursued.

Despite the pain, I managed to get a larger brick chunk into the bag and get it swinging before they caught up. I timed the blow perfectly—for my Wasteland body.

One of them snatched the bag from my hand and turned my makeshift flail against me. Fists pummeled me from every angle. Blocks and counterblows landed with neither the coordination nor force they should've delivered.

I managed a mostly glancing blow to Tiny's throat. He dropped gasping. Vindictive pleasure flashed through me a moment before Ugly locked my arms behind me. Mister Familiar went at me. I kicked his knee sideways, but the blow hit too low, only sweeping his leg away. He got back up and pummeled me with cautious lunging punches.

"That judge let you off easy, freak." He punctuated the last word with a fist to my gut. "We're not going to make that mistake."

Three days in a muscular stimulation tank being pumped full of growth hormones had barely rejuvenated muscles long-disused outside necessary conformation stimulus. The process hadn't even filled me out enough to fit my tailored suit once more. The underpowered delivery of my best, even underhanded blows simply couldn't compete with three angry, full-strength men.

The beating intensified until I could barely see. Pain punctuated every attempt to breathe. I kicked blind, swung as hard as I could for whatever it was worth.

"What the hell—" Familiar said.

I went down. Kicks slammed into me wherever I wasn't able to defend.

"Thought he," Ugly yelped. "Thought he couldn't touch magic."

"Get this thing off me," Tiny said.

The blows hitting me paused. High pitch cries filled the space between.

Ugly screamed in pain. "Hit him, make this stop."

Darkness pooled around my awareness, muffling the grunts, screams and strange cries. A kick slammed into my side.

"Shit, behind you." Familiar said. "And there."

Unconsciousness loomed over me, a starless night of growing dread lit by the occasional fireworks of pain. My attackers cursed and yelled, cried out and mumbled mad gibberish. Maybe they stopped hitting me, or maybe the pain reached a point where I couldn't feel any more.

Darkness rescued me from one nightmare but delivered me into imagined childhood horrors. Pain-induced hysteria drowned me in a grave of wet, writhing rats—a slithering sea of squeaks, urine stench and slimy fur.

I woke.

That in itself was a surprise. My body hurt, throbs big and small suggesting my continued existence was unintended and that correction might walk into the alley at any moment.

Death was a constant danger in the Wasteland but offered neither escape nor release from imprisonment. I lay on the hard, wet alley concrete unsuccessfully postulating what had made my attackers stay their final judgment.

The attack whirled in my mind, a confused swirling knot of pain, glimpses, and screams. They'd wanted me dead, but they hadn't finished the job. Some nebulous something had stopped them. Pain and anger pulsed like living entities of their own.

Stubborn pride forbade me wistful thoughts of an ignoble, undeserved trip beyond, but I couldn't help academic curiosity about whether I'd have been better off delivered to the afterlife rather than back to painful consciousness.

None of my speculations mattered. Whether Wasteland or real world, I'd survive whatever was thrown at me at least long enough to spit in the pitcher's eye.

Two mornings passed without the return of my attackers. I'd gotten hold of a couple dining chair braces, but the colder it got, the more tempting burning my makeshift clubs became. The temptation to revisit the Manger worsened too. More cardboard, a blanket, hell, even just their coffee drew me. The pain of my empty stomach grew louder than my other injuries, but I refused to submit to coercion.

Others might need that woman's help, but not I, not ever.

I tucked my cardboard into a recently-emptied dumpster and stretched stiff, frozen kinks from my limbs. I wouldn't have thought it possible, but I almost missed the sensation of biting ants crawling all over me produced by the muscular stimulation tank.

I steeled myself along the walk away from downtown. Injury and recovery had interrupted my plans, but I'd calculated how long I could allow my convalescence before I had to act. I'd held off as long as I could, but the time had come to break my hundred dollar bill and purchase the staple foods I'd decided best suited to my situation.

I'd been hesitant to break the bill. Once broken, it would become easier and easier to spend until I was as penniless as the other street people.

I already resemble them.

The beating and a week in the elements hadn't done my Armani suit any favors. All I had to do was roll up my sleeves, showing off the gold jack ports, to look like all the black homeless junkies I'd always pitied.

If I get really desperate, I could cut the jacks out of my skin and sell it.

The little store I found seemed mostly liquor store and newsstand. Grocery items stocked shelves at premium prices that took advantage of too busy office workers. A long trek out of the city center by foot or bus might've saved me a little money, but it probably evened out overall. I sought out the cheapest bread loaf and bologna he sold and got in line behind a midlevel executive assistant about my age. She caught sight of me in her peripheral vision, choked up on her purse and slid half a step closer to the old man in front of her.

When she positioned her fingers near the eyeSentinel charm on her purse, I took half a step back to accommodate her comfort zone and shook my head. Sunny might claim to be different, but judgment remained alive and well on the streets of Seufert Fells.

The lady paid, stuffed her wallet back into her bag and fled the convenience store.

The cashier checked my hundred with the marker four times. Rather than make a pointless comment, my sandwich makings and I returned to the cold streets. A wallet lay on the sidewalk just outside the convenience store. Several twenties peaked from hastily closed pockets. My left hand closed into a fist at my side. Knuckles rubbed against one another in an oscillating rhythm as if spinning a coin across their tops.

I picked up the wallet and scanned the street for the woman who'd checked out ahead of me. She hurried down the block.

"Hey, lady!" I jogged after her, holding up her wallet. "Hold up a moment."

She sped her walk, glanced back nervously.

"Ma'am, please stop." I picked up my pace.

She couldn't run well in the impractically high heels, but she turned a corner to flee my sightline. When I caught her, she whipped around with an eyeGuardian mace canister. I felt the surge in magic and hit the ground as hard as I could. Flame jetted through the space I'd just vacated.

I bolted back to my feet and snatched the canister from her hands with a snarl. "God damn it, lady. Are you just clumsy and inept or were you *trying* to kill me?"

I turned over the eyeGuardian. The new model had its flame rune placed immediately below the mace rune despite repeated memos warning development against just such a configuration. The two activation runes were placed so closely together that only tiny fingers couldn't accidentally activate both at once. I almost felt bad about calling her clumsy—until she thumbed her eyeSentinel charm. The shield's magic washed over me as it encapsulated her in the magical protection field.

"You can have my money," she said. "Just don't hurt me or—"

I held up her wallet. "I already have your money."

She blanched, clutching her purse and the shield charm tighter.

My calves prickled, hands itched and neck heated. I'd gone out of my way to help the woman, and she'd practically accused me of being a rapist. I didn't think about it. I pulled on the mananet and silently incanted the emergency failsafe on the eyeSentinel that let first responders help those walled off by the shield. Her protection sizzled away with visible sparks. She stared down at it in horror, poised to bolt.

I shoved the wallet into her arms. "You dropped your wallet. I just wanted to *return* it to you."

She did a quick inventory. "It's all here."

I rolled my eyes. "Yeah, screw you too, lady."

My left hand opened, rising to scratch my temple. As the imagined scenario came to its probable but undesired outcome, I stared at the wallet on the ground a moment longer.

Screw her, it's not worth the bother.

I turned toward where I'd spotted a Chick-Fil-A and marched away with an overcoat of lingering anger. I really couldn't blame the woman. She hadn't actually tried to torch me, but I'm sure she would have if I'd given her the chance.

Inside the blissfully warm Chick-Fil-A, I bought a coffee. While I waited, I collected a discarded newspaper, some condiment packs and a few saltine crackers. I settled in a back corner with fresh so-so coffee and laid the paper on the table.

When I couldn't stall any longer, I looked at the paper's date. I just stared at the year, unsure how to feel. Subjectively, the Wasteland had held me over a century. In reality, I'd been imprisoned almost nine years—less than a decade. In all probability, my parents lived in the same house they had when I'd been imprisoned. Adam, Thecia, and Darrin probably still worked alongside many of the same people at Thoth Corp as I had.

I covertly made a sandwich under the table, chewing over-salty bologna that was still somehow delicious. A Chick-Fil-A employee brought me another coffee, more crackers, and a wrapped sandwich. "Cook made a mistake. Would you be interested in a complimentary sample?"

My neck prickled once more. I wanted to throw the sandwich in her face, to demand who she thought she was. Truth be told, I wanted that sandwich far more than I'd ever willingly admit. I pushed down my anger and whispered my thanks.

She beamed and trotted back to her other duties.

I ate the hot, delicious chicken, egg and cheese bagel with added bacon unsure where the cook had made a mistake, but happy for it. I pulled a wilted, water damaged business card with partially-faded ink from my inner suit pocket. The release sergeant had given it to me with instructions to contact the woman on the card within seven days. It had been six.

I considered not reporting to her. Her card titled her a shrink, not a parole officer. I'd assumed she'd handle getting me in touch with my PO, but if I'd served almost nine years, then I wasn't on parole. I'd served my time. I was free of the courts save my magical retail restriction and one other legal obligation I had every intention to avoid.

The judge had branded me as surely as if he'd held a hot iron to my skin. I would forever be a criminal on the outside of society, a man with a country I couldn't claim unless I were willing to vindicate the jury by publically admitting guilt.

Not going to happen.

Fifty years ago, I'd decided that I'd rather be forever lost among America's homeless than bow before injustice. The rest of the world could burn for all I cared. They didn't need me, and I didn't need anyone.

When I was young and angry, Dad frequently quipped on the value of bridges. He thought he was funny, but his stubborn son eventually connected the dots. He'd worked his ass off, rising in affluence through hard work and never burning a bridge.

He'd repeatedly grinned through shit sandwiches from some ass only to earn the ass's respect through hard work and reliability. Though he rarely received an apology, Dad often benefited from maintaining an even temper. Asses became associates that offered Dad lucrative business opportunities previously closed to him.

"No point wasting energy on negativity, Elias. The world is what it is, but determined positivity will eventually make it better."

Dad was a good man. His advice landed me in prison so I couldn't recommend it. Just the same, I avoided bridge arson by heading to the shrink's office.

The new municipal building occupied a concrete island kitty-corner across Gateway Park from Thoth Corp Tower. The government building had been constructed with plenty of marble, brass and a plaque honoring Thoth Corp for funding its construction. The monument of municipal corruption joined the other towers ringing Gateway Park. Situating city headquarters within the bristling mananet thicket forced reliance on magically provided electricity, wizard eyes, and other magical amenities.

No doubt a none-too-subtle political statement to Adam's high tech competitors.

Entering the overlapped mananet smothering the towers nearly left me cross-eyed. Gooseflesh raised mountain ranges along my skin, temptation and torture invoked by power's caress.

Water, water everywhere and not a drop to drink.

4

THE PAST WON'T LET GO

Doctor Jessica Porter had emblazoned her name and associated alphabet soup across the fancy frosted glass. An alcove with too-low, too-comfortable pastel furniture sat opposite her office. Her assistant sat cross-legged on a wide pillow surrounded by a curved coffee table holding all her office essentials without interrupting the frumpy, hippie energy.

Whatever skills the assistant displayed in her interview, the burnt aroma from a nearby coffee pot exhibited an almost criminal inattention to vital details. She'd never have lasted as an executive assistant, certainly not at Thoth.

I disdained the furniture, preferring to stand rather than to sink into fabric-covered quicksand.

A woman who could only have been Doctor Porter appeared in the office doorway. Her business suit had been sewn together in a combined Easter egg and clothing factory. Her bob hairdo was dyed; any further description might suggest her hair displayed more native personality than the doctor herself. It was a close call.

Women in their late forties shouldn't sound like they've been sucking helium. Porter defied the convention. "Mister Graham, please come inside."

The interior of her office was all leather and not the fun kind they talk about in prison. Her office decorator had compensated for the waiting room with a monochrome motif that made me feel as if I were inside a bad noir film.

33

"Please have a seat."

Doctor Van Day-glow sat behind her humongous desk and steepled hot pink fingernails. I tried to scan her credentials, but her colors refused to allow anything else present substantial attention.

"I'd started to worry you were going to stand me up."

I raised my brows. "Why don't you start by explaining why I'm here?"

"As a prisoner released on...well, with such an unfortunate sentence, we must ensure the long-term safety of the overall populace. As such, as part of your release, the court has ordered extensive counseling."

"I served my sentence."

"Consider this an addendum."

"For how long?"

"Until I feel you are safely acclimated to freedom once more." She paged through a file. "I don't see an accommodation report from any of the state halfway houses. I swear, some people just refuse to understand the importance paperwork holds in proper societal governance."

I rolled my eyes. "Your point?"

"My, we are grumpy today."

"Why are you grumpy? Unicorn take a dump on your cloud?"

She frowned, but it melted away. She pushed a list across the desk. "Which house should I contact for the paperwork?"

"None of them."

"I have to contact the house where you're staying."

"I'm not staying at any of them."

Her hundred watt smile flickered a moment before returning to full power. She punched up a record on her pink laptop, taking exaggerated care not to chip her too-long nails. "I don't see your residence registered in the system. You know you're required to register, do you not?"

"I understand that I must register my address upon moving into a residence."

The bulb flickered.

"Was there anything else? I have a very busy day planned."

"Mister Graham, I don't think you understand how serious it would be for you to violate the law again."

"Nope, got that."

"Are you staying with someone?"

"No."

The wattage dimmed once more, apparently inversely controlled by the number of wrinkles across her forehead. "Are you staying in a halfway house?"

"No."

"A shelter? A hotel? That technically counts as a residence too."

I crossed my legs and did my best imitation of Adam in a boardroom meeting. "Jessica, may I call you Jessica?"

"Doctor Porter."

"I don't live anywhere, Jessica. Nowhere."

"Preposterous," she blustered. "You have to be living someplace."

"Do I? Is there a law against not living somewhere?"

She started paging through my file again. "Well, I'm not sure, but I am sure that you are required to register your address."

"And I swear that I will register the moment I have an address."

The wattage returned. She poised a pen above my file. "Excellent, when do you think that might be?"

I gave her the selfsame smile I intended for Adam and Thecia. "Right about the time when hell freezes over, Lucifer shacks up with a unicorn, and they start selling their cotton candy offspring."

"Mister Graham, I don't think you understand—"

"No, *Jessica*, I don't think you understand. You and your societal governance can go screw yourselves for all I care. You leave me alone, and I won't cause you the slightest problem."

"I told you to call me Doctor Porter."

"Is there a law against using your given name?"

Rather than answer, she forged on. "You can't divorce yourself from society."

"Why not?"

"You need society to help you, to instruct you on the proper way to live, the things you need to own and practices you need to observe to be a contributing member of, well, society."

"Is this the same society that sent me to jail?"

"Well, your crimes sent you to jail, Mister Graham, due course, just verdict, jury of your peers and all that."

I stood, holding back another colorful suggestion that would just wrinkle the perfect world washed into her brain. "Then you can keep it."

She chased me into the hall. "You're required to see me every two weeks until I release you as a patient. That's the law, Mister Graham."

I turned, cocking my head. "Am I required to let you see me when I see you?"

"What?"

I shook my head. "Words are important, Jessica. Look into it."

A full head of steam drove my exit. My encounter with the deluded public shrink had left me so angry that I didn't see the limo until it hit me. A grey, rainy sky filled my double vision, thunder either shaking the heavens or my head throbbing like a bass drum.

A burly security guy in an expensive suit appeared above me and glared down over top of his sunglasses. The square cut of his jaw and flinty glare made me wonder if he was somehow part gargoyle.

Satan's personal succubus appeared beside him in a tailored, crimson skirt suit. "Elias?"

"Thecia." The word exhausted a world supply of venom.

Her perfect, cosmetically enhanced chocolate eyes softened, leaving her flame-touched raven curls as the only evidence of her demon blood. "Are you all right?"

"Outside betrayal or Stony here hitting me with his limo?"

Her expression hardened. "You do know you are legally restrained from being within a thousand feet of any Thoth Corp property."

"Then you shouldn't have built the municipal building so close to the tower, or you know, *hit me* with said property."

"We-I didn't know you were out."

"Yeah, a century of starvation and suffering just flies by." Holding a hand to the back of my splitting head hampered my struggling effort to regain my feet. Stony yanked me the rest of the way.

She fished into her purse. "Here, let me give you—"

"Money?! You steal everything in my life, and you think a little pocket change will absolve you?" I stumbled away, picking up the worse-for-wear plastic bag of bread and bologna. "Go screw yourself, or worse, Adam."

I cut through Gateway Park, returning quickly to the griffon statue and his new phantom double. I paced around him, waiting for my vision to come back together while I seethed. "I might accept a free sandwich from an otherwise innocent corporation, but I'll be damned to hell for another century before I'll take the slightest help from *that* woman."

Unsurprisingly, the statue offered no comment.

The plastic bag toting my foodstuffs broke a block from my alley. My angry march back warmed me enough to notice the evolving stench of my suit. Considering all I'd put it through, only cold and frequent drenching had delayed the inevitable.

I need more clothes.

Four twenties and the crumpled fragments of the fifth remained to last me indefinitely. Before denting my monies permanently, I reviewed the situation in preparation for devising a plan. Isolating myself from humanity—particularly the other transients—hadn't allowed for much research into practical street survival. Without consulting the other homeless about their experiences, I had prevented myself from gathering a working knowledge of the best practices of transient survival.

The most obvious choice open to me required the unacceptable option of contacting family. Most of my friends deserted me shortly after I was charged and the rest vanished once I was convicted. I'd previously paid more than enough taxes to qualify for some kind of government assistance, but after my interaction with Jessica, that sort of thing also topped my list of unacceptable choices. In any case, applying for such aid probably required an address of some kind. Begging for scraps from either passersby or the government was out of the question, particularly after Sunny and Jessica had shown me what either cost.

I could've attempted to rejoin the workforce, but employing my degrees would probably put me back into the same situation that stole a century of my life. Besides, it seemed unlikely anyone would be interested in me as a consultant of spell design.

What do I need money for, anyway? It's not like I'm not going to live in a house or an apartment.

Once I had clothes enough to stay warm and a sturdy bag to keep my belongings at hand, food would be the only resource I'd need to renew.

My stomach grumbled. It did that too often. It would have to wait until I'd solved my wardrobe limitations. The most expedient solution dwelt at the Manger, but there had to be consignment and thrift stores somewhere around downtown Seufert Fells's halo.

"Elias?"

I clenched my ripped bag in a hard fist, scooped up one of my makeshift clubs and took on a defensive fighting stance.

Darrin stood in the alley mouth.

Great, must be "National People You Don't Want To See Dropping By" day.

My arms folded across my chest. "I told you to leave me alone, Darrin."

Hearing my voice quickened his steps. "Jesus, Elias, what are you doing someplace like this? What happened to your savings? Your investments?"

I shifted my meager larder behind my back. "Confiscated, frozen or spent in my defense."

"And what happened to you and your suit?"

"The local concerned citizenry felt it necessary to amend the judge's sentence with something more lasting." I frowned. "How'd you find me? Thecia have me followed?"

"Thecia?"

"She just hit me with her limo."

Darrin stared off into space a moment. "No, nothing like that. Just used one of your earlier, more effective tracking charms."

I nodded. "I saw Adam is hawking the short term charms."

"Higher repeat sales." Darrin looked at the charm in his hands. "Find your keys no matter where you left them, three charges only four ninety-nine."

Heat prickled my neck. "The components to fuel three castings couldn't cost more than four cents."

Darrin shrugged. "Seven now, though with the cost of the actual charm we're layering the spell onto, the whole thing comes out to about thirty-five cents."

I pushed away my anger. Other issues took precedence. Thoth Corp's pricing practices weren't my problem any longer. "Go away, Darrin. Don't come back."

"Eli, please, I really need your help."

"I don't help people anymore. Do I look like I can even fucking help myself?"

"People are being hurt. Please, let me bribe you a little. Lunch at Hunter's Glade in exchange for giving me a fair hearing."

Hunter's Glade had long been my very favorite place to eat. Just the mention of its name sent my stomach into Jurassic grumbling mode. They were hands down the best restaurant in Seufert Fells, four-star ranking notwithstanding, but calling it a bribe set my hackles on edge.

"I'm not for sale. That should be obvious to even someone as corrupt as Adam."

"This isn't for Adam, okay? Nice people are being hurt, and I can't figure out how to help them."

It hurt to tell him no, especially to something like that. I liked Darrin, and I'd made it my life's work to find magical ways to help people.

Right up until doing so cost me everything.

There was nothing wrong with rejecting him out of hand. I didn't owe anyone anything and certainly didn't have to explain myself to my old protégé. Just the same I didn't want Darrin thinking poorly of me. "I'm not dressed for it."

Darrin scanned the area around me. "Guess you don't have a change."

"No, my laundress absconded with my closet and went on holiday."

He chuckled. It wasn't meant to be funny.

"I'll buy you some clothes."

"I want neither your pity nor your charity."

"Jesus, Eli, I'm trying to help you, man. How many times did you have my old junker fixed so I could study instead of walking between class and Thoth? Stop being a stiff-necked prick and let me return the favor."

"You still got that car?"

"That was almost a decade ago."

"That's a no."

"Yes, that's a no. You know what I mean. I have a new car, why?"

"Is it Thoth property?"

"Oh, right. The restraining order. We'll use a Bluebox."

Blueboxes had barely been prototypes when I'd gone to the Wasteland. The brainchild of a British arcanologist with a sense of humor, they allowed for instantaneous transportation between boxes. They'd also turned a lot of test subjects into mutton stew. Even if I was willing to trust the Bluebox tech without thoroughly studying their final arcanology, they were too expensive to pop all over town so I could go thrift store shopping.

"You raise a valid point."

Darrin brightened.

"I do need to hit a thrift store, so I'm going to pass."

His expression turned almost as desperate as it'd been when Heather from product development had asked Darrin to a costume ball, but he wasn't begging for dance lessons this time. "Please, Eli.

I'll call us a LUX, take you wherever you need to go and then to Hunter's Glade. *Please*, hear me out."

I debated it. Lunch at my favorite restaurant and a ride to a thrift store bartered for catching up with an old friend and hearing his troubles. I didn't have to help him.

"Fine. A ride to a thrift store then lunch, but I promise nothing. One thing though, what's a LUX?"

Darrin beamed and pulled a crystal amulet from under his shirt. An illusionary display screen appeared before Darrin's face—the magical equivalent of a holographic control panel straight out of science fiction. He did whatever he needed to do to summon a LUX and headed out of the alley. "I have to grab something from the car."

"I can't go near it, remember?"

Darrin shrugged. "Can you tell a company car on sight?"

He had a point. I followed him to a luxury sedan. Whatever Darrin claimed about how Adam treated him, he wasn't exactly hurting. My former protégé pulled a duffel and what looked like a portfolio case from the trunk. We waited in awkward silence for our ride.

Darrin's amulet chimed. He turned toward approaching traffic. A tiny city car approached. Its round, ivory passenger compartment seemed just large enough to uncomfortably seat two football players or career couch potatoes. The undercarriage had been designed by an insecure character from a Ritchie Rich comic. Gold paint was embellished with delicate black lines, filigree and the letters "LUX-00143G." An additional glance found similar letters on the passenger compartment reading "LUX-00503P."

I frowned, giving Darrin a confused look.

He grinned. "You're going to love this."

After a comfortable ride, we arrived at a thrift store. Darrin waited in the car while I shopped surplus. I managed two sets of jeans, some thermal underwear, two long sleeve shirts, an old army jacket and an even older seabag to carry it all in. I'd considered my bathing options while standing in line to check out, ultimately stepping out of line to collect an electric kettle I'd have to somehow re-engineer so that it could pick up power from the nearest Edison node.

The LUX just sat there when I returned. I looked at Darrin, but he sat with a silent, smug expression. A moment later a hum drew my eyes to a golden, X-shaped drone the size of a car. It eased down over us, the rotor fan assemblies scissoring together into a rectangular shape the same size as our LUX. A thunk heralded a sudden spin of our passenger component. The drone rotor hum rose to new heights as we lifted off the ground. The golden sled that had driven us to the thrift store slid back into traffic headed for parts unknown. The rotors spread back out, banked to one side and lifted us into a sparse, nebulously-defined sky lane hidden from casual view by height and buildings.

"All right, Darrin, this really is cool."

"They've only just started moving into the area. The city isn't big enough to really need it yet, and they don't run the flyers during the rain, but I think it's a positive step."

Just as quickly, the drone lowered us onto a rooftop landing pad atop a satellite location of Corp-A D'Gym.

"Guest pass is waiting at the front desk," Darrin said.

My pride snarled silent objections.

"Look, Eli. I know how you are, and your pride's probably trying to find some way to object, but I get guest passes for free, and you'll be much more comfortable this way."

"All right, smart boy, since you've decided I need a nursemaid—"

"Eli—"

"Did you make any arrangements for soap?"

Darrin grinned, pressing a hand to his chest. "I'm hurt. As if Thoth's senior-most spell architect would use a gym without superior concierge services."

I glowered as I got out of the car. It was too easy to fall back into the young man's easy smile. I'd learned my lesson. There was only one person I could trust: me. The front desk hassled me a little, but I got my pass and a very nice grooming kit then made my way through the barrage of disapproval to the locker room.

Hot water should be considered a world wonder. The fancy little guest bag had all the amenities, but I left merely clean and dry.

Who do I need to shave for anyway?

Hunter's Glade probably hadn't seen a more mismatched couple. The hostess looked at me sideways but greeted Darrin by name. She was too young to have served me in the old days, so I assume she either thought I was Eurotrash or expected me to steal some utensils.

She could call Corp-A D'Gym, surely they counted the towels after I left.

Darrin ordered all my favorites without looking at the menu. He had the good graces to look guilty when my eyes narrowed. "This is a business lunch, Eli. You remember how it goes."

"Better get on with the sales pitch."

Darrin removed a phone from his inner jacket that could've doubled for a television. He placed it between us, offered me an earpiece and waited. The moment Darrin hit play, I knew why he'd chosen the phone over illusionary holograms. The sights and sounds he put in front of me definitely weren't for public consumption outside a criminal court.

I stared.

Women and occasionally men were mutated—that was the best word I could manage—by magic. Adam had perverted one of my most important spells and didn't care about anything other than his profits. I flipped the phone over and counted to a thousand over clenched fists.

"Glamour hit the market and rocketed to the top of our sales ranks. Then...this started."

"You didn't do thorough enough tests."

Darrin bristled. "Glamour is based on your spell which we both know you thoroughly tested. This variant went through similar testing. Initial tests worked just fine."

His tone filled in the rest of the story. Adam really didn't know Darrin had come to me. Darrin had kept him out of the loop, hoping that our relationship would help convince me to help. He was probably also banking on me feeling in some part responsible, or if nothing else, my love of a puzzle. "Then I can assume that you've already covered all the bases. There's nothing more to do. Pull the product."

"Adam's not going to pull it."

"Then what do you expect me to do?"

"Figure out what's wrong?"

"You may not have gotten a real good look at my place, but I don't exactly have a well-stocked lab."

"I'll take care of that. We'll get you set up in the industrial zone, loft apartment and worksh—"

"No."

"I don't understand."

"No, as in we will do no such thing."

"Damn it, Eli, I know you blame us, me for what happened to you. People are being hurt. Can't you just overlook yourself this once to help others?"

I found myself out of my seat before I'd realized it. I towered over him, white-knuckled fists on the table. "All I ever did was help others and look where it got me. I'm not who society says I am and I will not validate their claims by moving into an apartment, a loft or any other address."

He looked around nervously, waving off a hastily-approaching concierge. "Please sit down so we can talk about this rationally."

I sat, folded my arms and scowled.

"If I set up a lab for your use, will you please help me fix this spell?"

"No. It took a long time to learn to live without magic. I'm clean a hundred years." Guilty thoughts shot to breaking the woman's eyeSentinel until I remembered it hadn't actually happened. "I'm out, and I'm not going back for people I don't know."

Darrin's brows pushed together. "What are you talking about? Magic's part of you. You've been making spells since you were a boy."

"Components are regulated now, spells licensed. You know damn well I'm forbidden access to any place that sells them. The Wasteland's only kindness was the absolute lack of mananet. It taught me to survive without magic."

"You're an arcanologist. I'd kill for your sensitivity to magic."

"That man died, crucified by a jury of his peers. Let him rest in peace."

Darrin's gaze shifted to his bags, but he made no argument. He'd recovered a semblance of his usual smile by the time the appetizers arrived. He gestured for me to help myself, but I could see the gears still turning.

Hunter's Glade served us incredible foods that somehow didn't seem as enjoyable as they should have. Nostalgic memory might've been the problem, or maybe the horror film still lingering at the forefront of my thoughts spoiled my mood.

º 5 º

VIGILANTE VERMIN

Neither of us had much of an appetite. Darrin had the restaurant double-package the veritable feast. He helped me lug it into my alley when we returned, adding his two bags next to mine. "All you had as a kid was what you found. Franchise stores and spell libraries didn't even exist. The only thing stopping you from being you is pain and pride."

I opened my mouth to object, but he bulled onward. "I know you, Eli. You do care. These are for when you stop selling yourself short and remember that."

I jerked open the portfolio bag and yanked free some kind of laminated wood. Unfolding it revealed a pre-printed spell circle. Threaded and oddly notched holes had been spaced out at varying points along the inscribed circles.

"What the hell is this?"

"Our newest spell board. Component nodules are in the other bag."

I opened the other bag and went through the sealed octagonal containers labeled with component name, measurement, and retail price. "Five dollars for twenty cents worth of charcoal?"

"The containers, the instructions, the prepared node points fulfill current government regulations to limit usage mistakes."

I turned the plastic component containers over in my hands, noting notches in the interlock housing and no way to remove the components themselves from inside except by magic. I raised my brows.

"Proprietary component nodules. They're designed to interlock with only certain points on the board."

"Does that mean having to buy two different nodules for a given component since you can't just set two pinches of ash side by side?"

Darrin licked his lips. "Yes, Eli. It does."

"Adam's turned magic into paint by numbers for profit?"

"Thoth's made magic accessible to the least common denominator—like every other arcanology company."

"This is exactly why I don't want anything to do with society. Instead of using magic to serve the critical needs of the world, you guys dumbed it down so any idiot can walk around with a flamethrower." I patted my pockets for the eyeGuardian I'd taken from the woman.

"Eli?"

"A woman nearly killed me because development placed the eyeGuardian's flame rune too close to the mace rune. I can't find..." My angry expression slid away into embarrassment.

...the fictional mace canister from my scenario projection.

Darrin studied me.

"Take that and all this crap with you. I'm not helping Adam profit from one more spell."

"So people being mutilated and turned into ravening animals isn't important enough for you to help?"

I met his gaze, finding my young protégé as stubborn as his teacher. "Victims of their own vanity."

Darrin stormed out of the alley, leaving his crap behind and reciting a long litany of choice insults under his breath.

I turned my back on him. The alcove mostly sheltered me from a wind not yet satisfied by how cold the weather seemed already. The spell board boiled my blood enough that I barely noticed the wind that reached me.

Adam had given regular people a cheat sheet. He'd made it unnecessary for them to learn the basics of magic, leaving them too ignorant to avoid fundamental magical dangers.

I glowered up at Thoth's Eye.

Ought to march up there and punch him in the face.

Despite the casual evils of the spell board, it made a far better guard against the icy rain when wedged between walls above me. I rifled Darrin's care package. Beneath the component nodule, I found Darrin had also included a pleasant surprise. The bag's recesses contained varying width strips of differently colored high-quality paper.

Working through his earliest training, Darrin had learned bits about my childhood and the sickness that had kept me cooped up in the house. He'd witnessed the resultant habit derived of countless idle hours filled by instruction books Mom brought me about origami. My Thoth workrooms had once teamed with numerous folded shapes born out of book after book.

Once more, fingers folded while the rest of me stilled. Muscle memory quieted distractions, allowing me to focus on architecting the path ahead. Unfortunately, my fingers only controlled a portion of the old habit that had heralded emerging talent which eventually grew into a master's degree in arcanology.

I set a tiny pink crane down beside a baby blue frog and several differently colored spiders. The little paper avian didn't like the damp ground nor its hyperactive companions. It fluttered up onto a shoulder, perched to watch as folds brought about its brother. Spiders followed the bird up my torso onto the same shoulder but didn't leave their perch when the crane fluttered to the opposite side.

The crane's flight might not have disturbed the spiders, but the fluttering wings broke me from my reverie. My gut knotted. Even in the thin seam I'd found between mananets, mindless folding bliss populated my alcove with tiny, animated constructs.

A disgusted sweep of the hand knocked the evidence of Darrin's claims to the wet concrete. I shoved away the unused paper strips and dug into the leftovers from Hunter's Glade. Once more the delectable food satisfied my stomach but not my palette.

I dug the electric kettle from my seabag. Focusing on the appliance turned over and over in my hands helped me ignore my paper audience. Wasteland survival had bent my intellect toward salvage and jury-rigging. Each life in that hellish purgatory had been improved once I'd secured a means of heating water. In the real world, Edison blocks like the one I'd chosen offered even the homeless wireless power I could access if I could only engineer a receiver. If that task proved fruitless, cutting into building wires with bastardized scrap could still provide a means to power my kettle.

Puzzling over the kettle, I quickly determined the necessary parts and tools I'd need. It was too late to hike out to a thrift store. The Manger wasn't too far, probably had tools they'd let me use and table space to work.

Better to be patient than suffer ideological assault by that woman.

I stored the kettle for later, huddled beneath my spell board roof and pushed away any thought of the Manger. The Wasteland had been hard too. The harsh quasi-reality reinforced plenty of lessons I'd thought unnecessary in the real world—lessons I'd learned too late through the hardest means possible.

Sleep refused to come, and boredom consumed my leftovers. Paper strips dwindled, and the alley's origami populace crowded my small alcove. The rain lessened. The cold worsened. The air grew pregnant with malicious intent as a storm built up the strength to force its way over the Rockies and into our lives. Alley rats bustled in and out of their warrens, last minute hurried supply runs before the storm's descent.

I dozed.

An icy stillness woke me. My instincts jangled and I knew something was wrong before my eyes lit upon a scratched, bruised and bandaged man, watching me from the alley's mouth—Mister Familiar back to finish the job.

Old, yellowing light reflected off of his white bandages, standing out against dark skin to create a cockeyed checkerboard. He glowered in turns at me, the ground and at oddly still rats sheltering on fire escapes and beneath protruding pipes.

I remember him now, though I can't recall inflicting anywhere near that much damage.

Part of me couldn't believe my luck. His sister Eve had been on one of my project teams, a competent enough worker with a poorly hidden fetish for the magically sensitive. She hadn't hidden her jealousy nearly as well, but as it hadn't interfered with her work, I'd refused to have her let go despite Thecia's insistence.

I never touched her, but I understand why her brother might feel a need to avenge what he believes I did.

A new thought struck me.

Were Eve's accusation her idea or Thecia's own jealousy?

Eve's brother hadn't seemed interested in enlightenment during our first beating, so I didn't waste my breath. I'd experienced enough violence to last several lifetimes. As long as he left me alone, he could glare all he wanted.

He wandered off at some point when watching him stand there bored me into a doze. Rodent cries woke me just after dawn. The cat I'd driven off harassed a discarded chip bag. Distressed cries escaped his cornered prey, heating my otherwise frozen limbs. Leaping to the rescue abused my still sore body.

The cat darted tight circles around its quarry, hissing like I were the devil himself. I scooped up a rock and bounced it into the angry little beast. It recoiled and growled, but refused to retreat enough that its prize could escape.

My approach forced it away, but it darted in quick as lightning to bat the bag and retreat once more.

"You're just not going to learn, are you?" If I'd had chalk or a marker, I might've drawn a fifth resonance circle around the bag and let the cat beat his head against the impenetrable barrier. Instead, I fetched a handful of origami spiders and dropped them around the old chip bag. I stepped back, folding my arms and noticing an adult rat peeking out of their warren entrance.

Despite the cat's brave terror tactics to harry its trapped pray while I guarded the bag, my retreat made it suspicious. Yellow eyes flit from me to prey and back.

I waited.

The cat lowered its body and slunk forward. The adult rat squeaked objections and rushed out of its warren as the cat extended a paw toward the bag's opening. The minefield of paper spiders swarmed the cat, leaping onto its coat. Kitty leapt three feet straight upward. He growled and yowled, spun and batted the harmless animated paper away. A spare few moments of assault sent the cat bounding away, paper spiders fluttering off its coat to the alley floor.

I returned to my alcove. The adult rat warily wove through the spiders skittering around the bag and led its offspring back to the warren without any creepy gestures.

The storm fell, keeping the world in icy twilight. It's possible that my formerly pampered life had sheltered me, but the continuous rain and cold seemed out of character, even for the Pacific Northwest. I needed better shelter than the spell board offered, or at least a means of staying warm.

Wait, the spell board.

I lifted my eyes to the makeshift roof. The pre-inscribed circles offered me both shelter and a way to keep warm. I weighted desire against knowledge. If I didn't do something to protect myself, the elements could very well kill me. If I let myself dabbled in magic even once, rationalizing continued use would become easier and easier. The shivering of my origami entourage solidified my reality.

I have no choice. I'll do what I have to now then find a way to prevent needing to rely on magic in future.

I reached out to the mananet, drawing in power and a false warmth much like alcohol. A quick evaluation of my alcove recommended a cylindrical circle rather than spherical or conical.

A magical circle could really be any geometric shape based upon magician's will or, in the case of artificial circle constructs, the runes inscribed. They provided wizards of old with the magical equivalent of highly specialized containment—like a petri dish that acidic fungus couldn't devour. Thoth's spell board circle included no runes—flexible, but only for someone with actual magical know-how.

The limited strength of the mananet edges enveloping the area slowed the formation of my fifth resonance circle. A century without magic use further hindered the barrier's build up through the soft blue-white of first resonance to the milky white of fifth, but eventually, a magical cylinder encased me. The purely physical barrier kept splashing rain out. At higher magnitude, fifth rez could've blocked the wind too. There wasn't enough available magic to reach that magnitude, and even if there had been, there'd have been nothing left to allow air permeation so I wouldn't suffocate.

Since my fifth rez circle couldn't block the wind, I layered a translucent green sixth rez within the fifth to create a fifth-sixth combined circle undercut by a scent like burnt popcorn. I settled in, wistful of a book or something else to help me wait out the day. I couldn't help but smile as my little shelter slowly warmed, the sixth rez preventing the nonmagical energy of my body heat from escaping the circle's boundaries.

Protected from the elements and reasonably warm, I slept.

The first gunshot missed me but abraded my face with showering brick. Sleep fled a hasty retreat, not even leaving its remains in my eyes. A shadow loomed from within night's darkness at the alley entrance. The same tired streetlamp reflected from Eve's brother's bandages—Caleb I suddenly remembered, but Caleb's face remained in shadow.

Nothing in my upbringing prepared me for dodging bullets. I reached my will up through misgivings and rushed restoration of my fifth rez barrier not with the thin mananet but my own energies. Cylindrical light sprang down around me with an audible pop. Dizziness washed through me, almost sabotaging my desperate expenditure of my very limited energies.

The sudden magical light or maybe second thoughts over killing another human being slowed Caleb's next shot. His gun's thunder echoed off the alley walls. Concentric rings exploded along the circle's bend from a bullet impact that otherwise would've struck near my heart. He fired again, a less accurate shot with similar results.

Why is he shooting from the alley mouth?

His next shot was better, but his attention only stayed on me until the rippling light stopped it once more. My shield weakened. I drew on the mananet to stabilize my defense as best as I was able. Minimizing temptation by choosing a home almost bereft of mananet nearly cost me my life.

As one of the few humans capable of controlling magical forces without some sort of artificial construct, I could both use my own energies and hold magical power within me for spells. Had I been living well-fed inside a safe tower, maintaining the fifth rez circle wouldn't have been a problem. If I'd been within reach of a stronger mananet or in an intricately prepared circle designed for maximum mana efficiency, the barrier could've protected me indefinitely.

I was a homeless ex-con struggling to feed myself and fend off the elements. Fifth rez circles weren't all that costly, but dispensing kinetic energy of bullet impacts ramped the costs considerably— particularly using a crappy spell board.

Sirens filled the distant night.

My attention shifted back to my attacker. Caleb sidestepped, and the light illuminated a fearful expression. I followed his attention to a rat sitting up on a fire escape, and the glowing, glowering electric blue eyes fixed on my attacker.

My breath caught.

One set of glowing eyes became two then four then eight. Rats rose onto their back haunches around the alley. Eyes lit with magic, and the power behind my circle's magnitude intensified, thickening the shield.

The sirens sounded close when he turned and ran.

The glowing eyes vanished one at a time until only a single set peered at me from across the alley. The rat—still on its back haunches—stepped toward me. A police car rushed to a stop with a second on its tail.

Blue-uniformed officers scanned the alley from within their cars before exiting cautiously. I doused the circle. The sudden lack of light drew their attention.

"Don't move."

I hadn't planned on it but saw no reason for stating so. One officer held back while three others approached in a spread out pattern. Light flashed in my face, and I fought the urge to shield my eyes. It took a moment to realize my blindness hadn't come from a flashlight.

The lead officer spoke with exaggerated slowness. "Wheeeere... diiiiid... heeeee... gooooooo?"

"We must move you."

I looked down into a rat's glowing, blue eyes. Behind the rodent, a horde raced across the alley surface while another group scurried along an oblong infinity symbol. Whatever they were doing seemed to be to my benefit, so I resisted the urge to recoil from the little beast—well, mostly.

If my repulsion offended him, he didn't show it.

Up close the rat's fur resolved into some kind of cloak rather than a skin-tight coat. Beneath, the anthropomorphized rat wore short trousers, a tiny knife and a waistcoat complete with a silver chain leading to a pocket and possible pocket watch. He reminded me of a hyper-real, CGI Rattigan from the Disney cartoons.

"Please, Magus, into the dumpster." He gestured to the dumpster that had nearly killed me. Other rats boosted each other up its side in an elaborate cheerleader's pyramid.

"But I'm the victim. Caleb shot at me."

The rat speaking to me in English with a faint Germanic accent pointed at them. "These law keepers smell of fear and anger. You are safer hiding. Please."

"They'll search the dumpster."

"Trust us to see to that."

I looked once more at the police. They'd responded to the shots, but I didn't like my choices as a homeless ex-convict with Caleb and his revolver no longer on the scene. I didn't have a gun for them to blame for the shooting, but I was only just out of prison.

Rat might have a point.

I hurriedly climbed into the dumpster, thankful it had been emptied recently. A rat called me a nasty name when I almost trod on its tail dropping into the dumpster's recesses. "Sorry, sorry."

"Crouch or kneel, please." The first talking rat said.

It took a lot of will to crouch in the circling swarm of filthy creatures. Their spokesman didn't look like an actual rat, and plague-carrying vermin didn't typically have glowing eyes. Rationalizing the differences overcame the little boy screaming at me to run for my life.

Magic wrapped a swirling sphere of dark energy around me like an inky soap bubble, blocking out the lingering rot smell from the dumpster with the taste of cinnamon-spiced clover honey.

The first officer spoke outside in the alley. "Spread out and find him."

"And be careful," another said. "He may be armed."

"Jackson's right. Slow and cautious."

The spokesrat bowed at the waist, addressing me in a whisper. "I am Kenrith, father of this warren."

"Eli. What are you?"

"We are one of many rhet tribes whose lineage stretches back to the first ancient Rhoed."

The dumpster lid flew open. An officer pointed crossed wrists bearing gun and flashlight inside. His nametag labeled him Flowers. "Just a little garbage."

"Could he be hiding beneath it?" Jackson asked.

Flowers reached in, pushing empty air with this flashlight. "Nothing."

I shot Kenrith a look.

"Glamour." He mouthed silently.

Glamour?

Despite Kenrith's matter-of-fact expression, real glamour shouldn't exist in the world.

Dear God, they're fey. They're supposed to be extinct.

"Sergeant Donaldson?"

"Wha'cha got, Winslow?" Jackson said.

"Bunch of spell components, but no weapons," Winslow said.

"Don't touch anything else," Donaldson said. "Dispatch, this is sergeant Donaldson on the shots fired, I need SMILE on the scene."

I cringed. SMLE, Seufert Fells Magical Law Enforcement, had been the department that had arrested me before. They weren't exactly known for insightfulness—take their misspelled acronym for example. They'd arrive with the same Thoth-provided tech I'd created for them to locate and track magic. They'd find an ex-con at the sight of a shooting, decide I somehow magicked away the gun and arrest me—if I was lucky enough that Adam hadn't paid them to do something worse.

"Kenrith, can mage sniffers detect glamour or other fey magic?"

Kenrith frowned, glancing at the other rhet. His nod was slow in coming. "Yes, it is likely, but we can't hide you in our small spaces, and we cannot risk our matron to connect them into something big enough to fit you."

"What about a second rez, wrapped outside your glamour so the fey magic couldn't be detected?"

"It would be detected itself."

I sighed. "I'm surprised you're managing this with as thin as the mananet is here."

Kenrith gave me a flat look.

"What?" My brow furrow.

It isn't like they could store much magic in such tiny bodies.

A smaller rhet slid inside the circle, earning dirty looks from the others carrying his share of the glamour spell. "Father? What if we hid him in trash instead of the illusion of trash?"

Kenrith sized me up. "Good, Ahbnar. Eli, stay still and be very quiet."

Without a further word, the soap bubble popped, replacing sweetness aromas with rotten stench. The entire swarm scurried up and out the dumpster left open by Flowers. Curiosity about the lurking officers ate at me, but I had no way to see them without exposing myself.

SMLE is on the way. If they find me hiding here, especially using magic to hide—well, it'll probably be more damning than a signed confession.

Several rhet rushed into the dumpster. A small, previously-invisible soap bubble popped, dumping soaked, melting cardboard atop me as they fled once more. More rhet appeared. Each group popped bubble after bubble of garbage over me. In short order, they spoiled all my attempts to stay dry and doomed my effort to remain clean.

"What do you think, Sarge? He stole a bunch of magic crap at gunpoint?"

"Good suggestion, Flowers," Winslow said. "But who was he shooting at?"

"Maybe he shot at some homeless thief to take the magic crap back," Jackson said. "Like some kind of vigilante."

"Maybe the three of you should be quiet and stay on guard until SMLE gets here," Donaldson said.

I really wanted to tell them Caleb ran off when he heard the sirens—well, when the rats all started to glow. The problem was, the police wouldn't believe anything I told them. They certainly didn't seem likely to believe Darrin had given me the spell board and components.

A squeal of brakes overdue for new pads announced the latest car's arrival some six eternities later. By the time the door slammed I wasn't only frozen and soaked, the reek of the piled garbage seemed to have seeped in past my clothes to permeate my skin.

"Who's in charge? What've you got?"

"Sergeant Donaldson, sir. We got a shots fired call. Figure in that alcove was hidden under cover of a fifth rez, mag three circle projected from that wedged spell board. He dropped the spell and vanished a moment later. We've been unable to find him, but we did find a stockpile of component nodules in addition to the board."

"Let me get this straight, some homeless junkie invoked a fully opaque fifth rez barrier to protect his magical stash, and since you lost him and couldn't figure out where he went, you called me to do your job?"

Donaldson's voice hardened. "I'm sorry to disturb you, Detective Brooke, but a magnitude three circle is impossible on an Edison block. Additionally, his spell board is like nothing I've ever seen."

The SMLE detective's heavy footfalls stomped nearer. "You expect me to believe he managed all that without a mananet?"

He's right. Rhets must've upgraded the shield somehow.

The heavy footfalls neared. "So, where is this pile of magical paraphernalia?"

"It was right there," Donaldson said. "Which one of you idiots moved the evidence?"

The rhets?

"I see," Brooke said. "Disappearing man? Disappearing evidence?"

"I would not have called SMLE without good reason, Detective."

The telltale oscillating whistle of a mana sensor reached my ears. "Well, I'll say this for you. There's quite a bit of residual magic on that dumpster. Did you bother to check behind or inside?"

"Flowers checked it, nothing but trash," Donaldson said.

"You're sure? What about a bolt hole?" Brooke asked.

"Sure, detective," Flowers said. "Even with only a glimpse, he was a big guy. I shifted enough trash to be sure he couldn't be hiding. Then I did a thorough check under and around the dumpster."

"Donaldson?" Brooke asked. "You sure this block isn't covered by mananet? There's an awful lot of magic around this alcove; actually, I'm picking up higher than residual all the way to the alley mouth."

"I checked the department map," Donaldson said.

"Right," Brooke grumbled. "You people are always Johnny-on-the-spot when it comes to keeping on top of updates."

"What are those?" Donaldson asked.

"Forensic drones," Brooke said.

My brows rose.

A sound like angry hornets filled the alley. A few minutes later their noise stopped flat. Brooke swore. "You had a mage here all right. Alteration and illusion auras indicate defense—probably that fifth resonance circle—and that he hid himself and ran away. There's also a very faint aura of evocation, but too small for any offensive spell I've ever seen. Whoever this mage is, he's long gone."

"So what do we do?" Donaldson asked.

"Cordon off the alley and wait for the full forensic team. They'll already be on the way."

"You're not staying?"

"They don't need me second guessing them," Brooke said. "Besides, the trail's cold, and if I don't hurry home dinner will be too. I'll look over their report in the morning."

◦6◦

CANNIBALISTIC BEAUTY

Kenrith and his people dug me out as soon as SMLE had gone, but not before my whole body was shaking from the cold.

Kenrith placed a finger over his pronounced front teeth and whispered. "We must go, Magus."

All I wanted to do was sleep, but that was the cold talking. My limbs shook more than they had when I'd first jacked out, but I managed to climb from the dumpster. My right arm, weak with cold and slimy with trash, lost its hold. I tumbled to the ground. My head cracked on the concrete. Two drunkenly weaving officers between me and my bag of clean, dry clothes glanced over but quickly lost interest.

I reached a hand toward my alcove.

"We can replace your losses and warm your flesh, but we must go quickly. We need your help, and it may be too late if the law keepers take you away," Kenrith said.

Why do a bunch of fey rats need my help? What choice do I have? Darrin? The Manger? I gestured for him to lead on.

It took more effort than I'd like to admit just to keep up with the rats running circles around me down the alley while maintaining the glamour keeping me from jail. My legs fought my efforts, often flagging to nearly trod or kick a rhet behind me. Six thousand blocks later, Kenrith's people piled atop one another to open a side door in an old theater.

They ushered me into an immaculate backstage area. I think they wanted me to keep going, but I collapsed in the first dry open area big enough.

"Magus, we cannot linger here."

Chattering teeth garbled my words. "I can't go any further."

A long blink later scraping noises heralded five space heaters. Rhet settled them into position around me, equidistant coils already glowing glorious orange.

I lay in the heat, still shivering and struggling to keep my teeth from jackhammering each other flat. Exhaustion and hypothermia drew me down toward the bottom of a dark well despite the five glowing suns.

Kenrith appeared next to my side, lips pressed together in a way that made his long front teeth seem even longer. He nodded. "You can sleep a moment, Magus. We will watch and see you take no harm."

I knew better. Knew I shouldn't. My body didn't care.

The scent of warm food drew me from darkness by my frostbitten nose. Pins and needles stabbed both fingers and feet, and my gut seemed to growl from within a deep ice age. I blinked at my surroundings. The heaters had been pitched downward at paper plates piled with a mishmash of foods. Noodles, bitten hotdogs, partial pizza slices dotted with gravel—all of it originated in places I'd never have considered as a source to quell my hunger.

I ripped the bitten section off the nearest hotdog and sank my teeth into mixed cola-soaked bun and salty goodness. I chewed the disquieting combination of flavors as I removed stones from atop greasy, cheesy pizza slices.

"Refresh and regain your strength with haste," Kenrith said.

"Thought you said you didn't have a space big enough for me."

He apparently understood me despite my stuffed mouth. "This is not a closed theater. Your kind will arrive very soon, and I only brought you here under strenuous objection."

Father of his warren or not, someone else is in charge.

I stuffed noodles down my throat by the handful until a pause brought white, furry evidence that the mushrooms weren't its only fungus. I shoved the plate away, struggling to my feet. Somewhere toward the theater's front, a set of doors slammed open.

"I have arrived," A woman shouted. Her laughter followed a moment later. "You may now all fawn and worship."

Kenrith tugged my sleeve toward a metal ladder. "This way, hurry."

My limbs still lingered mutinously asleep. The tiny rungs pressed painfully beneath my soles and the rough, pitted iron abraded my fingers like thorny sandpaper. I shifted my grip to the side poles until rhet scurrying up them, forcing my hands back to the rusty rungs.

"Hurry, Magus," Kenrith said. "And beware the sixth—"

The sixth rung broke free the moment I pulled myself up it. I plummeted the length of my other arm, jarring my shoulder socket with more pain I didn't need as the metal bar clanged against the ladder then clattered to the floor.

"What was that?" The concerned woman's voice seemed impossibly near. "Who's there?"

Just a bunch magical mice. No one who cares about you acting the diva.

Any trespass report to the cops would likely connect me to the alley shooting. I'd talked my way out of a few trespassing incidents in the past, but something told me my current appearance wasn't up to the job.

I rushed up the ladder for all I was worth. I made the platform with chest heaving and mutinous limbs ready to collapse. I wanted to flop down on the catwalk and rest, but her clopping high heels warned me to keep moving.

Ahbnar frantically waved me forward, and I scurried along behind other rhets to another short ladder. I climbed, crossed another catwalk and climbed again, running a desperate war of haste and quiet. Luckily, while my arms lacked the muscle I'd built in the Wasteland, my feet—no matter how sore—knew how to sneak away in hurried flight.

"Oh, my god!" The woman squealed.

I froze, head sweeping down toward the woman who'd almost spotted me so slowly I'm surprised I didn't hear it creak.

"Magus, I am so sorry," Ahbnar said. "It was my duty to see to your belongings, but in all the tidying up to remove all trace, I ran out of time."

Relieved at not being discovered, I finished my climb atop the shadowy roof of a control room. Ahbnar wrung his tail with his bottom lip held firm beneath his teeth. A sudden dread filled me.

Far below, the blond woman bounced around Darrin's bag, flapping her hands like butterfly wings. She whipped out her phone, punched a few buttons then shrieked into it. "You are the best agent ever!"

"Magus?" Ahbnar asked.

The hair on my arms and neck prickled to life. She had the sample components and the spell board. Darrin's video flashed through my thoughts as she settled the board on the ground near one of the make-up stations. She scanned the directions and socketed the component nodules into place with practiced ease.

She hurried to the curtain, peaked through and hurried back to the board. My sister had been big into college theater. She'd said casts were hardly shy about dressing and undressing around each other. This woman stripped naked in a flash and leapt onto the spell board.

Doubt that's what Zahda meant.

"Magus, what do we do?" Ahbnar asked.

Sound escaping my lips sounded distant. "We should try to stop her."

My knuckles slid up and down against one another.

I abandoned my hiding place in a rush. "Stop, don't use that!"

She raised her face as I clamored noisily back along the catwalks. Her delight melted to horror. She had her phone out as my slide down the first ladder impacted the ground hard enough to cost me my footing.

She stepped onto the spell board and touched the Thoth Eye on the wand. The moment a fifth rez circle sprang up around her, she did her best to keep her phone at her ear while covering herself.

"No, please, stop!" I cried.

The words she spoke into her phone took a moment to process, first due to low volume and second due to my own shock. "Hurry, he's trying to murder me!"

The spell board was new to me. It had to have a disable command built in just like the eyeSentinel, but I didn't know it. I dove to her feet. She screamed for help.

Fingers scrabbled at the board's edges, managing after several tries to pry up one end. I hadn't studied Glamour's instructions, but if I could steal her balance and make her release the wand, the circle should collapse.

Her calls for help became incoherent shrieks. She held the wand mere inches from my face.

Weak arm strained to lift the board and all her weight. The cheap elm splintered and snapped, throwing my weight forward against the barrier. I'd barely recovered and turned my attention to the component nodules when the police crashed through the back door.

I seized the nearest component nodule, trying to yank it clear.

Another cop tackled me from behind, not bothering to give the homeless man at the feet of the screaming naked woman any warnings.

I didn't struggle under the cop's weight, but I had to stop the actress from invoking Glamour and transforming into a monster. "Please, I'm not attacking her. We've got to get her off that board before—"

A heavy boot kicked the back of my head. Darkness swallowed me. A plunge into burning fluid woke me in time to choke on chemicals. Gloved hands jerked me out of orange sludge and dragged me toward a door marked "Wasteland."

The SMLE detective's voice escaped speakers somewhere out of my view. "Maybe you'll learn to tame that sick predator drive. This time you'll get five hundred years to learn the error of your ways."

My screams faded into the actress's delighted squeals. I pressed a hand to my left temple, massaging away the irritating throb.

"How?" Ahbnar asked. "Magus? How do we stop her?"

I tensed to charge the ladder for real, but I seemed chained in place by phantom wires that once jacked me into the Wasteland.

If the vast amount of power surging into the theater was any indication, either Glamour required an unreasonable amount of power or brick shards had damaged the board. Every rhet's nose came up. They held eerily still except their quivering whiskers.

She swept the wand into position and commenced the spell. Swarming pink motes wrapped around the actress. The scent of spring rain confirmed Glamour as the progeny of the druid ritual I'd used to create my own restoration spell.

Kenrith appeared above me in a hole I hadn't noticed. "No. Stop her!"

Magic coalesced around the actress. Thoth's Glamour spell drew in power far and above what the druid restoration spell ever had. Moment by moment, the actress became increasingly subsumed in light until she was only a shape.

Ahbnar sprinted across the rafters in a literal blur, trailing honest to goodness fairy dust. He dove off directly above her. His little body plummeted the thirty-foot drop. A pained shriek filled the air an instant before the tiny, furry projectile called Ahbnar careened into her wand hand.

At first, I thought her screams signaled outrage, but they didn't stop. Blood escaped the actress's mouth, running down her chin and throat. Furious agony ripped from her throat in a bestial snarl exposing a mouth full of small, dark fangs. Shoulder length hair lost its golden luster, becoming a dark, stringy mane.

Tan skin lightened to wrinkled, ashy brown only to be subsumed by some kind of mottled green mold. Dark hair sprouted from atop her shoulders and spread down her upper back and upper arms.

More hair sprouted a furry line upward from her inner thighs, across her stomach and between her four breasts to join that atop her shoulders. Brown spots appeared on bare skin, swelled in size as they darkened. Limbs shrank and thickened. Lithe fingers became gnarled claws. She raked them across her skin as if bursting pustules of rancid puss and leaving bloody tracks were luxurious pleasures.

Dear God, Adam, what have you done?

She froze. Her dark, shrunken nose darted back and forth. The actress's eyes sprang open. Vomit yellow sclera glowed around small black pupils, falling upon Ahbnar's still form.

She seized him, shoved him into her mouth. Ahbnar—either dead or unconscious—didn't scream as blood sprayed across the actress's face and wrinkled, naked chest

Small mercy I guess.

She sprang back to her feet, Ahbnar half consumed, and searched the rafters with deep, rapid sniffs. She sprinted to the ladder. Her clawed feet negotiated the climb as if running naked along vertical surfaces was her favorite pastime. The rhet nearest me shoved me toward Kenrith's hole, forming up in a defensive formation with the others.

"What are you doing?" I asked. "Run, I'll..."

Stop her? How am I going to stop her?

"Magus! We need you to help protect our1 matron," Kenrith said. "Hurry, we need what you call a fifth rez barrier."

I was torn between answering Kenrith's call and guarding the ladder. The former actress raced toward me with rhet blood spraying from broken, bitten bodies in each clawed hand.

"Magus, please!" Kenrith said. "They can only hold off the demi-goblin so long."

Demi-goblin? She's human...sort of.

Three steps propelled my jump into the hole. I wasn't sure why Kenrith needed me to draw a circle when his people had done such an excellent job with the earlier one, but if nothing else I could guard the small hole better than the control room roof.

Kenrith and his people rushed me through the attic space. Spears and tiny swords passed paw to paw back toward the hole and the assembling defenders. Battle cries, death screams, and high-pitched snarls filled the area behind and below me.

We turned hard into a small outcropping of attic, and my heart stopped. A glowing, snowy-white rhet twice Kenrith's size held out a silver Sharpie. Tiny bronze chains and white gossamer veils did nothing to hide her naked beauty.

Kenrith snatched the marker from her outstretched hand, shoved it into mine then seized two curved blades from the walls of her luxurious bower. "Draw, Magus!"

A hundred reasons why I couldn't and shouldn't draw a magical circle flashed through my mind. None of them stopped my hands. Ink trying to soak into plywood was an even poorer medium for a circle than that imprinted into the Thoth spell board. Unlike the spell board though, my marker danced through all the accompanying runes that allowed me to tune the shape and resonant frequency of the magical energy like a musician might his instrument. Sharpie-stained wood encircled both the beautiful rhet and myself in the absolute fastest protective circle I'd ever drawn.

Rhet flew head over tail into view. The perverted actress bowled into sight. Too dark blood ran from countless spear wounds and slices. She slid through a hard turn, toe claws digging furrows in the attic floor.

Kenrith stood his ground, blades poised but immobile. "Now, Magus. It must be now."

I sucked in all the power the mananet could hand me. When my draw exceeded that limit, a sweet, heady magic rushed into me in a dizzying wave. My will locked on the task. A milky white cone sprang to life around us just short of the ceiling.

The actress slammed into it with a sickening crunch. Her flattened nose gushed bright red blood down her face to join rhet blood staining her mouth. More drained into her throat, turning her snarls into gurgles. She beat her claws against the shield and howled.

Ruckus and cramped space leeched my attention. Nonetheless, I activated runes in careful sequence, tuning frequency for mana efficiency and barrier effectiveness until it sang a sweet, pure magnitude two note.

Through the thickened wall of swirling milk, Kenrith sliced a sword across each of the actress's inner thighs, bathing himself in her blood.

Other rhet swarmed her. She lashed out, screams and cries mixing with the rhet battle cries. It ended in moments. The actress lay dead, flaps of gouged flesh gaping as limply as the rest of her.

They killed her. Killed a human being.

Except she couldn't have been human. Her spells should've collapsed with either death or unconsciousness. She didn't change. The claims of the bus station ad sprang to mind.

<...true beauty is no longer just illusion...>

I released the magic holding the cone and stared through tears. An effort of will confirmed that no magic lingered in her eviscerated flesh.

"Thank you, Magus." The rhet matron laid a paw on my arm. Warmth and magic eased into my skin, feeling like a bubbling, hot spring.

I jerked away from her touch before the feeling reached my heart and cleansed away my anger. The rhet had been thrice over decimated in mere minutes. A woman lay dead in front of me, in part because of my actions pinning her between the rhet and my magical barrier.

I crawled away from the matron, tiptoeing around and over the actress's blood. I found a clean, dark corner, pulled my knees in tight and cried like I hadn't since the first time I'd had to kill in the Wasteland.

This is worse. This is real life.

The remaining rhet tribe hurried through gathering their dead. A brush of magic drew my attention. It became quickly apparent that rather than a threat, they were applying magic to clean up evidence of themselves and the battle's gore. I dropped my face into my arms once more.

Kenrith cleared his throat. "Magus?"

I didn't look up. "What?"

"Thank you for the life of our matron. We are in your debt. Young and inexperienced though she is, many magics are at her disposal."

"I want nothing to do with you, your matrons, or your magic."

"Matron," Kenrith corrected. "She is the last."

My head shot up. "The last anywhere?"

"All the matrons in Seufert Fells have been killed or taken by demi-goblins like this one you helped us slay."

The matron stepped up behind Kenrith. "Magus, though we are now in your debt, we-I beg of you a boon."

Kenrith stiffened.

"No," I said.

Kenrith bristled. "You will do Matron Biuntcha the courtesy of hearing her out."

"The magus is weary and troubled, Knight Kenrith," Biuntcha said. "We shall speak of this with him later."

"With respect, Matron Biuntcha, we have no time to waste if we wish the magus's spells to find the missing matrons."

"I don't have spells. I'm not a magus or mage or whatever, not anymore." I struggled to my feet. "I just want to be left alone."

Biuntcha's face fell. "You cannot exit until nightfall when your kind no longer occupies the theatre—that is unless you know transportation magic."

A cold hand tightened my chest. "What happened to the spell board and components?"

"We were not quick enough to stop her using them," Kenrith said. "But we were able to remove your spells, instruments and Ahbnar's remains before the other humans arrived."

"Come, Kenrith, we must honor his wishes. We shall leave you in peace." Biuntcha returned to her bower.

Kenrith met my eyes a long time. "We were surprised when a magus took up residence in our alley, but you intervened to protect my children, so we did not drive you out."

Despite his size, I sensed no bravado behind his claims.

"I never asked for your interference."

"We saved you from your attackers to square that debt, but continued to protect you in the hope that you might help us in return. Protecting you and your magical instruments cost me many children tonight. You owe us a blood debt."

I opened my mouth to refute his claims, but despite myself, I felt partly responsible for his losses.

"You've seen the magic and the monsters your kind have unleashed on us. You can go more easily where we cannot. We need your help. You are a magus, the wise. Why don't you act like it?"

"I just want to be left alone."

Kenrith shook his head. His apparent disgust prickled my pride. "Very well, Magus. I will leave you alone. You may hide here under our protection until nightfall. After, you are on your own, but I warn you. Use your knowledge of us to advantage yourself, and we shall finish what we stopped your kind from doing. We will not suffer a warlock in our territory."

He left me in shadow.

My spell, perverted to provide shapeshifted beauty for the terminally vain, had transformed the actress into a ravening monster. She'd killed the rhet who'd helped me. Their bodies stacked on the far end of the attic beside the actress's corpse.

My hands are clean. Thoth perverted the spell. Adam refused to pull it from the market.

I turned my hands over. In the dim light, the stains from the rusty ladder were black smears easily mistakable for dried blood. Part of me had wanted to believe Darrin's little movie was an elaborate fake meant to covertly pull me back into working for Thoth without the benefits I'd owned prior. More, I'd insisted Thoth's crimes, if real, were Adam's problem for which Karma would eventually visit.

An icy light glowed from within Biuntcha's bower. Injured rhet bowed out of the alcove newly healed.

The last matron. Without her, how long before these fey join their extinct kindred?

I shook once more, cold from magic, shock, and rage. I didn't want any part of Thoth or other people's troubles.

Damn you, Adam.

∘7∘

HARD HOMELESS TRUTHS

K enrith appeared, a half dozen of his number depositing a camouflaged infantry backpack stuffed with clothes and a blanket at my feet. They presented a small duffel bulging with lunchroom milk cartons, apples and a ball of mashed together sticky buns. Behind them, the spell board and components lay beside the floor stains from the actress's corpse.

"It is safe for you to do whatever you desire," Kenrith said. "We go to our small places where your kind cannot reach our matron. I thank you for her life and protecting my sons. Goodbye, Magus."

They left me alone in the theater attic before I could answer. The attic itself offered far better shelter than the streets outside, but people would come looking for the actress sooner or later. I didn't know where the rhet had deposited the body, but a thorough theater search would eventually uncover her blood.

I'd rather not be present when they start looking for a killer.

It took several trips to safely transport everything down to the backstage area. I couldn't leave the spell board or components lest they link me to both murder and the previous night's gunfire. I opened one of the milk cartons and drank down the creamy liquid. Crunching the little ice crystals left my teeth aching. A shift of movement pulled my gaze into the shadows. Nothing.

They've gone to their small places.

I finished the milk and tightened my fist to crumple the carton. Kenrith's words tumbled slowly from my lips. "We can't hide you in our small spaces, and we cannot risk our matron to connect them into something big enough to fit you."

Connected small places?

I turned the carton over in my hands. Golden jacks on my wrist caught the light.

Kenrith and Darrin might have a point. Once a spell architect...what could a little magic hurt?

My envisioned future flashed through my thoughts once more, causing an involuntary shiver.

It could cost me five hundred years, that's what.

Folding the milk carton flat without breaking the container anymore, I slid it into my new backpack. Leaving set off the back door alarm. I hurried to the nearest street, turned onto the main sidewalk and took a circuitous route back to my alley.

Yellow police tape blocked either end of the alley.

Now where do I go?

A grumbling stomach convinced me to do my thinking while drinking another milk. I folded the container and put it with the first before heading up the alley toward the Eye. I crunched a sweet, red apple down to only stem and seeds to sate my still demanding stomach while I searched for a new home.

An alley half-way between the theater and my first haunt offered a slightly larger alcove. The space backed up against a chain-link fence made opaque by green slats woven into its mesh.

I peered over the fence top. If push came to shove and demanded rushed escape, the ten-foot fence could be scaled, but escaping required me to wade through countless years of discarded, rain-melted trash laying between my fence and its brother beyond.

Maybe I can clean it out later.

I scrutinized the fence. Suspended from bolts affixed to bricks on either side, there seemed no easy way to add hinges for quick egress. I set the spell board down against the fence, finding no damage to the inscribed circle from bullet-shattered brick. I settled atop the board and considered a fifth-sixth rez circle to protect me from the elements. Instead, I wrapped myself in the olive wool blanket and settled in for sleep.

"Finally." Sunny's voice woke me. "There you are."

I blinked up at her, trying to bring her into focus in the waning twilight.

"I was worried when you didn't return. When I saw the police tape where Grace said he'd seen you, I feared the worst." She extended a foil-wrapped ball. My sideways glance at the ball evoked a pretty little laugh. "We ran out of Tupperware."

She peeled the foil back to expose a cracked hamster ball filled with leftovers. My stomach grumbled on general principle.

"I don't want anything from you."

"Hope you don't have an issue with your food touching." She shrugged, set the ball down and dug into an oversized purse. She placed thick wool socks and a rain poncho atop the ball.

"I said I don't want anything from you."

"I heard you, which is why I'm just abandoning these things right here." She tucked away hair fallen free when she bent. "Hope they're found by someone who appreciates them."

"You have got to be the most stubborn woman I've ever met."

She let out a low whistle. A smile filled her face. "Wow, Mister Pot, tell me more about myself."

Something small shifted in the shadows. I let my irritation show. "Why are you here, Sunny?"

"First timers don't last long on the street. Normally, you might have time to develop your survival skills, but not with this weather. I wanted to make sure you had what you needed."

"Why didn't you send Grace or someone? It's not safe for a woman to be out in the alleys at night."

"God protects me."

"Faith is hardly protection against—"

"Violent criminals?" She smirked. "His rod and staff, they comfort me. Not to mention my eyeGuardian, Sentinel and a Smith and Wesson .38 special."

My gaze shifted from her to the goodies and back.

She dug Styrofoam cups and a thermos out of her bag. She laid another poncho on the ground, sat opposite me, poured steaming dark liquid into a cup and offered it with a smile. "Coffee?"

Heavenly odor caressed my nose, vapors spreading warmth deep into my lungs. "You're not just going to go away, are you?'"

She set the coffee in front of me. "How are you?"

"I still don't need a friend." The coffee tasted as good as it smelled. Warmth flowed down my throat to spread out from my stomach.

She chuckled, adding a plastic thimble of cream and two sugars to her own. She sipped, eyes brightening. "Everyone needs a friend, Elias."

A scowl overwhelmed coffee's warmth. "How do you know my name?"

"Probably irritate you if I said God whispered it into my ear."

"Yeah, it would."

She shrugged. "Grace dug up your name from one of those rags that publish arrests and releases."

"My past is none of your business."

"True." She sipped her coffee. "Would you like to talk about it?"

"No, I don't want to talk about it."

"Not even what you went through in the Wasteland?" she asked.

My cup hit the ground hard enough to slosh over my hand. "No."

"I can't really imagine." She shook her head. "Some say the Wasteland is a custom hell, designed with the convict's crimes in mind."

If looks could kill, I'd probably have ended up in jail again.

Despite my expression, she smiled and didn't let her gaze waver.

"I don't want to talk about it."

She glanced around. "This where you intend to stay? We still have a bed, and there are other halfway houses."

"Here will do."

She finished her coffee and stood once more. "Well, when the loneliness gets to you, I'm a good listener with a warm dining room and an always ready coffee pot."

"I don't get lonely." I glanced at the abandoned ball. "Stay safe, there's a lot of bad elements around."

She cocked her head. "You included?"

I shrugged.

"Stay warm." She spun toward the nearest street and strolled away, humming merrily to herself. The woman was all kinds of too cheerful. A sudden urge to trail her—solely to ensure her safety—tickled the hair on my neck, but I let her go. She had God on her side after all.

The next day was cold enough my food didn't need a refrigerator. Even so, between Kenrith and Sunny, I ate like a king. When my stomach was full, I wrapped the blanket around me and the poncho around that. I drank and saved another folded milk cartoon then heaved myself up to collect all my things. On a whim, I scaled the fence, found a black garbage bag without any apparent holes, dumped its contents and returned with it to my alcove.

It took quite an effort to assemble all of my belongings, explaining why shopping carts were so useful to my fellow homeless. I lugged my belongings uptown to Gateway Park. The public restroom had a deadbolt which could be activated from the inside. I locked it, turned on the sink's hot faucet handle and stripped off my shirt while I waited for the water to warm.

It didn't.

I washed in haste and cleaned the garbage bag. My shirt clung to shivering skin seated beneath the stubbornly cool air of the hand dryer. When the bag and I were mostly dry, I returned to my alcove. I arranged the component nodules on the ground. They watched me reprovingly as I ate sticky buns, procrastinating as long as I could.

My walk back and forth to Gateway Park allowed me sufficient time to dwell on what I'd learned about and from the rhet. True, their help had been meant to force help from me. No one likes being manipulated. Regardless of where the scale of favors and debts tilted, I felt responsible for all the rhet that had died to protect me.

I picked up the nodules, turning them over in my hand while my gut twisted like it was connected by sympathetic magic. Glamour had killed the actress and Kenrith's people. My perverted spell secretly imprisoned countless others behind Thoth Corp's benevolent façade. I was involved whether I wanted to be or not. The plan to remain separate from magic had been meant to encourage building a new life far from temptation that might land me back in prison. Sticking to the plan should've been easy.

Unfortunately, Dad taught us the importance of squaring our debts.

I took a deep breath and extended my will into the mananet. Warmth flooded into me that had nothing to do with the temperature. It wrapped me all at once a warm, comforting blanket and a childhood pet—reassuring, accepting and capable of biting my hand off.

Glamour created demi-goblins. Demi-goblins killed the rhet and took their matrons. Whatever corrupted the spell was to blame. I had no supporting evidence, but it seemed logical that if the matrons were still alive, they'd be near the source of the corruption.

Troubleshooting a problem is a craft composed of two parts logic and one part experience-derived instinct. Divide the problem into possible causes. Query it so that the resultant answer rules out one group of possibilities, and repeat until you derive the solution.

Glamour was composed of spell board, component nodules, wand, and runes. Wands weren't much more than wireless mananet receivers, so ruling it out seemed prudent. Runes employed in the wand were the magical equivalent of computer chips. They could be part of the problem, but I didn't have the equipment to check them, and Darrin would've started there. My spell board was new. It hadn't corrupted any of the circles I'd used, ergo the board wasn't part of the problem. That left the components.

I sighed.

My initial inspection of the nodules offered me no clues as to what had perverted Glamour. I daren't cast the spell again without further information. The nodules were designed to prevent tampering with the components within, which meant tracking down where the nodules were assembled.

Find the components, I find the corruption. Find the corruption, I find the matrons, deliver the information to Kenrith, and I never have to deal with the rhet again.

The government-regulated seeking spell Thoth sold consumed simple thread to create a connection from the magic user to the sought item. The thread couldn't survive the energy required for seeking long distance or over an extended period. Unlike the thread connecting caster to object, the components in my hand had been part of a greater whole. They'd been born and imprisoned in their container in a particular location.

My will wove a magical cord, anchored on one end to the material components inside the nodules. I stowed the spell board inside the garbage bag with the rest of the elements and hid the bag with the detritus beyond the fence.

I hitched the rest of my belongings onto my back and trudged North toward the seeking spell's riverward tug. Daylight filled my trek with even more storefront illusions hawking things I deserved and couldn't live without. Crowds bustled around me, faces wooden and purposefully looking past me. Other homeless sat along the way against city buildings, hats and cups and cardboard signs begging for spare change.

I would not join the ranks of beggars, but I inclined my head in acknowledgment as I passed each. The tracking spell throbbed behind my eyes as mananets waxed and waned. I drew in power to fuel the spell across leaner blocks. Delight welled up within me, forcing me to struggle against the whispered siren song of joy from holding power within me.

Don't get used to this. Seeking spells are easy and don't take components. I need to stay away from magic. Hell, if SMLE catches me using any *spell, they'll assume I violated my restrictions.*

A shiver shot through me at the thought of returning to the Wasteland.

The buildings around me shrank gradually, melting from glass high rises to concrete industrial buildings over dozens of blocks.

Sidewalks ran a zig-zag path rather than always paralleling the tug's demands. The pull drew me to the rebuilt riverfront area along the edge of the Columbia. Most of Seufert Fells's industry had been rebuilt on the Washington side of the river. I cursed myself for not thinking ahead.

I'm looking for a factory. Should've headed for one of the bridges from the start.

With a sigh, I trudged eastward keeping to the sidewalks edging the river as far away across a grassy strip from the tourist shops and peoples' dirty looks as I could manage. I snacked another small apple as I headed toward Fells Overlook Bridge.

Upstream awaited the rusting girders and hulking concrete remains of Seufert Fells's once-essential and long-destroyed Pacific General Electric hydroelectric plant. The old accident had long ingrained Seufert Fells's people with the belief that magic and technology were antagonistic to one another. Technology and arcanology companies decrying each other's evils had reinforced the belief to support their propaganda supremacy war.

The whole thing was wrong thinking. Technology and magic weren't antagonistic so much as early understanding of each hadn't yet evolved to an understanding of ways they could cooperate. Magic was merely science we hadn't yet worked out.

Not that the truth matters...not anymore.

Riverfront that had grown up as industry in The Dalles had been replaced after an experiment blew up The Dalles dam, hydroelectric plant, and the countryside for thirty miles. Usually, hydroelectric power is safe, but a bunch of Pacific General Electric executives— without any knowledge in engineering or arcanology—decided to make it otherwise.

They insisted that if the mananet could be used to power buildings, they could divert that revenue back to themselves by electrifying magic for The Dalles's citizenry. Since most bodies of moving water swept magic from some upstream source down their riverbeds in a kind of undercurrent, they figured they could somehow collect that potential cash flow along with the turbine-pushing waters. PGE engineers—may their scattered pieces rest quietly—did their best.

Boom.

There were probably people who knew what had caused the explosion. Rather than educate the populace, they let fear and rumor rule the day, fueling the ignorance about magic and technology.

Probably just to keep hobby arcanologists and survival nuts from trying to use raw magic to power their own little generators.

My eyes drifted to the hydroelectric plant's remains just upriver. The concrete spillways gaped open. The concrete supported in the maintenance road had been blown apart on the southern end nearest the power generators. Even after so many years of rain, burn marks lingered in the dam's jagged remains, progressively lightening the further they got from the explosion's center.

Too late in the year, the fish ladders for spawning salmon offered little activity, though a private boat sat in the locks waiting to be lowered downriver. I stopped to watch the operation. I'd seen it all before, but not in over a century. I wasn't over the moon as water lovers go, but nothing in Wasteland's frontiers matched the Columbia.

A screech of tires and blaring horn whipped me around. A twenty-something woman leaned backward from an orange convertible, flipping off the white panel van that had apparently stopped suddenly. A LUX containing two wide-eyed teens stopped just in time to avoid both before following the convertible. Fishing was prohibited on Fells Overlock Bridge, so I checked the van's tires.

Doors sprang open. Three masked thugs seized me. Two threw me inside, jumped in immediately after and started pummeling me. The third leapt into the driver's seat, slammed his door and floored the gas.

Caleb ripped his mask off and spit in my face. "You aren't conjuring help against us again. I checked. Magic doesn't work over running water."

What? That's horseshit.

My backpack held off some of the damage until it was ripped off and hurled at the closed backdoors. Motion and a low ceiling minimized the amount of room they had, but they made the best of it kicking me from both sides. The driver seemed the smallest, leaving me to fight back against Caleb and Ugly. The confined space worked for them but not me. Every time I uncovered myself to strike back, the other went to town. "Caleb, stop. I never touched Eve. Ask her if you don't believe me."

"After what you did to her, she'd say whatever your magic brainwashed her to believe." Caleb turned his next kick to my face. "Besides, I can't ask her, and you know it."

Blood gushed from my broken nose, muffling my yell. "What are you talking about?"

The van slid to a stop on some kind of gravel. Ugly threw me at the door. I bounced off, so he did his best to throw me through the old steel cargo van again. Tiny got one door open. I hit the middle, tripping over my backpack and sprawling out the door onto the southern end of some riverfront construction project. Tiny took advantage of my slow reactions to get in a few kicks of his own.

Caleb shoved Tiny away. He yanked me up by the old army jacket and slammed a fist into my already screaming face. "She's dead. Car accident right after the trial."

"Kind of suspicious," Ugly hit me. "Don't you think, sicko?"

Oh, God, did Adam kill her to keep her from changing her testimony? Is Eve dead because of me?

"No witness for the appeal," Tiny kicked me. "How could you do that, and to your own kind?"

"He ain't one of us." Ugly drove a fist into my gut. "Nobody who makes it big like this traitor came up in our neighborhood."

"Unless they sell out their own," Tiny added.

"Like how you did my sister," Caleb said.

Caleb still wanted blood rather than truth. I tried to fight back, but the van ride left me in bad shape. Ugly and Tiny seized my arms while Caleb went back to the van. He returned a moment later with massive, thick chains.

They're going to drown me. Think.

Several scenarios played out in my mind, a fist or kick snapping me back from one death after another. Finally, one scenario offered a chance at survival. I summoned all the strength I had, kicked out at Caleb. I twisted free of Tiny, stomping backward onto his instep to encourage his release of my arm. I shoved the heel of my freed hand toward Ugly's throat.

He blocked.

No, that should've—

Caleb swung the chains over my head and yanked them back into my neck, effectively ending my riverward escape. Tiny kicked me in the balls. White hot pain shoved nausea toward my constricted throat, and a high pitched whine filled my ears.

Chains wrapped me thug to thug until I was trussed up with zero chance of wriggling free. Caleb's fist slammed into a kidney exposed between chain loops. His Mexican-food stinking breath heated my neck. "You be sure to apologize to Eve on your way to hell."

A brand new, oversized diesel passenger truck threw gravel, skidding to a stop between us and the river—two wheels on the retaining wall separating the site from the river. The first man out the passenger door addressed Caleb with a thick European accent. "Let him go."

"This is none of your business," Ugly said.

"We are making it our business," he glanced at two Ugly-sized men with bulging, tattooed biceps stretching their polo shirt sleeves. "Yes?"

The first cracked his knuckles. "This looks like our kind of business to me, boss."

The boss narrowed his eyes. "Maybe we're wrong, Mihail. Maybe they should tell us what their problem is with him."

"Look at him," Ugly said.

"He's a filthy criminal," Caleb said. "A blight on society that needs to be sent to hell."

"I'd be careful who you call a criminal," Mihail growled with an even thicker, more eastern European accent.

"Particularly when attempting murder in broad daylight," the boss said.

Caleb closed the distance looking down at my would-be savior. "Look, whoever you are. This is a family matter."

"You may call me Duval." Duval gestured at me "We're family too."

"You don't look related," Ugly said.

Duval shrugged.

I didn't catch the signal, but Ugly let go of me and decked Mihail at almost the same moment Caleb slammed a fist into Duval's gut. Tiny grabbed me around my midsection from behind, lifted me off my feet and fast shuffled to the retaining wall over the Columbia.

The truck's driver gunned the truck engine. The bed shot backward into Tiny and me, sending us tumbling along the edge. The driver leapt out without killing the engine. He grabbed Tiny around the head. Tiny kicked me with both boots.

The water swallowed me within a moving wall of icy wetness. The current did its best to take me, but the heavy iron chains dragged me down. I careened off a sunken lip of wall, rolled off the concrete and sank deeper into Columbia's muddy heart. I writhed side to side, struggling to hold my breath and somehow free myself from the anchor wrapped around me.

The chains refused to release me. My lungs strained against held breath. Tiny might as well have nailed me into my coffin.

Think!

⋅8⋅

ANGRY GUARDIANS

There wasn't enough breath left in my lungs to wait for a rescue that probably wasn't coming. Physical means wouldn't free me in time. My above-average intelligence came up dry when it came to thinking my way out of the restraints.

What does that leave me?

The answer might've been less palatable if I weren't dying. Construction and expansion of the Washington side of things should've meant a mananet.

Please let there be a mananet.

I reached upward for magic, but no mananets answered me. Before resigning myself to drowning, I reached into the river for whatever the PGE executives had hoped to harvest. A small amount of magic coursed around me in the water, but a somehow muffled yet more potent source tugged my attention deeper beneath near the riverbed. I gave the new source my attention.

Drawing in a sip, a firehose of power shot into me. My extremities burned like a body-wide throat searing from cheap tequila shots.

A fire hose...the emergency breathing charm!

The idea and possibly approaching death left me giddy, almost as if I were high—not that I'd ever jeopardized my one true resource with drugs. One of the early emergency services spells we'd produced had been an emergency respiration bubble patterned off old deep sea diver helmets.

The short-term spell filtered air, collecting the carbon and ash on the globe's exterior until air blockage nearly cut off the user's oxygen. We'd engineered the incantation from a hollow, walnut-sized glass bead inscribed with Egyptian hieroglyphs representing their god Shu. Inside, we'd included a bit of cheesecloth, ostrich feather and a chip of dry ice.

Except cooling and filtering already present air won't help me underwater.

A giggle released little bubbles to tickle up my face.

Bubbles? I'll boil the water and slurp in the bubbles like what that SCUBA divemaster taught me to do with a stuck mouthpiece surge valve. What was his name?

Something slipped by in the water, stealing my train of thought. The distraction barely had to work to peel away my fractured thoughts.

Something's wrong. High? No nitro...nitrogen...what kind of idiot am I?! Heating river water won't release sufficient oxygen to save me. It will just leave me breathing steam.

Circles dominated the lives of first-year arcanology students. These most elemental exercises gave them the tools to experiment safely with different kinds of magic and were almost immediately abandoned. As a research mage, I'd employed them extensively.

A magical circle is essentially a line without beginning or end. Research into the topic never revealed definitive evidence of why the construct was called a circle, because it didn't have to be a circle at all—certainly not a perfect circle. The shape wasn't as important as a complete circuit and the controlling will behind it.

I closed my thumb and forefinger and conjured a fifth rez cylinder the thickness of a quarter. Shaping the circle to the degree necessary required a flexible imagination and steady focus. Imminent drowning steeling my will, I grew my cylinder without ever letting any more water in than what it had initially contained. Will slowly expanded the shape into a long bottle. The larger it grew, the more water it displaced. Before I managed to flatten the construct and bend it beneath me into a vague gondola shape, buoyancy dragged my construct and wrist painfully upward.

A dark shape half my size shot past me in the water. Another followed it and another, these later nudged the milky white balloon barely gripped in my hand. A dark round face appeared right in front of me.

If I hadn't been struggling so hard not to breathe, I might have yelped at his sudden appearance. The dark head cocked sideways, turned away making a weird, high pitched bark. *River otters?*

Natural curiosity about the oddly-shaped balloon shimmering in my hand made a certain degree of sense, but they seized the chains still wrapped tightly around me. Swimming together, they turned me feet first presumably downstream. Teeth sank into the hand holding the circle. I lost my concentration with a yelp of pain and surprise. The small amount of water that I'd tried to breathe set me choking. I allowed the outward coughs meant to expel the water but fought any involuntary intake of breath.

An otter holding onto chains around chest pressed his mouth to mine and shoved fishy tasting breath into my mouth. Before I could tell him I only wanted to be friends, he shot upward out of sight. A moment later he returned, shoved more air into my mouth and laid his belly against my face, aborting any more attempts to breathe water.

Silt pressed against my underside. Otters tugged my legs side to side. River bottom grew slowly up and around my legs. If the otters took me into whatever their den was called under the water, I'd never get to air. Despite what could only have been two intentional transfers of breath, panic rose up. I fought to get away best I could in chains. The otter covering my face spun around. The sudden removal of his suffocating bulk almost caused me to inhale. He bit my ear.

I jerked away from him.

He bit me again as others pulled me waist deep into river bottom silt.

Wait, they're mammals. They breathe air. They can't sleep underwater so any den will have air. I stopped fighting. The otters wriggled me deeper into the mud, an otter digging frantically on either side of me.

The movement stopped. Mud and earth squeezed my already tight chest while I still fought to cough up breathed water into my mouth without inhaling.

Without the slightest bit of warning, I shot forward into the mud. A moment of panic set in as earth closed over my face. Gravity took me a moment later, and I fell in a deluge of water to a concrete floor ten feet below. The impact forced my held breath. I choked and gagged on my face as the flow of water deluging me tapered away.

When the fit subsided, I turned my head and might as well have swallowed water again. Among my other magical studies in college, I took great pleasure exploring obscure texts about cultures, belief systems, and other societies devoted to magic. I'd read accounts of what it felt like to tap the flow of ley lines sometimes referred to as mother's arteries, but until that moment I had never *seen* a river of wild, floating, raw magic.

Tapping into the source beneath the river—probably the ley line before me—had afflicted me with the relatively minor disorientation that I'd mistaken for nitrogen narcosis. The power pulsing from 'Mother's artery' overwhelmed me, leaving me temporarily nonsensical.

I stared dumbfounded and dizzied by a stream broader than I was tall that undulated in the air back and forth, up and down like a liquid abalone shell. Pearly white rather than merely milky and shot through with swirling rainbows of light, the free-floating energy coursed through the air down a tunnel of rock. Whenever undulation drew the ley line into contact with PGE's concrete, the artificial stone melted down the wall like tallow. I might've been able to crawl through the tunnel dug by the writhing river of magic, but if the magic pounding against my senses was anything to judge, the slightest brush of that power would leave me a burnt husk.

An otter raced around me, carving a sizable, oblong line onto the concrete with half an empty shell. A moment later a soft blue-white cylinder—dim in the ley line's brilliance—sprang up around me blocking the incoming waves of magic.

First rez circle.

A clink of chains alerted me to otters struggling to remove my bonds. I had no ideas as to their reasons, but I wouldn't argue. I had to help them untangle me. My shivering limbs slowed our progress despite the room's warmth. When the chains fell to the ground with a rattle, the otters crossed out of the circle without breaking it. They scurried to the far end of the room and sat all in a row on their haunches.

Struggling to my feet took more effort than I'd like to admit, partially complicated by the slick cement floor. I braced myself, exited their circle and stepped nearer the ley line. Even trying to wall myself off from the magic, the dizzying waves throbbed against my skin. I'd like to claim I'd done so to warm myself faster, but truthfully, my curiosity streak is far more substantial than the common sense Dad tried to beat into us.

Stepping a bit too close made the largest otter bark a harsh, "Hah."

I backed away and glanced at the nearby wall. The far wall had been built by some daredevil laying it closer to the undulating river of power brick by brick. This wall had been made from a single humungous square of stainless steel. Two mammoth magical circles had been inlaid into the metal. The first seemed to have been deeply etched and filled with copper.

I leaned closer.

Not a single seam, must've built it laying down.

Thick glass rippled like a rock had been dropped into its circular surface an instant before the liquid glass froze solid. Runes surrounded both circles. The outer copper runes were a simple fifth resonance tuning set. Inner runes of polished crystal exactingly inlaid in the metal encircled the glass lens in a confusing tangle of the familiar and runes I'd never seen before. I untangled the symbols enough to recognize fifth, sixth, second and third resonances arranged around the unfamiliar runes.

Physical barrier, energy barrier, magical barrier, linking. Holy shit, what madman tried to redirect a ley line?

My fingers traced the runes, glided across the metal onto the perfectly smooth glass lens, and I had to wonder if the waves had been caused by tapping the ley line or been built to diffuse the energy.

An otter bark reminded me of my audience. I turned to find them sitting abnormally still. The otters reminded me of the river I'd escaped which should've flooded the chamber through the same hole I'd used to enter. I turned toward my entrance point.

My heart stopped.

My gaze didn't travel upward to what logic insisted must be a thoroughly clogged hole keeping the Columbia at bay. My eyes locked on a wall of shimmering, liquid silver.

What the hell?

The ley line slid from the center of the gravity-defying wall without a ripple. I turned to examine the junction, but movement drew my attention back to the otters. The six otters formed a pyramid much as the rhet did when trying to reach something. The wet, oily brown and black fur started to run like poured tar. Pained whines bounced off the warm, close confines as the otters melted together into a vaguely human shape.

The indistinct mannequin resolved into a man—gender quickly becoming apparent. Clothes and furs formed around his body. Paws from several different animals hung on his belt beside a beaver tail. Feathers from hawks and owls ringed his neck on a thin strip of leather. Dark long hair framed darker eyes, a long hawkish nose, and stern chiseled features.

When he showed no inclination to attack me—he had saved my life after all—I turned back to the liquid mirror. I pried a penny from the change pocket of my water-tightened jeans and swept it through the silver. The liquid rippled but the penny came back undamaged, unsoiled and untarnished where it had touched the fluid.

Tucking the penny away, I extended a fingertip. I hesitated. The ley line which emerged from what looked like melted silver had undoubtedly melted rock and concrete block.

I glanced at the man, as I edged my finger forward. He neither moved to stop me nor made a discouraging noise. Ice cold liquid rippled beneath my touch.

Why doesn't it ripple for the ley line?

I withdrew my finger and verified my digit was undamaged, then slid my hand into the liquid. The liquid seemed to end only a few inches, but my reflection offered an image of me and my mirror self connected at the bicep.

"Before you go, I would speak."

Go?

I whirled back to him, barely recognizing his perfect, unaccented English. "What is this place? How did you find it? Why did you bring me here? How is there air to breathe? What is that stuff?"

His laughter echoed in the confines, a boisterous warm thing almost possessing a life of its own. He gestured to a tarnished plaque on the wall behind him. "Pacific General Electric power tap room four."

My eyes shot back to the mammoth circles carved into the side walls, tracing their runes. "They built this? Were they insane? Did tapping a ley line for power cause the explosion which destroyed the Dalles?"

"Their greed destroyed many things, not least of which my people's trading place," he said.

"Celilo?"

He nodded. "We were surprised to feel a magus tumble into our waters. We knew your appearance signified a great foreboding. We saved you so that you might save us."

We? Us? Is he a man that can be many animals or many animals that can be a man? How does that work? The magic in here was too thick to tell what he used, maybe if he changes again and I pay more attention I could unravel his spe—

He cleared his throat. "We see greed in your gaze, though a different one to that which destroyed Celilo. You hunger for knowledge so we will gift you a tidbit, and then you will hear us."

I nodded.

He gestured behind me. "The air seeps through the Silver, for our world is an Asian twin with the world on the opposite side."

Asian twin? Another world?

It hit me. "You mean Siamese twins."

Our world is Siamese twins with another world? What is it like? Can I breathe on the other side? Of course, I can, he just said I'm already breathing the air. I wonder—

He tapped his foot.

I reddened. "Sorry, I'm listening."

"Something has disturbed Celilo's spirits. Dark tidings of foul plots whisper from the world beyond. The ancient trading paths are blocked. You will open them up once more."

Sure, I'll go right out and restore trade routes to a buried and drowned village for a bunch of restless dead Indians.

I rung my hands. "Look, I don't know what to call you—"

"You could not pronounce my name. Your attempt would bring insult, and I would be forced to rip your throat away."

"Good to know. What you should know is I'm homeless. I have no access to components. I'm not anything like the mages in fantasy novels, and I'm swamped—"

He'd crossed the room in an eye blink, lifted me off the ground and pushed my head incredibly close to the undulating ley line. "You will help, or I shall give you to the wild blood."

"Fine, I'll help you. I promise."

He yanked me back from the ley line, shoved me against the metal wall and yanked up my palm. In another flash of movement, blood welled in my palm. He raised it toward my face. "You will promise to this blood."

I blinked.

He shoved my hand closer. "Promise."

I glanced down at my hand. "I promise, I will help restore the trading paths so Celilo's spirits can rest."

He dipped his face forward, deeply inhaled and then slurped up the pooling blood. His smile was all red. "If your promise is worth a white man's word, I will hunt and devour you. Now we go."

Before I could object or even take a deep breath, we plunged back into the Columbia's cold. Six otters sped me to the surface. We broke the surface. I gulped air and blinked away river water only to get rain stinging my face.

The otters deposited me in knee-high water and vanished.

I wadded onto the shore behind an old half-demolished high-rise. I flopped down exhausted and shivering in the heavy rain. I wanted to cry. I wanted to just lay back and howl my frustration. I'd survived only to die anyway.

Why not.

I howled. It came out more an adolescent whisper. I gave it up as a bad job, closed my eyes, hoping whatever came next was warm and dry.

"Magus, thank the Old Ones I found you, but what are you doing with the Ottiren?"

"K-k-kenr-r-rith?"

"I must say, Magus, I've never known a mortal from African climes so disturbingly fond of tilting lances against hypothermia. I trust these choices are not evidence of suicidal inclinations, for you are needed."

"W-what are you d-doing here?"

"You must come this way." Kenrith trotted away without waiting for my response.

Supreme effort managed shaky footing and allowed pursuit. Kenrith strode into the partial high rise and turned around a corner and out of my sight. I glanced up at concrete which swayed but didn't totter.

No way am I going upstairs in a concrete weeble wobble

Kenrith appeared once more and waved me inside. A few quick turns took us down a set of concrete stairs to a boiler room. Following the little rhet knight forced me to wriggle through pipes to a secluded alcove. I felt the campfire even before I saw its light reflected off of old plumbing.

The rhet's fire crackled and popped just inside the opening of an old boiler. Wood comprised a pyramid of warmth rather than use the gas intakes. I shuffled over, blocking the door to absorb as much of the emanating heat as I could. Eventually, I turned my backside to the flame, finding the rhet lined up much like the otters. They stared just as intently.

"Why are you here? I told you I wasn't going to help."

Kenrith's lips pressed together into a grim line. "I was ordered to see to your wellbeing, safeguard you if you suffered trouble."

"Ordered? Matron Biuntcha?"

"In the end, she too declared that you would help us of your own accord in betrayal of your claims."

"If your matron wasn't the first—"

"The sooner you achieve the goal, the sooner you are rid of us."

My gut twisted and not just from hunger. "Look, Kenrith, I didn't mean it quite like that. You can't understand what I've been through, why it's better if I don't get involved."

"No, nor do we know why you act against your own best interest, but here we are. Are you recovered sufficiently for us to continue?"

"You're coming with me? In broad daylight?"

"We will be near. That is all you need to know."

I threaded my way out of the boiler room, grumbling under my breath. What glimpses I caught of Kenrith's expression left me thinking he felt about the same as I did. I backtracked upriver until I found my backpack. I chewed down another mouthful of food from the hamster ball and invoked the seeking spell once more.

Before I let it lead me away, I stepped to the river and reached out to the source of underwater magic that I'd learned was a ley line or it's otherworldly shadow. I drew in magic to carry with me into the Edison zones. The wild power washed into me unlike any tamed magic I'd ever pulled from the mananet. It burned the same way as good liquor and twice as heady. The seeking spell guided me drunkenly through a labyrinth of construction sites and factories.

At long last, the seeking spell brought me to the fence line of a large factory complex. I circled its perimeter until I'd triangulated confirmation and let the seeking spell fade. "No trespassing" signs painted in angry reds and oranges hung on chain link beneath layers of barbed wire.

I crossed the street, flopped down against a facing building and removed my shoes. Thumb and fingers massaged a slow line of sore toes beneath Sunny's thick wool socks.

"This block is claimed."

I looked up at the speaker. He dressed in much the same clothes as I'd seen others wearing in the Manger, though something about the stains and rips seemed too symmetric. Huge smokestacks behind him drew my attention. Puffy, white clouds of condensing steam joined darker clouds threatening evening rain.

"Can't you read? This territory is occupied."

My attention shifted back to him, following his extended finger to a series of strange marks scratched into the back of a traffic sign.

"What are you talking about?" I asked.

He narrowed his eyes and spoke with exaggerated slowness. "This block is assigned to me. Go back and tell Duval there's too little traffic to support another."

"I don't know any Duval." The moment I said it, I remembered three men attacking Caleb, Tiny and Ugly on my behalf.

He tightened his fists. "Begging in Duval's territories without his permission will get you broken. Move on, now."

I put my shoe back on, voice hardening. "I don't beg."

He kicked my legs sideways and invaded their vacated space. Hard lines and a harder expression glowered downward. A line of clean skin under his hairline explained all I needed to know about his puzzling appearance. "You got a problem with begging?"

Using an arm to help me up, I met him nose to nose. "I'm not a beggar. I'm only here to investigate—"

He paled. "You're a cop?"

"No. Look, whoever you are, it's been quite the journey getting this far, so I was resting my feet while I try to figure out how to get inside that factory for a look around. I am not a beggar."

"Christ," he swore. "Thought I'd screwed the pooch on that one. Name's Wayne. I've paid to hunt this territory. I'll give you the benefit of the doubt, but if I catch you poaching, Duval will hear about it."

He said it as if it were the ultimate threat. My attention shifted to the scratches. Slashes, shapes, scrapes—I had no idea what they all meant, but I'd remember them if only to avoid trouble in future.

"What do you mean by hunt?" I asked.

"Panhandle. You know, that thing you seem to have a problem with."

"Fine, you mind if I eat a little while I rest?"

"Suit yourself."

I unwrapped the hamster ball, twisting open the lid. "Want some?"

He wrinkled his nose. "These blocks aren't *that* lean."

He strode over to a corner up about a block and a half. I ate from Sunny's care package, unsure why her cold leftovers tasted so good. Despite the excellent taste, a feeling of being watched I didn't think was entirely due to Wayne kept me on edge.

Who the hell are these people? The begging mafia? Organized panhandling?

I wasn't sure who Duval, Wayne or any of the rest of these organized homeless were, but I certainly didn't need another source of trouble.

Just need to find the corruption to find the matrons and then Kenrith can take it over and I can...

I sighed.

I can try to figure out how to restore trading routes to an Indian village destroyed decades ago.

My attention returned to the factory. Only three cars hunkered together at one end of the parking lot. Security cameras watched the fence and parking areas, but no one came in or out.

Edison block, makes sense.

Preparing components within a mananet could cause problems if the right protections aren't maintained.

Now, how do I get in?

Feet rested and belly satisfied, I circled the block in a slow trudge. The factory took up about a three-by-four block area. Black painted wood covered all the upper windows, broken in only a few places and none big enough for me to slip inside.

The empty parking lots suggested that the factory employed few if any humans to manufacture the component nodules. The fence offered me a sign declaring the company a wholly-owned subsidiary of Thoth Corp.

Shit.

·9·

MAGIC REKINDLED

Thoth was manufacturing their own components, making Glamour's problems entirely Adam's responsibility. That also suggested that the matrons had been taken onto property I couldn't enter without seriously jeopardizing my freedom.

I can turn back.

Even as I thought about returning to my alley, I could feel Kenrith's eyes on me. I could almost hear his smug condescension telling whomever that they'd been wrong about me.

Damn it, I just want to be left alone.

Every inch of my being wanted to turn my back on the factory. It wasn't worth the risk, no matter what I owed Kenrith. I argued with myself, guilt and debt warring for superiority when the light prickling against my skin finally registered.

Aversion spell?

I retreated to the opposite side of the street.

I still didn't want to trespass on a Thoth property.

I still wanted to go back to my alley and work on my own survival.

Neither desire overwrote the guilt hamstringing me with a undeniable sense of responsibility

to warn me off. That would affect the workers too—unless it's keyed to just me. No, they have to have some ward token.

That Adam had used aversion magic or something like it to protect his secrets increased my certainty that the matrons or some other malevolence had been concealed inside. Pushing aside my curiosity wasn't easy—particularly when an opportunity for revenge might be involved, but the thought of being strapped back into the Wasteland's horrors soured the possibilities.

Do I really want to risk imprisonment for creatures I barely know—no matter how helpful?

In the end, Dad's stern glower broke my indecision. I exhaled a heavy breath. Even without a lecture, I knew what he'd say about me leaving a debt to my nearest neighbors unrepaid—especially after Kenrith's rhets built a fire to warm me.

Besides, I might find something to ruin Adam.

A thick European accent turned me around to a brand new, oversized, diesel passenger truck. "Who the hell are you?"

Duval glared at me through an open window.

My brows shifted toward one another. "No one?"

"Well, no one, you want to explain why I had to save you from those guys back there?"

"You didn't have to save anyone."

"You work for me, I protect my own. Wayne bring you in to work this territory?"

"I don't work for you." Wayne's reaction when he'd thought I was police sprang to mind. "I'm investigating this company."

The truck's driver shifted a glance my way and then to Duval.

"Oh, case of mistaken identity." Duval frowned. "Still, I saved your ass. Don't forget, cop."

"Forget what?"

"That you owe me one, a big one. Drive on, Paul."

The truck sped down the street, leaving me curious and confused. I forced my attention back to the factory and did another circuit. A midsized cargo truck with Thoth Corp logos pulled through an automatic gate on the opposite side of the parking lot. The complex was big enough to serve as both factory and warehousing—especially considering how small the nodules were.

I hurried around the perimeter to the other side and considered my approach.

Traffic around the factory wasn't heavy, but there was enough to maintain a steady trickle of witnesses. Climbing the fence through the barbed wire would either hurt or take lengthy caution, exposing me to discovery. To protect my identity and minimize chances of a trip back to the Wasteland, I'd have to cover my face making me even more suspicious.

If instead I waited and slipped through the fence line just after the truck departed with its cargo, but before the gate closed, I minimized discovery and wouldn't have to mask myself until absolutely necessary.

The sun's position offered hours left before its bedtime. A nighttime approach might be better, but based on the parking lot, Adam probably had whatever automation was preparing the nodules running day and night. The neighborhood seemed to be patrolled by organized homeless like Wayne, but it could turn dangerous once he left for his bed.

If nothing else, Caleb and his friends might come back.

In the end, I chose the truck's exit. Waiting dragged on enough that I started to think it was in for the night. The slam of a driver door woke me from my doze. I hurried up the block, across the street and back down the opposite sidewalk trying to time my stroll with the truck's departure. I ducked my head inside my poncho, covering my face in the blanket. Slipping in through the closing gate, I immediately ducked behind an obsolete old power transformer.

My pulse raced in response to the sudden rush as my anticipation grew in equal measure to the uneasy feeling pressing against the rabid gooseflesh prickling my skin. Nausea tightened my gut, though whether from fear or too many cartons of milk while I waited, I couldn't be sure.

An almost-empty shipping dock offered me no cover. Ducked low against the dock lip, I closed to the warehouse access door the driver had exited.

I opened the door and peeked inside, preparing to bolt to the nearest cover. A wave of magic hit me like nothing I'd ever felt. It wasn't overpowering like Gateway Park. It wasn't the overwhelming wild power of the ley line in PGE tap room four. It was like biting into an imported, dark chocolate-covered cherry only to get a rotten eyeball inside instead.

I cursed silently. The magic pressed against me changed nothing and everything. Darrin's problem was still Adam's to sort out, but Glamour's components had definitely been corrupted. With so much magic involved, the corruption had to be intentional. *Just how complicit does that make Adam for the attacks on Kenrith's people?*

The blare of an impatient horn wrenched my attention to a limousine waiting outside the gate. Cursing silently didn't slow my headlong dive inside and behind the nearest stacked crates. Plunging into the magic-gone-bad stole my breath. My heart slammed against my ribs, demanding flight from whatever tainted the factory.

No amount of handling the component nodules had given even the slightest hint of corrupted components, but inside the factory, there was no mistaking the source of the problem.

Heavy footfalls clomped closer, but rather than exiting to welcome the limo, the considerable stone automaton picked up the entire palette of crates I hid behind and marched deeper into the warehouse with it.

Golems.

The automaton hulked a quarter again my size. Rune marks carved into its skin as belts and armbands clothed the anatomically-neutral green clay man. He took no notice of me beyond lifting my cover and trudging away with it. I sprinted to the next hiding place, making sure the crates weren't stacked on a palette for sudden, easy relocation.

Golems made perfect sense when it came to mass producing magical components. While magic empowered their animation, almost none of that power would bleed out of their bodies. They were chemically and magically sterile. They'd work day and night without break or illness, repeating their tasks exactly as trained.

They would never steal. They couldn't be bribed or cajoled into industrial espionage.

Only extreme carelessness or a magic user of vastly overwhelming power could change a golem's allegiance. Bought once and their value amortized over a basically infinite lifespan, they were Adam's perfect worker.

I slipped from cover to cover through the warehouse until I had a view of the factory area. Assembly lines filled the factory interior, stretching further than my vantage allowed me to see. Where I could see, Golems worked more production lines than just those for the components Darrin had given me.

From the mismatched assortment of golems, Adam had dredged them up from a bargain basement sale. They'd been constructed of everything from green clay like the first to the brick and concrete remains of demolished buildings. A few even seemed cobbled from gravel-thick asphalt. Most were only basic, humanoid shape with no facial features beyond twin divots that gave humans something to identify as eyes.

The automatons performed innumerable functions in lieu of robotic automation. They transferred raw components into vats. They arranged component nodules for injection and operated the injection machines. Golems with broken and missing limbs even worked quality check positions, removing flawed nodules.

Movement caught my eye, freezing my breath in my throat.

Even with the warning provided by the limousine horn, seeing Adam and Thecia in the well-dressed flesh across the factory floor sent a monsoon of emotions through me.

Where Thecia remained Lucifer's unnaturally beautiful handmaiden, Adam had aged, but only for the better. Men in lab coats and hard hats bowed and scraped—flapping sycophants swarming Adam's feet.

"With all I've invested, why are our stores unable to fill Glamour orders?" Adam demanded. "We must move this product before some competitor reverse engineers our spell."

"Even though it's hurting people," I grumbled.

A nearby golem raised its head. Ancient clay shoulders covered in intricate runes turned slowly around. A fully detailed face met my gaze with glowing acid green eyes. Its head shifted ever so slightly left and right, making my flesh crawl. Golems on assembly lines to either side of me stopped what they were doing, green light flared to life in their eyes, and they marched up nearby stairs.

"Where are they going?" Adam demanded. "Who told them to stop working?"

My gaze broke the ancient golem's lock to find Thecia looking right at me. Adam slapped the nearest hard hat. "That thief is stealing my golems. Do something about it."

I bolted back into the warehouse. A pair of golems became a wall of twin glowing glowers fixed on me. They grabbed for me and being made of rock or stone did nothing to slow them. Diving from their reach deposited me between them and the former assembly line workers. I jerked this way and that without avail.

"Stop where you are." The eighty-year-old security guard had a gun in his shaking hands, but he couldn't possibly get a shot at me without hitting a golem. The gun barked anyway, bathing me in a shower of exploding brick fragments.

Another golem charged into view behind the two that had walled off the warehouse. Light filled his shallow eye sockets in the flickering yellows and reds of flame as he careened through them, creating a gap in his haste. I sprang through without hesitation. My shoes lost traction in the full sprint turn, sliding my feet out from under me.

The security guard fired until empty.

Adam cursed and shouted. "What are you doing? Stop shooting the equipment and kill the thief."

I hit the exit door at a full run. My rebound filled the air with cracking sounds and shattering glass. I lay stunned at the door's foot, freedom just beyond the metal mesh that had once been a window. Large automatic bolts locked the otherwise cheap door in place.

I'm trapped.

Heavy feet thundered my way. I struggled to a crouched position and faced my attackers. The clumsy golem charged ahead of the others, a tile-patched broken clay juggernaut.

I dove out of its way.

It slammed into the wall behind me. Its patchwork body shattered with the impact. Momentum took its crumbling right side through the roll down loading doors. The golem's head bounced onto the pavement outside and tumbled to a stop along one side.

I gave my run through the broken entry everything I had. My headlong flight nearly turned into another tumble when the light in one of the severed golem head's eye sockets flickered for a two count. I pushed the weirdness from my mind, focusing instead on escaping.

The closed gate blocked my escape.

I leapt off the loading dock onto the transformer and again into the barbed wire across the fence top. Barbs seized my pant legs, turning an awkward fall into a high-speed face plant that drove the breath from my lungs and gravel under my skin.

Gun barks spurred my legs to scramble back into flight. I veered through a broken fence leading to the construction site across the street. I paused at a huge concrete section of water pipe to snatch up my belongings and resumed my flight. Pain exploded in my right shoulder. My backpack careened ahead as I shot left. Another shot creased the ground at my feet.

I doubled back for the pack. I couldn't have left it behind as identification even if another shot hadn't forced me to change directions. The few steps I took to reach it let me see the shooter wasn't the old security guard anymore.

Adam shot again, the bullet tearing into my backpack and nearly costing me fingers.

Reloading bought me time to put most of the construction site between me and his gun. I hid behind a stack of new bricks, snatching them up and arranging them in a low circular wall around me. I couldn't catch my breath. I built the wall up higher. If I could make something that looked intentional, I might be able to work some kind of magic to hide me from search. Maybe I could employ my blood for some short-term decoy I could order to dive into the river.

"Magus."

I looked up into Kenrith's electric blue eyes. He perched on the brick stack, a half dozen of his tribe beside him.

"Save your strength, Magus. Just be still and quiet."

I threw up bloody mucus instead.

They formed a circle around my pitiful brick wall, and fey glamour cocooned me from view.

Cold reached into my bones while pain in my shoulder blade burned like a miniature sun. My legs shook beneath me, and I still couldn't manage a breath even though I was no longer running. I tried to speak.

Kenrith's rebuke offered no room for negotiation. "Be still."

A weight pulled down on the back of my coat. A moment later my agony doubled. I cried out, and Kenrith sank his long teeth into my nose.

The nose contains a lot of nerves. Sudden pain at the forward point of my face distracted from the agony of my gunshot wound long enough for Kenrith to spit my blood and several curses I didn't understand.

"Be still and be *silent*. We are trying to keep you hidden while stopping your bleeding and you're jeopardizing both."

I mumbled an apology.

"One more word and I'll bite you again," Kenrith said.

I opened my mouth. Kenrith's eyes blazed to light, and his voice shifted into an oddly harmonic chord. "*Sleep.*"

A battering ram of magic sent me into dreamless darkness.

Sluggish thoughts climbed out of deep slumber into warm dreams. I lay curled on my side. A thousand tiny mouths bit my skin and twice that many feet scurried over my flesh. Urine scent overwhelmed my throbbing nose. A moment later I realized I wasn't asleep, but instead buried beneath a writhing swarm of rats.

Disgusted panic shot through me, rocketing my heartbeat into maximum overdrive. I bolted upright, snatching rats and hurling them away. "Stop, I'm not dead. Don't eat me."

My attempts to clear them and escape being eaten alive only slowed their assault. The rats scurried back onto my body, covering and smothering me so they could eat their fill.

A large rat shimmered. Rat skin rippled and peeled away from its body. The bloody, skinless red muscles and organs lightened. Clothes flowed around human-like flesh covered in a powder thin layer of fine, fuzzy hairs. Kenrith met my eyes, his expression a mixture of pain, disgust, and disappointment. "We *are not* eating you. Be still, you'll interrupt our working."

Working?

I raised my hand from the swarm to find the Ottiren's cut healed. Kenrith's form shifted shape once more into something only a hair more humanoid than a regular alley rat, and he rejoined the swarm. Examining the rhet more closely offered glimpses that left me with the impression they'd changed shape into a rat version of movie werewolves.

The urine reek intensified once more.

I squeezed my eyes shut and pictured being beaten unconscious in the Wasteland—a far happier thought. Fighting my desperate need to throw the foul creatures off of me took all of my will and reason.

I really don't want to understand how this works.

It was dark by the time they finished. Kenrith's people numbered dozens more than had first appeared. They watched me in silence, shoulders slumped with exhaustion. Kenrith gestured, and all but the original number split off into shadow.

I tried not to reveal how relieved their departure made me. "You, your matron and your people have my thanks. You saved my life, though your method will probably haunt my nightmares for months."

"You find too much trouble, Magus."

"Yeah, thanks to you. I only wanted to—"

"You will not blame your troubles on us," Kenrith said.

"Why not? You're why I'm here." I pointed. "The taint creating demi-goblins came from over there. My guess is your matrons are there too."

Kenrith's gaze shot toward the factory and back to me. He scowled.

"I thought they were wrong, but you did help us in the end." Kenrith bowed to one knee and clasped a fist to his chest. "I ask your forgiveness for any insult, Magus. I resented that you wouldn't help us even though we brought our troubles to you unbidden."

I wasn't sure how to answer him. I resented being dragged into their mess even if in some small part his problem had originated with my spell. Rats were filthy, horrible things, but Kenrith and his rhet weren't rats. They'd helped me out of a sense of honor. It was only right to push aside my misgivings and finish squaring my debt.

"Did you find our matrons within? Where were they inside?"

"I was ejected before I found them. There's definitely something foul going on inside. The magic in there feels wrong, and—"

"It smells of infernal creatures."

Infernal? As in demons and the Devil?

Golems, even fey I kind of understood. Golems were a fact of life. Myth, folklore and corroborated testimony certified the existence of the fey. Even so, I just couldn't comprehend something as absurd as real demons.

It can't be true, can it?

Fear took three swallows to get down. "I need another look inside."

"They've intensified their watching, and law keepers now circle."

No way for me to get inside then. "Could your people slip in?"

"We lack the numbers to keep you hidden and spy within."

"What about the others? The ones that were helping heal me?"

"They belong to another warren, and the working has exhausted the favors owed to us."

Reaching my feet took exhausting effort and staying upright as the world dizzyingly wove around me cost almost double. Rhet magic healed my flesh but seemed to have stolen my strength to do it.

And who knows how much blood I lost.

I bent for my food ball and toppled. I sat where I fell and shoved food into my mouth without thought of separating or identifying flavors. Milk kept cold in my bag by weather washed down Grace's cooking as if it were little more than the paste dripped into my stomach by a feeding tube. I folded the used cartons away and dug through my mind for some kind of solution.

A cat's yowl sent a shiver through Kenrith's people. It also gave me an idea. I sprang to my feet, nearly toppled and rushed to the nearby construction dumpster. Loose sheets of paper stuck rain-glued to the empty bottom. A simple trailer near one fence line contained what I needed, but breaking and entering with police circling the block seemed a bit beyond my daily limit of stupid choices.

"Kenrith, are there any restaurants or convenience stores nearby?"

"What need you, Magus?"

"Paper, mostly."

"Have you not paper strips in your bag?"

"Yes, but I need bigger pieces and doll accessories."

Kenrith led us over several streets.

A small strip mall offered a convenience store so marred in advertisement posters it would've looked boarded up if not for glowing, neon beer signs. An old DQ repurposed into a Tacky Burger franchise faced off the store from the opposite corner.

I rushed around Tacky Burger to its dumpsters. The reek of rotting sugary drink made me think twice, but I threw open the trash to discover a treasure trove.

"Have you not already eaten?" Kenrith asked.

I snatched up to-go bags and crumpled waxed wrappers. I stuffed enough into my pockets to forbid more when a heavily tattooed youth in a Tacky apron appeared with more trash. "Get away from there, old man."

I opened my mouth to argue, but I had what I needed, so I fled.

"Filthy beggars." He called after me. "Eating garbage is unsanitary!"

Kenrith's sudden words from my shoulder made me jump midway across the street. "Your people waste much that is good. Even what has begun its corruption can be cleansed."

"Could you please stop doing that?"

"What have I done that distresses you, Magus?"

"You keep appearing out of nowhere and speaking without warning."

Kenrith showed me his teeth. "The fey are a subtle people."

"Even knights?"

Kenrith stood straighter. "The Knights of Rhet exemplify the best of the chivalrous qualities, particularly stealth."

"How is stealth chivalrous?"

"Would it not be the height of rudeness to wake a king when abducting his daughter to make her your wife?"

"Do rhet have wives? Are you married to Biuntcha?"

Kenrith gave me an exasperated look that had often graced Dad's face. "The Code of Chivalry applies to all fey equally, whether or not their tribe practices marriage abduction."

"Gotcha."

·IO·

HEADLESS HIJACKER

The convenience store had its aisles arranged so tightly I almost felt claustrophobic between them with no one else nearby. Rhet circled my feet. Perhaps they changed my appearance for the security camera, or maybe they offered me some kind of invisibility. The small selection of overpriced toys provided a generic wizard student doll with thick black glasses. The old woman behind the counter didn't look up when I took the toy to the register, cringing inwardly at spending six of my very finite dollars.

"She cannot see you," Kenrith said.

"I need to pay for this."

"A knight may take anything he needs in his service to the greater good."

My snort distracted the cashier from some phone game. "That's a slippery slope if ever I've heard one. Let her see me so I can pay."

My sudden appearance sent her sprawling backward. She fell into a pile of cascading cigarettes and adult magazines. Dislodged cover protectors released a war of illusionary and holographic pornography. The cashier grabbed her chest.

She pulled herself back up. "Don't sneak up on a person like that."

I shot Kenrith a pointed smirk. "May I buy this toy please?"

"Oh my God, you've got a rat on your shoulder."

"Yeah, he likes it up there."

She looked me up and down, eyes narrowed. "You're not going to lure children with this, are you?"

My neck prickled. "Just what do you mean by that?"

She pulled the toy to her side of the counter. "You should go."

"I need that doll."

"Are you buying it for a relative?"

"No, I'm buying it for myself, not that my reason for purchasing something is any of your business."

"We may refuse service to anyone. Someone like you—"

I cut across her, tone pointed. "Someone like me?"

"You're obviously a vagrant. You could be a serial killer wandering the country abducting children, and I won't take that chance."

Where the hell did that come from?

She shook her head. "I won't be an unwitting part in whatever weirdness you and that filthy rodent have planned—"

Kenrith stiffened. "I beg your pardon, madam?"

"It talked!" she shrieked, falling back into the writhing porn.

I slapped six dollars onto the counter, snatched the doll and exited. Before she could follow, I opened the toy and removed the plastic glasses and tiny wand taped to the packaging. I'd barely pulled free the tiny accessories that'd cost me so much before she stormed out of the store, threw my money in the air and snatched the doll away.

Kenrith retrieved my money and returned to my shoulder in a flash of magical rhet speed. "A knight is humble, Magus, never pointing out when he's foretold truth to another."

"How very gracious of you," I grumbled.

"You should have just requisitioned it by noble right."

As we walked back to the factory, I flattened, creased and folded burger wrappers together to create the size and shape I needed. We detoured to the river, washing out a few discarded jugs and filling them with river water pregnant with the wild, raw magic beneath its current.

I knelt beside the banks with my fingers in the cold water. One deep inhalation at a time, I drew Mother's wild blood into myself once more with an eye out for the Ottiren.

I'd eaten. I'd drank mother's milk, but I still hadn't felt genuinely full until creation's power filled my every cell. Thrumming invincibility summoned my anger. Adam had chained the wild, free miracle of magic for use by the ignorant masses solely to fill his own pockets. His indiscriminate spell peddling to the ignorant had forced the government to regulate magic in order to protect people from their own stupidity.

Adam was the guilty one. His betrayal had seen me imprisoned without magic only to have my freedom restored into a world where law caged the magic away from me.

Magic is for the magi, the wise, a miracle to help all, not some cheap bobble to enable laziness.

My temper took us back to the brick ring in haste.

Since I'm sending in a construct, I might as well get component samples to confirm contamination before shipment for Darrin.

I finished folding my large origami spider around the black, plastic glasses. I folded small paper envelopes and fitted them into waiting recesses in the spider's back. I poured the magic-permeated water into the ring's bottom, tapping the tiny wand from the same packaging against each brick in widdershins order.

Animating origami creatures had been a thoughtless accident as a kid and had grown into a simple enough construct by comparison that I'd barely paid attention to the magic after college until I'd accidentally done it again in the alley. Tying the brick circle and water, wand and glasses tapped deeply into my stored power, but peering down into the shimmering pool left me looking up into my own face.

I pointed and willed the spider. "Go and see what must be seen."

The spider scrambled through the circling rhet toward the factory. Kenrith peered down into the pool and then back up at me. He bowed at the waist. "Despite any claim to the contrary, you truly are and always have been *Magus.*"

"Yeah, I guess so."

I turned my back on the strange Fey rodent, concentrating on the viewing spell rather than face him. Despite my belief that so many legs would even the construct's gait, the pool's view moved in a way no one could describe as smooth. Size exaggerated little obstacles and terrain inconsistencies. My animated spy took too long to cross the intervening spaces, ratcheting up my tension. It ducked out of the path of a passing police cruiser only to be deluged by a puddle's contents. The wave of dirty water blinded our view in the magical pool. When it cleared, the world shook confusingly up, down and side to side A small droplet obscured some of the view, clinging to a nonexistent lens.

Scaling the fence proved so disorienting that I had to look away. I turned back to the pool to find the spider climbing toward a patch of stars playing hide and seek behind fast, grey clouds. My spy slipped into the dimly lit warehouse through a high window. I willed the spider to follow a golem lugging a pallet into the factory floor.

It rushed through metal rafters, down a concrete wall and back up, leaving me dizzy and nauseous. We scanned the factory from a shadowy perch. I saw no indication of the human workers from earlier. Golems worked the factory lines mechanically. They unboxed raw component bags and dumped them into the dispenser bins. Others unloaded nodule casing parts onto trays, aligning them by stony hand into precise rows before slotting them onto conveyors for loading.

Everything looked like what I'd expect. Not a single golem eye glowed anywhere in view. My spy crawled along the rafters until it perched above a vat of the first target component. I cursed.

"What is wrong, Magus?"

"Poor planning."

I'd given my enhanced origami creation the ability to share what it saw. Enchanted to be a spider, magic gave its paper legs purchase enough to climb and cling. I'd given neither thought nor any mechanism to spin a web or lower itself directly down from the rafters.

Undaunted by my own misgivings, the spider let go. My stomach swooped as the spider fell in the rapid spinning descent of a poorly folded paper airplane. It hit the ground scurrying and ducked beneath the conveyor belts into an unswept wasteland of chips broken off of crumbling golems and spilled components.

I turned away once more as my spy sped up the conveyor's legs and across its underside. I looked back in time to see it leap from the conveyor onto the dispenser's side and scurry into a bin filled with red spice. The same magic that allowed it to cling to surfaces made grabbing one of my pre-prepared envelopes simple, but complicated filling said envelope. It raised a leg into view in response to my desire.

I imagined how I would refold the foot's top into a scoop and the paper mimicked my will.

It filled an envelope and then refolded its foot. The spy cached the packet out of sight beneath the conveyor.

Damn thing's smarter than I am. I didn't even consider how it would get full samples tucked back into those tight pockets.

More disorienting springs, jumps, and orientation shifts brought it to the next target vat. We'd obtained and hidden our third and second-to-last sample when I caught a glimpse of glowing green eyes through a partially obscured doorway in the background.

I willed my spy to investigate. The illuminated eyes shifted left and right, into view and out. We crawled along the upper lintel into the room's ceiling. A broken golem lay in the room's center, a head propped atop cracked and tile-patched clay. Flickering flames glowered from its sockets at green-eyed guards. The large archaic golem with the intricate face paced back and forth.

For all the silence, it looked like an interrogation.

Perhaps they communicate another way since they don't have mouths.

The flame eyes flicked up to fix on me. A snarky tone echoed eerily from the pool. *<Your spy has no ears.>*

I shot Kenrith a glance. "Did you hear that?"

"What was there to hear, Magus?"

My attention shot back to the pool, a question poised on my lips. The glower of angry green eyes distracted me. The intricate, angry clay face blocked my view of the broken golem I only then realized had helped my earlier escape.

The view from my spy's eyes shot sideways, wall streaking by in a rush. Whatever survival instincts the origami spider possessed didn't prove enough. Massive clay fingers slapped into view. They tightened into a fist, opened to replace darkness with dazzling light and let my spy fall broken to the ground.

I cursed.

The angle of my fallen minion canted the world, the vision pool riddled with cracks in the lensless glasses. My golem nemesis returned into view in a chrome distorted reflection on the surface of the breakroom refrigerator. Their adversarial conflict resumed within cracked, silvery swirls.

I spared no attention for an interrogation I couldn't hear, bringing my focus to the spider. My injured spy had dwarfed its many predecessors, but the basic folds that gave it shape were etched into early childhood memory. I imagined each of the folds that made its body and willed each into the pool.

Come on, refold back into a functional shape.

My view wobbled. It righted, pitched downward for a glimpse of crumpled but restored limbs and then up to the broken golem head. Flames in one eye died a moment. Both raised their fury upward, and more red intensified their glow.

Go, get out of there.

A heartbeat before my spider scurried for the exit, both eyes died in the severed golem's head. A flash of red light obscured everything then cleared to show the construct racing for the door with all the speed its legs could manage. I urged it to reach the last component vat for a hurried sample, but instead, it zig-zagged beneath the conveyors, down a hall and somehow beneath a door. It climbed onto a desk, snatched up a half full Doritos bag and dove into a wastebasket. A moment's burrowing into discarded paper and lunch leftovers proceeded to yank the chip bag over top of itself. The pool offered us a dark view of orange tortilla chips.

"What is it doing?" Kenrith asked.

"It sure as hell isn't doing what I want it to do."

The snarky voice of what could only be my construct filled my mind. *<Shut your gob, human. We can't risk being discovered.>*

"Why isn't it searching for our matrons?" Kenrith asked.

Kenrith's right. Stop what you're doing, search for the rhet matrons. If you can't find them, then bring the components.

<Thoughtless barely-evolved ape,> it groused.

The pool darkened. White letters floated into view atop river water turned oily black. They swirled into three rippling lines: Connection interrupted. Experiencing technical difficulties. Please stand by.

Slamming my fists onto the brick ring did nothing but shoot pain up my arms and worry Kenrith. "Magus, I do not understand this."

"You and me both."

A sudden crash proceeded one of Kenrith's scouts by only moments. Rather than wait for the report, Kenrith scurried up a support beam.

I looked at the rhet scout. "Well?"

"Golems, Magus, they're—"

A flatbed trailer stacked with construction materials interrupted the scout's report, careening through building supports toward us. I dove sidelong from the barrage of splintering beams. Four green-eyed golems crashed through a solid concrete wall the trailer hadn't removed from their way.

Kenrith shouted from above us. "Flee!"

"Flee?" I asked on the run. "How does that fit in the Code of Chivalry?"

Kenrith streaked past me. "Knights must be valorous."

The bricks I hadn't used arched through the sky toward us. My feet managed to keep traction despite a sudden hard jog right behind another concrete wall.

I glanced around the opposite end of the wall. The golems changed direction to pursue. None were the ancient model filling my life with havoc. "What's valorous about running away?"

Two rhet swung a third by his tail in a tight circle. The undoubtedly dizzy rhet let loose with a brick and a battle cry to make

Genghis Kahn proud. His projectile shattered a green clay head, causing the golem a moment's pause.

The thrower grinned, drunkenly weaving to keep his feet.

"Discretion," Kenrith said something to the throwers and led me back the opposite way than that of his people. "It is the better part of valor."

In the typical manner of my life, the headless golem recovered its senses—if not its head—and stomped toward me in the wake of his brothers.

"Where are we going and why are we splitting up?"

"I do not wish my people in harm's way when you unleash your magic at these automatons."

We ducked another barrage of hurled building materials.

"Think these things are a little big to scare with origami creatures."

"Release your wrath, Magus. Shatter them with your power's might."

"With what?"

"Combat spells," Kenrith said it in a way that suggested a waning in his faith of my intellect.

"I don't have any combat spells."

"What kind of magus has no war magic?"

"A nice magus who only ever wanted to *help* people."

Kenrith scowled. "If you survive this and intend to keep challenging evil, I suggest you help *yourself* by learning some."

"Can't we just hide in Glamour?"

"Glamour will not fool a golem."

A cement mixer bounced across the yard like a runaway bowling ball. I ducked behind the trailer for protection. The mixer left a hole big enough to drive through but fortunately continued on to flatten the chain-link fence behind the trailer.

I rushed through the welcome hole. My attackers were big and strong, but unless smashing through concrete walls stole significant speed from them, they weren't fast. The open road offered my panicked legs room to stretch out our lead and escape. My vivid imagination sent flashes of lamp poles or abandoned cars through the air, but it hadn't envisioned the police cruiser that screeched to a halt across our path.

I spun away as officers jumped from the car and leveled guns at me from behind the protection of their open doors. I managed to pull the blanket over my nose before they shouted for me to freeze. Four golems picking up the construction office trailer turned their guns from me. A postal service truck screeched around a nearby corner. The aroma of burnt rubber filled the air as the truck slid to a halt, barely missing the closest officer as it sheared off his cruiser's door.

Rhet choking on resultant dark smoke waved me inside from their Rodent Pyramid of Driving cheer formation. I hesitated. Kenrith leapt inside and locked angry glowing eyes on me. "Get in."

Gunfire busied both police and the golems.

If I do this—

"Magus, duck!"

The headless golem cut off my train of thoughts by swinging an Edison pole at me like a baseball bat. I hit the ground just in time, the pole catching my hood enough to tug me sideways before it ripped. Rather than lose my head, I dove into the vehicle. "Go! Go! Go!"

Rhet have mad driving skills—Mad Hatter mad. Sirens rose in the distance.

"I can't believe you stole a car. Do you have any idea how much trouble I'm in when they catch me in this thing?"

"*If* they catch you, Magus."

Kenrith dispensed orders in his native tongue. The driving pyramid pulled the vehicle over and piled out onto the sidewalk. I felt the magic rise around us.

"Glamour, Kenrith? How long can they even keep that up after all they've had to use already?"

Kenrith gave me a steely glare. He drew both swords, and I couldn't help a hard swallow. The sword display started with a slow, simple flourish, building up speed until blade motions could only be tracked by the sparkling magical dust trailing in their wake.

Power hit me like a limousine. I stumbled backward, tripping on the driver seat and hitting the back of my head against the door. Kenrith didn't cut me, but when the dust ceased its sparkling, my clothes had changed into bright colors one might wear if running at night. I'd be obvious at a distance.

But obviously not a burglar hiding from notice.

Kenrith led me away from the stolen truck through block after block, turn after turn until we returned once more to where his rhets waited around the brick circle. Lights flickered from the direction of the golem altercation with the police. SMLE would doubtless be on the way. I needed to get what I came for and be long gone before that happened.

Breath held, I turned my attention to the viewing pool. The single portal through which we looked had been segmented by interwoven paperclips giving us a confusing, facetted view of the world. Spindly limbs wrapped with inside-out chip bags opened up their scoop tips to display a Doritos logo. Scoop open or closed, the legs picked through the contents of a desk drawer. My spy gathered paperclips and rubber bands then rifled a sewing kit, taking needles and several spools of thread.

<*Helloooo, human. We are back on the air!*>

"What the hell is it doing?" I asked.

<*You gave me pockets. Anyone who knows anything knows that string must always be carried in pockets.*>

"I'm unsure, Magus, but please make haste."

He heard me?

<*Of course I heard you, with thoughts that vulgarly loud, the real question is who didn't? Speaking of, did you get rid of your new friends?*>

Did you find any rhet matrons?

<*Can't find what's never been there.*>

Shit. I needed to find them so I can get out of this mess. Where else could they be?

A gun report reminded me of reasons for haste.

<No idea, but I got your samples> Four envelopes fanned out into view.

That's something I guess—a bonus objective if nothing else.

The components might allow me to help Darrin, but staring at them didn't find the matrons or square my debt. I noted for the first time that cracks no longer shot through the vision spell.

Can you meet us on the opposite side of the factory or do I need to maintain this vision spell for you to remain animate?

Contemptuous laughter underpinned its response. *<Meet you there>*

I doused the vision spell, praying that taking advice from a construct gone haywire wouldn't cost me my prize. We hurried the long way around the block, heart caught in my throat. Between police and SMLE, golems and infernal magic, more terrifying dangers stalked me than in my first nights in the Wasteland.

Kenrith drew his sword, holding up a hand. "Hold, Magus, something awaits ahead."

"Hopefully my spider."

"Allow us to scout this."

I nodded.

Kenrith hadn't failed me yet. Nothing in my education—formal or otherwise, equipped me to judge the age of a fairy rat. I watched the rhet knight, breath held against the next jack-in-the-box waiting to spring. Kenrith, Knight of the Rhet, slid his blade away and cupped a hand over his face. His groan reached me from there.

"Can I assume it's safe to approach?" I asked

"At your own risk, Magus. You're the one who summoned *this.*"

Closing the distance brought me into view of my origami spider, except no origami spider I'd ever folded had displayed the detail level bobbing up and down over my sample packets. Tiny foil mandibles rubbed together over sewing needle teeth. Red flame swam through small, yellow eyes behind the hexagonal paperclip mesh covering the doll's glasses.

The whole surface had been wrapped with inside-out chip bags giving it a shiny skin. Paper shredder leavings sprouted all over the foil skin. Street lights reflecting through the tiny hair created a hypnotic effect everywhere except the two tile shards tipping its front legs.

"Hello, human."

"You can speak?" I asked.

It rolled its fiery eyes. "Obviously, though I had to heavily correct your *horrid* design. No ears, no mouth, how do you expect me to hurl fitting insults at those letting stupidity leak out of their gobs?"

"Magus, we mustn't linger." Kenrith vaulted onto my coat and took his position on one shoulder.

"Kenrith's right." I retrieved the component envelopes. "Thank you."

The spider's shrug made me queasy. It took the other shoulder, mimicking Kenrith. I tucked the component envelopes deep in my backpack and swung it into place trusting Kenrith and my spy to dodge or be dislodged. The weight of the day joined the burdens of my backpack and passengers. With a last glance at the factory, I trudged away from the river.

·II·

BURNING BRIDGES

Thunder cracked overhead a bare moment before the heavens opened up. I pulled my ripped poncho hood into place, and Kenrith hunkered into his fur cloak. The spider bobbed jauntily, rain beading on its foil but soaking the shredded paper hairs.

"So, human, you wouldn't happen to have any skill at sculpting by any chance, preferably superior to your folding abilities?"

I regarded it out of the corner of one eye. The little automaton was and was not my construct. The fiery eyes hinted to the helpful golem's spirit stowed away in my little spider.

I skipped the obvious questions. "What and who are you?"

Spiders shouldn't smile, particularly at night with a lightning storm backdrop. "You may call me Razcolm, human, or master until you have paid your debt to me."

Kenrith sounded unsettled. "What debt did you agree to, Magus?"

"I've agreed to no debt."

"I fetched your packages," Razcolm said.

"The components weren't the main objective. If you hadn't hijacked my construct, I'd have been able to ascertain whether or not Kenrith's matrons are being held inside."

"I told you they are not," Razcolm said.

"Well, I don't know you. Your trespassing prevented me from seeing for myself."

"Trespassing? Me?" Razcolm pressed a leg tip to his chest. "Would your name be Kettle by any chance, human?"

I shook my head.

"Your construct is assembled from naught but discarded filth. Your property claim on it is weak at best," Razcolm said.

"Magus Elias claimed the materials comprising his spider, knave."

"So, I'm trespassing in the construct, trespassing in another's factory and stealing its inventory."

"Enough," I growled. "I've no time for word games. I accede to no debt. You brought me what the body you hijacked would have without you."

"I stole from that factory, you've burdened my conscience by forcing my complicity in theft," Razcolm said.

"You cannot steal what is rightfully yours," I snarled.

"Besides," Kenrith said. "Stealing is much of your very nature. Your kind considers anything they can grab abandoned."

The spider stuck a tongue out at the rhet.

"What of his kind?" I asked.

"I may not speak his kind's secrets freely on this side," Kenrith said.

"All right, then you owe me a debt for saving your life at the cost of my body." Razcolm clapped the legs tipped in tile and rubbed them together. "Actually, that's two debts you owe me come to tally."

Huh, he might have a point.

<Of course I do.>

"Stay out of my thoughts."

"Stop thinking so loud."

I grabbed my head, releasing a deluge of icy water through the poncho's hole. I turned us beneath a storefront awning and closed my eyes against the throbbing. "Could you please grant me a couple minutes of quiet?"

When they didn't object, I sat cross-legged before a reflective window, dropped my food ball into my lap and set to eating. It'd been a long day. I'd often studied to the exclusion of all else in college, eventually learning not eating as the source of my headaches. I chewed slowly, trying to enjoy the vivid flavor of real food. Cold with its fats congealed, my meal filled the stomach but my love of food left pangs in my heart.

"Rhet called you a Magus," Razcolm said. "Heat it."

"I don't have a spell for that."

The spider crawled over my head, turning back toward me once before addressing Kenrith. "He's kidding right?"

Kenrith eyed me over the construct. "He doesn't even have any combat spells."

The spider's voice became dubious. "You're sure he's a magus? What? Oh, right. I suppose this construct could be construed as evidence."

"If you two are not going to be quiet, want to tell me why you were in that factory?"

Moments passed.

"He's addressing you," Kenrith said.

"Oh, you know." Razcolm climbed across my back onto my left shoulder. "Saving your butt at the expense of my body."

"No!" I softened my voice. "No. Saving me wasn't the reason you were there. For all I know, whatever you were doing was what got me spotted in the first place, so no debt unless you can prove otherwise. You arrived before I did, tell me why."

The spider narrowed his eyes at Kenrith. "Are you a Knight? Can you...you know?"

Kenrith smiled.

Razcolm cursed. "Very well, His Majesty ordered me to investigate a disturbance on this side of the...um... river."

Kenrith's gaze hardened.

"All I can say without violating the old rules," Razcolm said.

"Fine, I'd like to speak to this...king" I glanced at Kenrith. "His Majesty is the proper title for a king, right?"

"Indeed, Magus."

"I'd like to speak to this king," I repeated.

Spiders shouldn't sneer either. "Well, you can't, *human*."

"My name is Eli, and just why can't I?"

Razcolm rolled his eyes. "Even the babies we steal know *that*."

"Kenrith?"

"Moon's wrong," Kenrith said. "The Silver's too thick."

The question slipped absently from my lips as I remembered the liquid metal wall beneath the Columbia. "The Silver?"

"A protective barrier between...us and His Majesty," Kenrith said.

"So I have to wait until the full moon?"

Razcolm rolled his eyes and thumped my throbbing head with sharp tile. "Hello, moron, a full moon is the most magical time in her cycle. Any real magus knows that's the best time for high magic. Does your master know his idiot apprentice is wandering around Seufert Fells making you both look like fools?"

"Starting to think I need to work out a fire spell," I grumbled. "You were looking into that rotten smelling magic?"

"Yes."

"What did you learn?"

"Not to waste a good body helping you?"

"Show respect, knave, or I'll be forced to defend his honor."

Razcolm rolled his eyes. "And what? Cut this body into confetti? I'll just find another...like one of those beautiful silver swords."

I slammed the lid back on the almost empty hamster ball and lurched to my feet, marching toward home. I'd been attacked four times—five if you included the police. I'd nearly been drowned. I'd channeled more magic than I had in the past century. My head felt like the inside of metal shop, and a hitchhiking entity kept insulting me. Planned or not, I didn't even have a bed waiting for me at march's end.

Adam, whether intentionally or by willful ignorance, had unleashed a malicious spell into the populace with no intention of pulling it until he'd lined his pockets. Envisioning his imprisonment gave me a certain vindictive pleasure, but SMLE wouldn't take my word, the word of a disgruntled ex-partner, against the upstanding CEO whose testimony had put me away.

Besides, what would I get for the trouble but the very attention I don't want?

The source of the spell taint had been in the factory, but I'd found no evidence of Kenrith's matrons—assuming Razcolm's word was to be trusted. The presence of the corrupted magic on site basically assured the component tampering occurred within the factory. Once I'd confirmed that by testing my samples, Darrin could investigate the factory from there.

Eliminating the spell taint would abort more demi-goblin births. I knew Adam would never shut down the factory, but that was really SMLE's problem. I needed to find Kenrith's matrons and leave all this behind.

Well, maybe not the magic.

"Razcolm? If there were no matrons back in that factory, did you at least witness any signs which might lead us to them?"

Kenrith's attention returned from wherever it had wandered.

"Not one, why? Have you lost one?"

"Many have been taken," Kenrith said.

"Do matrons share anything I might be able to use to create a thaumaturgic connection to track with a seeking spell?"

Kenrith shook his head. "Warrens are fiercely independent."

I waited in the rain for the crosswalk signal to change. Thunder echoed off the buildings as they rose in height the deeper into downtown we marched. All three species of city car rolled through the night near us: Edison, mananet or increasingly obsolete vehicles still powered by fossil fuel. It might've been fair to include the crossbred hybrids like the LUX drones as their own species, but I didn't. Outside long distance vehicles forced to travel beyond the range of both mananets and the projected power perfected by and stolen from Nicolai Tesla, few cars had reason to depend on the old fuels. The irony of a crime boss of the beggars driving a solely diesel vehicle wasn't lost on me.

People are their own worst enemy, not even myself excluded.

Police tape blocked off my first alley home, but we stopped there anyway. "You know where to find me."

Kenrith leapt from my shoulder, stopping to bow. "I thank you for not abandoning my people. Shall I seek you in the morn so we might continue our search?"

"I need rest and time to think. I'll also need to test what we brought back to repay Darrin. Guess I'll need time to find an animal of some sort for that too."

"Why do you have need of an animal?" Kenrith asked.

"The original spell only worked on living creatures. I assume the Glamour variant works the same, so I'll need an animal to test it on."

"Then I shall volunteer," Kenrith said.

"Better him than me," Razcolm chuckled.

"Don't think you count," I said.

Razcolm's laughter stopped. "One. Two. Thr—"

I snatched the spider from my shoulder and hurled it away. "A smart-assed whatever you are is *exactly* what I don't need. Keep the spider, I'll make another."

"If you don't know what I am, how do you know I'm exactly what you don't need?"

"What I need is for you and everyone else to go away and leave me alone. That's all I want. Just leave me in peace." I stormed around the block toward my alley. A twinge of guilt suggested my outburst at Razcolm might've offended Kenrith. I shoved the guilt away. I had enough weight on my shoulders. Having Razcolm and Kenrith off my back, even if temporarily, lightened my burden.

A restless night of dark dreams haunted my waking hours. I'd nearly drowned. I'd been shot, chased, and almost crushed by a golem I'd later learned had been possessed by Razcolm. Worst of all, I was no nearer finding the rhet matrons. My last milk hadn't been enough to fill my stomach.

I need to buy more bologna, but first I should probably deal with the rhet watching patiently from across the alley.

My dissatisfied stomach twisted. "All right. Tell Kenrith I'm ready."

The rat scurried away, blurring as it exited the alley. A screech of brakes and crunching metal brought me to my feet. The rat sat upright atop a metal trash can on the opposite alley. It lifted a little paw in wave.

I cradled my head all the way back to the fence. I wasn't sure where to go next in the search, so I set my mind to the only task readily apparent. I dug out the spell board and Glamour's ritual instructions. I read them three times, set the board mid alley and measured out the components taken from Adam's factory.

I sat in the board's printed circle, weighing pros and cons in testing the spell on Kenrith or myself. The rhet knight wasn't human, and the incantation had been designed for use on human beings. The origin spell had been tested successfully on animals. I'd always tested on animals first—especially spells I'd found through research.

God, that was a lifetime ago.

Even though it pained me to remember, it brought a smile to my face too. Jetting around the world, hacking my way through forests, delving into tombs like some action hero, it'd been a wondrous, surreal life. After our first few successes at Thoth, I'd explored the globe for old spells carved or painted in exotic hidey-holes. Lost and forgotten knowledge had sent me down lines of thought I might otherwise never have considered. The emergency room stasis spell had been one such success. It'd saved countless lives.

"And it would've saved more if Adam hadn't jacked the price so high."

Therein lay the crux that brought my disaster. We'd come to loggerheads time after time over Adam's greed. I had no problem with a small profit to keep us afloat and fund further research, but gouging hospitals for the means to save people's lives was unconscionable.

Adam had enough foresight early on to insist we include Thecia in our endeavors. Having the beautiful love of my life as part of our dreams, if only as a deciding vote, had seemed a fantastic idea.

What could ever have gone wrong? Oh, just about everything.

"Magus?"

I looked up at the small knight, hastily blanking the pain from my face. A group of variously sized rhet waited in a line against the far alley wall.

"Am I disturbing you?" Kenrith asked.

My head lied with a back and forth motion.

He straightened, holding his head high. "I stand prepared."

"I'm concerned about using you in this test, Kenrith. That woman killed how many of your people without the weapons or skills of a rhet knight?"

"Magus are wise, so it is that I brought my sons to put me down if necessary."

The rebellious recoil in my heart nearly broke my chest wide. I couldn't risk Kenrith. His matron needed him. His people needed him. Hell, I needed him. "No. We'll find a stray like that, well, no, not like *that* cat, but a stray of some kind."

A soft voice turned my head to a small rhet with a disfigured face. Parallel scars peaked out from beneath his shirt where the crutch beneath his left arm pulled it open. "I volunteer."

"Tunoh, I forbid it," Kenrith said. "Go home where you are safe."

He limped forward on his only leg and stood before me like Kenrith had. "I volunteer, Magus, for the good of my warren."

Kenrith rounded on me. Fury bent his face, but fear pled with me from his eyes. "Tunoh must go home, Magus. Risking Tunoh is not acceptable. We agreed it was to be me."

Tunoh met my gaze, pointedly not looking at Kenrith. "If something happens to me or I must be slain, it costs the warren only a burdensome mouth to feed. All would be lost without my father."

"Magus." The word carried entire dictionaries worth of meaning. When I didn't answer right away, Kenrith drew one sword—another silent declaration far beyond the simple action.

Too many factors stared me in the face. I would not experiment on Kenrith, but I needed to test the spell. I needed to see and feel all that was Glamour for myself. A stray would eliminate the sword soon to be at my throat and any factors using the spell on the fey-blooded might introduce. Until Tunoh had volunteered, the stray had been my choice.

Glamour was a variation on another spell meant to restore the grievously injured. Tunoh fit the purpose of that magic. Glamour could give Tunoh his life back while offering the answers I so desperately needed. Dad would've been the first to praise slaying two birds, but I had the impression Tunoh's father might do more slaying even if the spell succeeded.

"At what age does a rhet become an adult?" I asked.

The accusation in Kenrith's eyes echoed the pain I'd seen in the mirror after sentencing. He pressed his lips together and did not answer. The rhet behind Kenrith folded their arms and refused to speak. Tunoh probably could've told me, but his answer wasn't enough.

I rose to my feet. "Biuntcha will answer."

"Tunoh is more than old enough," Razcolm said. "Warren father or not, Kenrith cannot gainsay his offspring's choice."

Kenrith's resemblance to Rattigan returned at double strength. He pointed his sword. "I shall not forget this, imp. There will be blood between us, you have my word."

The paper spider stuck its tongue out.

"Knight Kenrith." All eyes shifted to me. "Your son shows both the courage and wisdom of his father. As a magus, I choose Tunoh—unless you wish to withdraw your request for my help."

Not that testing the components is about helping him exactly, but I'd be free to...to what exactly?

Kenrith focused his hard expression on me. If this went wrong, I had no doubt the small knight would do everything in his power to make me suffer. At long last, he turned to Tunoh. "Stubborn as your mothers, I salute you as an honor to matron, warren, and me."

All the drama apparently settled for the moment, I gestured for Tunoh to step into a smaller circle in one corner of the spell board. I'd rather have drawn my own circle, but I limited the deviation in spell recipe to target alone.

I reread the spell. I checked and rechecked component amounts and positions. I reached into the weak mananet. It felt worse than just flimsy and thin, it felt flat—almost lifeless. Willpower helped compensate, forming our swirling cream and orange spheres and closing the thaumaturgic link between them. Ironically, I once again regretted my choice of alleys. A stronger mananet field could've afforded me power for a fifth rez cage around Tunoh.

I took in a deep breath and cast Glamour.

Like in Darrin's video, the overwhelming wash of magic enveloped Tunoh in blinding, pink light. Tunoh shrieked. Pain lanced my heart in sympathetic agony.

I turned my guilty gaze to meet Kenrith's astonished expression. Tunoh's shriek stuttered, except it wasn't a shriek but high pitched giggling. Tunoh jumped up and down in the circle, transformed into a whole and wholly gorgeous rhet.

Damn.

Realization of failure stole shared elation.

Damn, I just disproved my theory. I'm back to square one.

I had no ready way to reach out to Darrin. Kenrith was ill-disposed to deliver a message for me, but Tunoh gladly planted a note summoning Darrin to me. Dumpster scraps helped lure a stray mutt who nearly bit me when I tied her to my alcove fence.

A rock allowed me to scratch an imperfect circle next to the spell board. I took great care drawing runes into the alley floor for the fifth-third rez I needed for testing on the dog.

Maybe I can get Darrin to bring me chalk or a permanent marker from Thoth.

Movement drew my attention from my careful preparations. I expected to see Tunoh or Darrin or perhaps even Kenrith. I hadn't expected to see a mirage from my past.

Thecia looked around, dressed in clothes like she'd worn in college rather than the high-end outfits she'd so craved back then. "Eli?"

The sound of my name on her lips stiffened my back. I rose, folding my arms. "I told you, Thecia. I don't want anything from you."

She closed anyway, eyes locked on the shoulder Adam had shot. Kenrith's people had healed me, but cloth around the bullet hole was still blood-stained. "I...I wanted to make sure you were all right."

"Perfect, not a scratch on me," I said truthfully despite the suggested evidence.

"That was you, wasn't it? In the factory?" Piercing worry looked deeply into my eyes. "Adam might not have recognized you, but I know your body language."

"I don't know what you're talking about."

"Why were you trying to steal our golems? You should know they're tagged with GPS asset management—" Her eyes fell to the spell board. Her voice hardened. "You were stealing components. You're going to figure out Glamour and go into business for yourself."

I opened my mouth to tell her that I didn't need to figure it out, that I was trying to fix Glamour, but doing so might incriminate Darrin. "Taking my share of what we both know is rightfully mine is hardly stealing."

She shook her head. "I don't know what you're trying to do, but Adam has SMLE and private security scouring the city for the missing golems."

My stomach knotted.

Missing?

"If they show up on a tracker with you nearby, he's going to send you back to prison."

"What do you care?" I demanded. "You lied on the stand. You betrayed me, for what? Nice clothes? Money?"

Her mouth worked soundlessly a moment. Tears collected in the corners of her eyes and I felt compelled to apologize, to hold her, to make it better.

That's just what she wants, idiot.

I cut across her, voice harder and colder than even I intended. "*I don't want anything from you, Adam or Thoth—not money, not warnings and certainly not pity. Go away and leave me alone.*"

Whatever I'd interrupted remained unsaid. She turned, hair whipping around and stormed out of my alley and hopefully my life.

"Probably for the best," Tunoh frowned at Thecia's back. "Darrin's on his way."

"Thank you."

I turned my attention back to my preparations. Darrin would arrive. I'd cast Glamour once more. Either I'd eliminate Tunoh's fey magic as a purifying factor, or the mangy little bitch would turn monstrous and rip out our throats.

·12·

SLIPPERY SLOPE

Darrin stared at the gorgeous stray mutt. My second test resulted much as the first. Tunoh had become a particularly handsome version of his father, but the mutt looked nothing like any dog I'd ever seen.

Darrin mouthed, extended a hand at the mutt and mouthed silently some more. When his voice finally returned, it transformed into laughter. "Well, now we know what an elven dog looks like."

I didn't bother to laugh. "Unless you can tell me that you had real elves to sample or some other spell that offered you—"

Darrin held up his hands. "I'm sorry, you're right, Eli. I created the elven component to Glamour."

"You care to explain how you got a spell to recreate something you don't have a component sample of?"

"Didn't you used to tell me there was something alive about magic?"

"No," I snapped. "I told you the texts alluded that magic had a mind of his own. I never claimed it as a scientific fact."

<It is a fact, human.>

"Shut up."

"I didn't say anything," Darrin said.

"Not you," I growled.

"No one else is talking."

"How did you do it?" I asked

Darrin tapped the crystal on his wrist, summoning its illusionary screen. He removed a rune chip from the wand and had the illusory screen zoom in. The marks on the chip hadn't been familiar, but my adventures had discovered new runes, so there was no reason to believe Darrin hadn't done the same in my absence. With the strange runes blown up by the screen, I saw they weren't runes at all. Darrin had arranged lines of text into rune-like shapes.

"I told the spell a story," Darrin smirked at me. "It was an accident really, old paperback accidentally kicked under the counter where I was testing the spell."

"So instead of the DNA sample component, you replaced locks of hair in my spell architecture with a story?"

"A particularly eloquent description of elves."

"How can that even work? What's the science behind it?"

Darrin shrugged. "It worked, hell, can you imagine if Adam found out what it can do for pets?"

"No. If you're going to use my help just to—"

"Whoa, hold up, Eli. I was just thinking out loud. I swear on my mother no one at Thoth will find out about this from me. Once the spell expires, there'll be no trace of this change."

"Wait, the spell expires?" My thoughts shot to Tunoh.

"Of course, you didn't think Adam would sell beauty when he could merely rent it out, did you?"

Of course he wouldn't.

It appeared I'd done myself no favors testing on Tunoh, regardless of success and now Tunoh's restoration wouldn't last. My Glamour tests offered no insights into the spell's corruption or the tainted magic surrounding the factory. I'd exhausted the stolen components, managing the spell perfectly each time.

"Can you get me more components?"

"You used all the nodules?"

"No, just what I took from the factory."

Darrin scrutinized me. "So that was you. I'd wondered. Adams in a tizzy."

"So I hear."

He frowned. "You know, I gave you the nodules so you wouldn't have to risk being arrested again."

"And I hadn't intended to break into a Thoth facility, but after seeing the product of your spell murder dozens of..."

"Whoa." Darrin held up his hands as the color of his skin fled. "Murder? Who got murdered? What did you do with the bodies?"

I opened my mouth but hesitated.

Darrin was a good kid and talented intern back when, but what do I know about him now? Moreover, do I have a right to reveal the existence of fey in our world? He's right about what Adam would do if he learned how Glamour affected pets. How much damage would he do if Darren told Adam there were fey available for the hunting?

Another thought froze me in my tracks.

What did Darrin test Glamour on if no one at Thoth knew what it would do to pets?

I pushed my curiosity and dread away. There were bigger problems. Something had brought tainted magic into the factory where the components were prepared. I hadn't gotten close enough to the pertinent vats to test each component, and either the ingredients I'd taken away weren't tainted, weren't contaminated yet or I'd possessed too little to detect the source before I started testing.

"The dead were dealt with."

"So, you *do* want friends," Sunny said. "You just have a problem with me for some unknown reason."

The groan escaped me before I turned all the way around to face her. "No, I don't want friends. What are you doing here?"

She raised a small bag. "Breakfast leftovers."

"You're feeding an army of homeless, how do you have leftovers?"

"Maybe God keeps playing loaves and fishes in the Manger's kitchen." Sunny turned her smile on Darrin. "Hello. I'm Sunny."

Darrin extended a hand. "Darrin. He keep trying to get rid of you too?"

"Bit of a Grumpy Gus," Sunny said.

"Tell me about it," Darrin said.

The elven dog sniffed at Sunny's care package. She knelt, cooing affectionately. "Who's a very pretty girl?"

The mutt licked Sunny's face.

"Great, now you've got a friend, you don't need me." I gave Darrin a meaningful look. "We need to get back to something, Sunny, so take your leftovers and your new friend and go away."

Sunny ruffled the dog's ears, talking to her like she was a baby. "No wonder he doesn't have a lot of friends, huh? Well, we'll just have to love him anyway, won't we?"

"Jesus, woman, can't you take a hint?" I snapped.

For a fraction of an instant, Sunny's smile grew brittle beneath hard eyes. "What is this animal? Is she yours?"

"She's a stray, all right, we tested a spell on her."

Sunny cradled the dog. "You tested magic on an innocent animal?"

"How is this any of your business?" I asked.

"Eli's helping me," Darrin said before Sunny or I escalated the argument. "He used to be my mentor. We're having problems with a spell based on one of his designs, people are getting hurt, so I convinced him to help me so that—"

"Why are you telling her all this?"

Darrin shrugged. "I don't know. She just seems trustworthy, easy to talk to. You won't repeat what I told you, right?"

"Repeat that Eli is helping people out of the goodness of his heart?" Sunny asked. "Who'd believe it anyway?"

I drew a hand down my face in disgust. "Darrin, can you get me inside the factory long enough to run tests at the source?"

Darrin's shoulders bunched and his nose dragged his face in the general direction of his shoes. "I don't know, Eli. I've gone pretty far out on a limb already, and Adam's bumped the security up. Escorting you in is going to be hard to explain. I could get fired or worse."

"Worse might already be in your future. In fact, you've got bigger problems than you know. The golems are—"

<I'm starting to like you, human. You've got a real flair for dramatic irony.>

What are you talking about? He needs to know about the golem possession.

<*Oh, just point him there to see for himself*>

Even without Razcolm's prompting, I couldn't have missed the two golems marching into my alley much longer. Darrin followed my gaze, the last of his skin color fleeing for all it was worth. He locked terrified eyes on mine, mouth moving soundlessly and one hand rising slowly to point over my shoulder.

"What the hell?" Sunny gasped, then mumbled, "Sorry, Lord."

Two more golems boxed us in from the alley's opposite end.

Shit.

<*And you never got around to making any war spells.*>

Oh, hell, he's right.

I grabbed Darrin, activated his eyeGuardian and shoved him toward my alcove. "Get the both of you out of here, scale that fence then run."

"She's right," Darrin said. "What the hell?"

"I told you the golems from the factory attacked me."

"You were trespassing," Darrin said. 'They defended the plant."

"Maybe, but they attacked me because they're being possessed."

The golems were too big to easily navigate the tiny, fenced off space. They were also way too big to fight.

As soon as Darrin and Sunny are over, I'm right behind them.

Despite their slow march, there'd be little time for my own escape after the other two scaled the fence—especially if they kept delaying. I had to do something, but I hadn't the first idea how to slip away with my head still on my shoulders.

Slip?

Dungeons and Dragons had enjoyed a short stint as an online game right after college. Of course, I'd soloed a wizard character and used his grease spell to slow or incapacitate enemies for easier kills. I sprinted to the nearest dumpster, careening into it harder than I intended. There wasn't time to whine or lick wounds. I threw open the top, scanning the trash and scooped a fistful of slimy noodles from the nearby Mongolian-Italian fusion place: Genghis Kahnoli's.

Truth be told, on the fly magic wasn't my thing. I'd spend months researching an old spell, reverse engineering and then planning exactly how I'd adapt it for modern use. That didn't even take into account the final product development team I didn't have or the century I'd spent without magic. My will milked the mananet for power, and my fist squeezed the rancid noodles.

The heady, warm rush of power stole my breath and almost my concentration. It seemed more than I should've gotten from the thin mananet, more like the wild magic I'd tapped near the Columbia. There wasn't time to check whether Kenrith's rhets were somewhere bolstering the sudden wash of power coursing through me. Runes and sigils swam through my mind, crashing like trailers in a tornado into a hastily-assembled spell.

The golems were almost on me. I had only moments.

Darrin leapt in front of me, waving his arms. "Stop. As Thoth Corp's chief architect, I order you to stop."

A fist comprised of rough, road debris and concrete slammed into Darrin. The shield took the brunt of a blow that should've shattered Darrin's spine, but conservation of energy still hurled Darrin into the alley wall with a crunch of bones audible over Darrin's truncated scream.

I squeezed my eyes as tight as I could, holding back tears of terror and grief as I focused on the spell litany. It tumbled from my mouth in a syllable-garbling rush. My eyes sprang open in response to the sudden outrush of power, seeking the magical lubrication spell meant to steal the golems' footing.

Personal lubricant jellies should be reserved for private intimacy. No one—certainly not me—should have a dumpster-sized KY gelatinous cube suddenly dropped onto their head, especially not in the presence of a religious prude. To say my lubricant spell had gone wrong ranked up with the biggest understatements of all time.

Sunny darted across the alley to Darrin's side. "The shield's keeping me from checking him."

"*You* have medical training?"

"No, but you're busy."

Add that to the other gigantic understatements.

Sex Jell-O robbed the golem's blow of power, but physics still threw me and my petroleum overcoat sliding. Another golem seized me with massive, asphalt hands. I shot up through his fingers, tumbling sideways submerged in lubricant. I scrambled to right myself and wipe enough glop away to breathe. Stone hands tried to help, but I slid out of his grip too. Wading through all the slime, grabbing and trying to hit me coated us all in the same glop.

Razcolm bounced up and down atop a nearby dumpster, front legs swinging pantomime blows as the little jerk giggled madly. "Yeah, grab him! Whoopsie! And another goes down! Queen of Night, this is better than the Three Stooges."

"What in God's name is that?" Sunny demanded.

"A spirit-possessed origami spider." I dodged another blow. "Do us both a favor. Cast him out."

Four huge golems and I slipped and slid in the world's worst Jell-O wrestling extravaganza. No surface had traction, but at least I had air. I pushed off an attacker, both of us sliding toward opposite alley walls. My trajectory dropped me hard near Darrin. I struggled to his side, neutralizing his protective shield and rifling through his belongings.

"Strange time to mug your friend," Sunny said.

I knew almost nothing about medicine, and as much as I wanted to check my old protégé, the best way I could help was focus on the golems. If Sunny helped him, great, but the hospital wasn't on the menu until I'd finished off the golem course. My search for a lighter turned up an eyeSentinel instead. I turned it toward my approaching attackers.

Sunny slapped down my arm. "Are you out of your mind?"'

Her rejoinder kicked in blessedly smarter than me second thoughts, halting my fingers a millimeter from the activation runes. Magical petroleum jelly coated everything including us. Activating the flame rune would send the whole alley up in a fireball that'd kill us and probably burn down nearby buildings.

The stone golems would stroll out of the alley singed but triumphant.

I tucked the eyeSentinel away.

<Aww, that would've been glorious!>

"Shut up and help me."

<You told me to leave you alone.>

I pushed myself away from the wall, leading the fight away from Sunny and my no-longer-shielded intern.

If you were planning on listening to me, you wouldn't be here now!

<True, so true.> Razcolm snickered. *<Still, maybe I'm only here for the entertainment value.>*

"Magus!"

Kenrith's cry drew my eyes upward. A golem fist slammed into my thin coating, filling my world with pain. To make matters worse, I somehow managed to be at the exact wrong place at the exact right time to be deluged with icy water.

I cursed the sky as blue as my frozen skin.

"Now, Magus, show thy valor!"

It took a moment to realize that the water had been blessing rather than a curse. Dripping, frozen and teeth chattering, I'd been freed of the lubricant. I wasn't sure how being the only one not coated in slime helped me, but Kenrith had some kind of plan.

I raised my fists in preparation to attack, trusting Kenrith— warrior to my scholar—to know something I didn't.

"No, Magus, retreat! Live to fight another day."

<Moron.>

Sunny screamed. "No, go away, get off him."

Darrin.

I spun to find Sunny gaping and Darrin vanished. His absence stole my balance and hollowed my stomach.

"Rats stole Darrin," Sunny pointed.

"Thank, God."

"Are you kidding me?" Sunny asked. "How heartless can you be?"

Once more I trusted the little fey. I raced back to her, seized Sunny by the bicep, turned tail and ran like demon-possessed golems chased us. The problem was, I had no idea where to go. I suppose the golems could've found me by systematically searching the city street by street, but that seemed a delusionally optimistic possibility. I could try running them around until SMLE or Adam's security tracked us down, but since they hadn't found four huge golems tromping around Seufert Fells, that seemed equally deluded. Like it or hate it, I needed help to get Darrin medical attention. I stopped six blocks from where I'd started, leaning on my knees and searching for Kenrith between chest-piercing gasps.

My spell-gone-wrong hampered pursuit, but the glowing green eyes of three golems still chased in the far distance.

"Ken...rith."

"Here, Magus."

"The rat just talked," Sunny said.

All fury and frustrations rumbled out of me in a snarl. "You're safe for the moment. Go back to your Manger and stay that way." I turned toward the grim-faced rhet. "Darrin needs a doctor. Where did you take him?"

"To our matron."

Biuntcha wasn't a doctor, but I offered Kenrith a grateful smile nonetheless. I wasn't sure how her healing magic differed from how the rhet had healed me, but I didn't care so long as Darrin kept breathing.

I stood taking a few sharp, deep breaths. "See, Kenrith's one of the good guys. Biuntcha will heal Darrin, and he'll be fine, now could you *please* get out of here so I don't have any more distractions trying to get me killed?"

Her expression was so confused as to be unreadable, but she turned tail and jogged away, pulling her phone from her pocket.

"All right. Any idea how we can defeat these things?" I asked.

"Golem magic can be defeated in two manners," Kenrith said. "Destroying the body can either destroy the construct or force it into prolonged convalescence while it rebuilds."

I resumed our flight at a more leisurely pace. "And the other?"

"Unwrite the spell that empowers it."

Unwrite, not erase. That sounds easier said than done.

<And only solves half the problem if they're possessed by a magical spirit.>

I cursed. The golems chasing me differed from others in the factory. They didn't merely obey their instructions and assemble component nodules. Their eyes glowed. They tracked people and staged full-on assaults.

I managed another question between labored breathing. "How can we stop them if they're possessed by some kind of magical spirit?"

"We'd need to know more about the spirit."

Somehow it didn't seem as if the golems would agree to a cordial meet and greet. Freedom really made me miss the Wasteland. Our flight took us through the perimeter of a mananet cluster of blocks. Already lightheaded, the power was intoxicating, but I somehow doubted anyone had ever constructed an energy drink spell.

I stumbled to a stop, my legs equally unwilling to keep running or stop moving. I knew from college that I should keep walking, cool down the muscles gradually, but I flopped to the ground.

"Magus, they still pursue."

Nodding was all the response I could muster. My lungs screamed louder than my other pains, but I had no time to baby them. "Chalk, can you get me chalk?"

"You have a plan?"

"An idea."

Kenrith sped away.

A groan escaped my effort to crawl back to my feet. Blinding pain crumpled me back to the concrete half way up. I tensed, worsening the cramp as I argued with my limb, trying to get it to relax. The knotted leg muscle burned like it was aflame.

When I managed my feet, the leg muscle remained knotted around the cramp, though it allowed partial, pained motion. I set about clearing the alley of debris from building to building. Kenrith returned before I finished. He handed me a box of colored sidewalk chalk and took over my cleanup.

I drew a magic circle in the center of the alley, encircling it with runes to enable all the circle resonances I knew. When I completed the first, I drew another around it and another until I had a series of concentric circles systematically grown to span the alleyway.

"Magus."

I hobbled to the other end of the circles and faced the approaching golems as they exited the far alley, waded through the busy city street and strode between the buildings bracketing my circles without the slightest alarm from pedestrians or commuters.

"Kenrith, we're missing one. Watch my back."

The little rhet knight drew his swords for all the good they would do.

Golem steps sent vibrations through the concrete I could only have been imagining. My eyes remained locked on their leader's, but my attention focused on the mananet and my outermost circle.

The last stepped inside the alley-spanning circle, and I threw up a spherical fifth rez barrier for all I was worth. The golems stopped—not in the good way where their eyes went dark and they crumbled to dust surrendering me an easy victory. They studied the ground.

My plan wasn't much more sophisticated than a castle wall, but they built castle walls for a reason.

I didn't rest on my laurels while they did whatever they did. I drew more energy, readying the next sphere. The moment they moved forward I threw it up, tightening their cage. Ring by ring, I threw up fifth rez circles. I misjudged the timing on my fourth wall. Milky white magic sprang to life, scything away half a golem arm.

I gaped.

What the hell?

Fifth resonance circles blocked physical matter from passing their confines. If a fifth rez barrier collided with body parts, it knocked them away—a source of many a college injuries and the proscription against carelessness when using the fifth resonance.

Why would a fifth rez cut through a golem but not a person?

My hopes leapt as it occurred to me that something about the innate aura of a living being must prevent fifth resonance from doing to living flesh just what it had done to the animated but not living golem.

I have a weapon.

The golems seemed less impressed. They hardly paused.

The amount of magic involved in my plan soaked my furrowed brow in sweat. I dropped the two peripheral walls and activated the next ring. A backlash of energy doubled me over when it sliced into two golems, but I managed to hold the circles—barely.

Let me be brief. I shook like an addict coming off a long overdue fix when the innermost ring caged the last standing golem. Only two of my fifth rez rings remained energized: the one that surrounded all of the golem pieces and the innermost that caged the last standing golem.

"Not the most elegant solution, Magus, but a mighty display of strength."

"Thanks," I gasped.

I studied our situation. I hadn't know which chalk circle would end up the smallest containing my prisoners, so I'd designed them all like the magical circle equivalent of a Swiss army knife. I'd intended to add a first rez to cut my prisoners off from outside magic. The dismembering had seemed a bonus, but I feared to drop the outermost ring lest the parts become a whole and beat my ass. Any number of results seemed possible if I cut off magic to only the innermost ring. I didn't want to kill my captive or whatever spirit inhabited it until I got a chance to examine it.

How likely is it I'd get another chance?

I invoked a second rez, surrounding the innermost ring in a dazzling shower of sparkling blue power that prevented magical energies from exiting. Just in case, I called up a fourth resonance circle around the second to stop ectoplasmic entities from crossing in either direction. A barely visible lemon-lime shimmer heralded a sharp bite of peppermint that almost always made me sneeze.

All combined, the amount of magic I was channeling through the circles, probably risked browning out the cluster of mananet powered blocks.

"Magus, you look none too steady on your feet."

"I bet."

I dropped the outside circle and trudged forward, stepping carefully to minimize damage to the chalk markings. A bit of manual labor that left me missing my Wasteland body lined up the various golem chunks across as many of the chalk rings as I could manage. I stepped back once more and threw a flash of fifth rez energy. Cylinders sprang up, dicing the golem pieces and dropping me to my ass.

One more round turned diced into minced. I held the innermost barriers by dumb, stubborn will, sat and breathed. Circles require a minor power drain overall, but I'd used a lot of huge circles in a very short period after not really using magic for a very long time. Paranoia kept the innermost circle bolstered at mag five strength—robust enough to stop a stampede of elephants. I wasn't taking any chances.

Three things interrupted my break in short order.

Darrin's body arrived still broken and looking worse than ever.

Tunoh sped in close on Darrin's heels. "Father, the other golem. It followed us and took Matron Biuntcha."

SMLE-marked cruisers screeched to a coordinated halt to block either end of the alley.

·13·

THWARTED
INTERROGATION

The SMLE interrogation room was too cold, overwhelmed by cleaning chemicals and brought back nightmares. A wizard eye hovered in one corner of the room, recording everything with an unblinking orb that made my eyes water. In the opposite corner, a dark dome housed a security camera that provided a means of ensuring defendants couldn't argue footage tampering.

After all, everybody knows magic and tech don't work together, so criminal mages can't adjust the tech footage.

Idiots.

Plain brown paneling served as the backdrop for an early forties cop glaring at me over an unlit cigarette. It'd probably been a one-way mirror once upon a time, but viewing magic allowed anonymous witnesses without weakening an interrogation room wall. I'd lawyered up the moment he'd arrested me. Neither of us was going anywhere until a public defender showed up.

I'd give the SMLE detective one thing, he hadn't roughed me up or abused his power in any way. When a younger officer bumped my head on the car door frame, he'd nearly skinned the kid alive. Everything had been letter perfect by the book.

The door opened. My eyes swept up the table along a pair a lean legs in dark nylons, up a black pencil suit skirt, further to a white silk blouse bracketed by a black suit jacket, past a modest bosom and gold crucifix necklace to Sunny's smile.

I dropped my head and groaned. "What are *you* doing here?"

"Who are you?" Detective Brooke asked.

"Marisol Terrel, Mister Graham's attorney."

I scowled at her.

"Unless you really *want* a public defender who'll only offer an ex-con a lip service defense," Sunny said.

"You're a real attorney?" I asked. "With a real law degree from somewhere other than a cereal box?"

"I managed to graduate law school and pass the bar if that's what you want to know," Sunny said.

She slid into the chair next to me, pulled a sheaf of papers from a very expensive leather briefcase and tapped them on the table. "Would you care to begin your questioning, Detective, or should we just move to releasing my client?"

"Your client—"

The door slammed open, and the devil himself leapt inside despite the restraining hands of two Thoth legal goons. "Why isn't this criminal on the way back to the Wasteland?"

Sunny tilted her head at me and raised a single brow that needed plucking. "This is going to be one of those fun cases, isn't it?"

I tightened my interlocked hands to hold my tingling fingers still and away from Adam's throat. My neck heated. My calves prickled, and I sucked in magic fast enough the wizard eye bobbed.

I locked my jaw and focused on a scorch mark on the table. Whatever Adam's dubious reasons for inviting himself to my interrogation, his ulterior motive would be my destruction.

"Detective," Sunny said. "Would you mind explaining Mister Mathias's presence?"

Adam pointed at me. "He was caught red-handed with my stolen property under his control."

The first Thoth goon answered, Ester, Easter, something like that. "Mister Mathias is the injured party in this crime."

"Which gives him absolutely no rights to attend a police questioning session." Sunny turned so I couldn't see her expression, but sharpened steel entered her tone. "Which your lawyers *no doubt* told you, but you decided to flout the law for some reason. Should we file a harassment suit against you, Mister Mathias?"

"There's already a restraining order in place," goon two said.

Sunny smiled at Detective Brooke. "Please note for the record, Detective, that this means Mister Mathias has knowingly and forcibly placed my client in violation of said order without my client's complicity."

"He broke into our property and stole our golems. We have GPS of them where he was arrested. He tried to kill our chief spell architect when Darrin tried to reclaim our property. He's probably the one that tampered with our spell," Adam snarled.

Detective Brooke's chair slid backward across the linoleum. The aging white guy moved his intimidating bulk with relative ease. "Councilors, remove Mister Mathias before I have him arrested."

Adam's expression hardened. "You're paid to—"

"Enforce the law," Brooke growled.

"Then enforce it," Adam pointed. "Put him away."

"Mister Graham is being questioned as a person of interest. You are breaking the law right now, right in front of me. I suggest you remove yourself to a distance in compliance with the restraining order. Now."

The legal goons managed to drag Adam out.

"Thank you, Detective," Sunny said.

"I did my job, nothing more, just like I'm going to do with your client once I have all the evidence."

Sunny raised her papers. "My client isn't guilty of these charges."

"So he'll no doubt claim."

"No, Detective, so I'll claim as I was present when the golems attacked Mister Graham, Mister Silus and myself."

A dark chuckle bubbled from Brooke's lips.

"What do you find funny, Detective?"

"That why you don't practice anymore? People found out you were shacking up with cons?"

His sudden vitriol knocked Sunny off guard. The perky, preachy woman mouthed silently a moment.

My barely restrained temper snapped several chains.

"Did you know this criminal before we put him away last time?"

"She didn't, not that that's any of your business," I growled.

"It is my business, criminal. I have to establish the veracity of the witness, determine any motive she might have for perjurious testimony. You obviously knew her before she walked in the door."

"She runs a homeless shelter, and she talks about God too much. We met the day after my release when I got breakfast there."

"Your file doesn't have you registered residing at this Manger, that's a violation of the law, criminal."

"Only if I'm living there, and stop calling me criminal."

"Are you or are you not a convicted criminal?" Brooke asked.

My knuckles cracked under the pressure of holding my hands together.

Sunny's tone rose higher as words tumbled from her lips. "My relationship is strictly based on my charitable activities running the Manger. I have no personal relationship with Mister Graham, in fact, he's repeatedly demanded I go away and leave him alone." She tapped the papers against the table several times. "Nonetheless, the homeless and especially former criminals who've squared their debts to society occasionally suffer poor representation by overburdened public defenders. Since I have been trying to help Mister Graham get on his feet and am a licensed attorney, I chose to offer him assistance pro bono. I was also a witness to the incident and called SMLE to deal with the runaway golems attacking *innocent* citizens."

She called SMLE? They didn't show up because of the trackers Thecia warned me about.

"Do you have any other questions about our relationship, Detective?" Sunny asked. "Or may we move on to these charges?"

The cheerful Jesus freak proved to be a shark. She pointed out every hole in the barely circumstantial evidence. Darrin had been hospitalized, so without him to offer counter testimony, Sunny's claims couldn't be refuted. A senior someone watching the interrogation through a viewing spell decided the evidence insufficient to charge me.

"You're free to go, criminal," Brooke said. "I promise, I'll catch the person responsible."

"A commendable attitude," Sunny said. "Let's go, Eli."

As we turned a corner, I caught a glimpse of Brooke with another cop. "We'll get him. Once a criminal, always a criminal."

Sunny led me out of the police precinct into late evening. She had a lawyer suit, a lawyer's briefcase, but the car she drove reminded me of Darren's old college car. She shrugged when she caught me glancing her way. "It gets me where I need to go."

Despite the beat up exterior appearance, the electric motor emitted only a purr of soft chirps. We rode in silence for several blocks. "I should probably thank you."

"That's nice. Are you actually going to thank me?"

"You butted in by calling SMLE. I imagine that's why you felt you had to come to help me out, but if you hadn't called them, I might've gotten some answers."

"That must be very frustrating. I know I'm frustrated not knowing just what the heck happened in that alley."

"You heard what I told the detective."

"I did," she said. "But this was more than just a random attack. Mister Mathias claimed that you broke into his factory, tampered with his spells, and abducted the golems."

I admitted nothing. "You were there. You saw them attack us."

"What about the rest? And what about magical rats? Eli, tell me what's going on. I can't help you or defend you without a clear picture."

I stared at her, my jaw clenched. I didn't want her help. I didn't want her involved. I certainly didn't want to tell her about Kenrith or any of the rest. She'd been of immense help in the interrogation room, and I could tell by the way she had defended me, that she was a dyed-in-the-wool Crusader.

In some ways, that was good. If Sunny found out what was happening to Thoth's customers, Adam might get his due, but Darrin might get hurt in the fallout.

Darrin. I should really check on him.

"You're not going to tell me, are you?" The tone of her question held more shark than sunshine.

I sighed. "I need to check on Darrin, buy—"

She pulled the car to a quick stop along the side of the road. She turned, gaze hot and fierce. "Eli, I want to help you."

"And I've told you before that I don't want your help."

She growled as one fist slammed the armrest between us. "Dammit, sorry, Lord. Mister Graham, you are the most stubborn, pigheaded man I have ever met."

My own temper rose in response. "And you are the nosiest woman I've ever met. I don't want you involved."

"Too late."

"That's exactly the problem. I lost a whole day in there. The longer I waste time answering your questions and sitting here, the more likely a ma—that other people are going to get hurt."

Those intense eyes bored into me. Dozens of gears turned behind them until they seem to lock into place. "Where'd you need me to take you? Hospital?"

I shook my head. "No. visiting hours are probably over, and I really can't spare the time. Take me back to my alley."

She opened her mouth to say something else, but whatever it was never escaped her lips. She pulled back into traffic and said nothing more, not even when she stopped in the alley. She reached over me and unlocked the old car's door with her dark eyes tight and lips pressed tighter.

I got out of the car.

She didn't drive away immediately. Whatever her internal wrestling involved, she settled it, put the car back into gear and drove away.

·14·

THE HOLY WATER HEIST

I dragged my feet down my alley and collapsed in the alcove.
Just need to sit down a minute, then I'll eat something...somehow.

Exhaustion stole my consciousness without granting a spare thought toward easing my hunger. When I awoke, the rain had washed away some of the badly-executed lubricant spell. Steady drops had disintegrated Sunny's so-called, golem-flattened leftovers, leaving a discolored smear across the alley concrete.

A shift of movement across the alley caught my eye. "Kenrith?"

Tunoh appeared. "He is hunting, Magus."

"Is there any way to find out where he's gone?"

"Couldn't you use magic?" Tunoh asked.

Tunoh was right, but whether to track Kenrith, Biuntcha or the golem seemed the most significant question. Thanks to Sunny's interference, the last rhet matron had been taken hours ago. Kenrith was no doubt on her trail. Following his matron would doubtless lead him to the others.

I exhaled, the weight of it all falling away, letting my thoughts escape. "Then he doesn't need me anymore."

"Not so, Magus," Tunoh said. "My father is a mighty knight, but alone against so many golems..."

I finished the sentiment. "He'll be hard-pressed to survive."

Something about the set of Tunoh's gaze seemed fragile, as if he were younger than he appeared even though he'd reached the age of majority. At one time, I might've moved heaven and earth to help a friend, but my friends had sold me out.

Kenrith came to my rescue. He watched out for me even though he personally didn't believe I'd help his people.

I met Tunoh's gaze, and somehow the small rhet made me feel even smaller.

<You're going to be smaller if you charge off unprepared; think smeared golem toe jam.>

Shit.

Razcolm had a very definite point. I'd managed enough of a lead to allow drawing circles to trap the golems, and it had been a happy accident that a fifth rez wall invoked at the right moment had sliced through them. I couldn't count on such serendipity again.

But what in the hell can I possibly throw at these golems?

My stomach grumbled. While I thought, I dug into my bags hoping to find some morsel of food I'd missed on the previous six searches. A slightly squashed yellow snack cake hid in the bottom of one bag. The package seemed sealed and the cake remained within date. I frowned at it. Sunny didn't seem like a sugar coma snack cake kind of woman. I didn't look the gift horse in the mouth, but even homelessness failed to make greasy yellow sponge cake taste good.

<Oh, that's a face that'll definitely freeze the golems in their tracks.>

"What are you doing back, Razcolm? Surely, you'd rather find a better body and be on your way."

<More than you know, but His Majesty thinks you are my best chance at eliminating the disturbance. If you ask me, old buzzard's been in his cups again.>

"I thought you said we couldn't talk to your king until the new moon."

<You can't talk to him, human.>

"Fine, did he send any suggestions on how I might help you?"

<None.>

"You possessed one of the golem, are you and they the same?"

<Here I thought working with you couldn't get any more insulting.>

"What can you tell me about them?"

<Nothing.>

"Magus, should I destroy that construct for you?" Tunoh asked.

"What? No, why?"

"Your tone and body language suggest its presence troubles you."

"Not the construct as much as the possessing spirit, but he'd just move—maybe into something less useful."

Tunoh inclined his head and retreated across the alley.

I tried to review what I knew, but my stomach's snarls demanded my full attention. The previous day's activity had forced me to forge my way forward without stopping to eat at all. The mananet provided magical energy for spells, but shaping and controlling that magic too personal energies. Whether because of starvation or my own hubris, I had nothing.

I'd known other companies made autonomous workers to cut their bottom line, but I'd been in the business of helping humanity, not putting people out of work.

I'd had no time to research combat magic. Some kind of sound weapon might vibrate the golems in worse repair apart, but I had no idea where to start on a spell like that.

A bell? Maybe a megaphone?

Kenrith had called the magic around the factory infernal. Employing divine magic to eject the infernal spirits sounded great in books. If it wasn't all confidence scam fodder, I had no idea how to tap into that kind of power. Like it or not, I had to trust Biuntcha to Kenrith a little longer, see to myself and hopefully experience a moment of inspired genius in the process.

I crossed to Genghis Kahnoli's dumpster. Throwing the lid open hurled a snickering Razcolm against the brick wall behind it and revealed mixed to-go containers, open-mouthed garbage bags oozing plate scrapings, celery tops, onion peels and other ingredient waste. None of the visible dinner remains looked rancid, but the scent of rot clung to the dumpster's interior.

Razcolm scurried onto the other lid, peering in with me. "Oh, sifting through that's going to be *fu-un.* Sure you wouldn't rather go see your girlfriend, raid her cupboards and her skirts for dessert?"

Heat prickled down my neck. I turned my gaze to my hijacked construct. Razcolm had wrapped the paper with foil chip bags for protection from the elements. I opened the hamster ball and set it between the plastic ribs of the dumpster's lid.

"You're going to love this." Will suffused my voice. "Fill this vessel with unspoiled foods from this dumpster."

"Screw you, human."

I drew on the mananet and focused harder. "Construct, do as I command."

Razcolm yelped as one of his legs jerked forward. "Stop. I won't."

Tunoh giggled from across the alley.

The spider climbed into the dumpster, its motions a jerky fight for control over its limbs. Razcolm had pointed out the dual nature of the golems, suggesting that while he'd hijacked control of my construct, the construct's animating magic remained underneath—magic I'd invested into it, magic that worked for me.

"Two choices, help the spider finish the task to get it over with quicker," I folded my arms, "or get out and be gone."

To my surprise, the spider started digging through the trash like a mad thing. Razcolm took the ball into the dumpster after dumping the first load into the ball. In no time he'd filled the ball to the top with leftover food. He plopped the ball onto the dumpster top, forcing me to lurch forward to catch it before it smashed on the alley far below.

For a moment, I thought I caught a smug grin on his mandibles.

I capped the ball and rolled it around, searching for the trick hidden beneath his obedience. The contents were thoroughly mixed in a way that meant a mishmash of flavors, but I didn't find any sign of rot or mold.

So what's he trying to pull?

Razcolm shrugged in response to my narrowed gaze, doing all he could to emanate an innocent aura.

Come summer the food in these dumpsters will go bad in far less time. I need a way to feed myself year round. If this is my new life, I need to learn new means of survival. I am a magus, a spell architect, why not make my own way with magic?

I dug through the to-go containers littered across the refuse's top until I found one holding only smashed breadsticks. They left a tiny, dried puddle of garlic and oregano, but an otherwise clean container.

I made a note to obtain a canteen of some sort and set about drawing with Kenrith's sidewalk chalk. Pink lines formed three circles similar to a Mickey Mouse head, but with the ears inside the biggest circle. I sat down inside with them, set the hamster ball within one of the smaller circles and the to-go container in the other.

<Oh, this ought to be ri—>

A soft blue-wife field enveloped the outermost ring, cutting off incoming magic and whatever else Razcolm had to say as a bonus.

Interesting, he communicates magically, not telepathically.

Swirls of orange and cream rose around the smaller rings. Magic can do a lot of things that technology can't, though I'd heard something similar to what I was about to attempt had been mimicked recently with tech. Regardless of whether our best minds had developed tech versions of arcanology's miracles, magic adhered to rules—even if we hadn't figured them all out.

The more old spells I'd reverse-engineered, the more it had become clear that conservation of energy ruled magic too. Spells were built upon ideas. A caster's will and the components employed molded the magical energy to achieve the desired result. The end result always equated to the combined mass and energy introduced minus the energy expended to create the change.

The hamster ball contained food.

Good, bad or rotten, the contained food equated to the ingredients of the blended paste dripped into my stomach all those years I'd been jacked into the Wasteland. Heat was used in cooking, among other reasons, to kill bacteria. With exceptions like soup, most foods could be burned—more often than not in the case of my sister Zahda's cooking.

Just have to blend and heat the ingredients without emulating Zahda.

I scoured my mind for the arcanology terms best suited to my desires, taking time to double check both meaning and order to avoid repeating the Great KY Gelatinous Cube incident. When I'd architected the spell's structure and the mantra's framework, I invoked the biomass conversion and purification spell.

I'll have to work out a better name later.

Energy washed from mananet to me to hamster ball. A peach glow wriggled into view along the cracks between noodle, meat or vegetable. On my left, like light sparkled along the interior of the of the to-go container's clean lid. The food in the ball drained away as the new food built up layer by layer like an object built by a 3-D printer. I cut off the spell when the ball's interior crisped and blackened, leaving me with a food brick the size of a small, microwave lasagna.

My stomach groaned with anticipation.

I extinguished my circles and picked up the new food. The heavy brick smelled brown, but not rotten. I bit into it tentatively. Elements of the original food remained, giving me a sanitized, incredibly dense meatloaf-lasagna hybrid that desperately needed salt. The first few bites stayed down, quelling my gut under a thick, reassuring blanket.

Just like Mom's meatloaf—tasteless, dry and dense as concrete.

I collected the hamster ball and my remaining food brick. The brick went into a plastic retail bag, and I tucked the ball behind the fence with my other belongings.

Not only had my experiment filled my stomach, but it'd also reminded me of Mom's Sunday meatloaf after church. It also brought to mind that our church's sanctuary had had a cleansing pool in its entrance.

As solutions went, using holy water against infernal creatures seemed pretty iffy, but legends usually had some basis in fact. Since I had no idea how they created holy water, there was no way to know if divine spring water equated to a strange kind of chemical weapon brewed to antagonize some demonic allergy.

Either way, it seemed a pretty good bet Sunny would know where I could get my hands on some.

Sunny folded her arms, pressed her lips together and tapped a single foot. "No, absolutely not."

Her posture was doubtless meant to leave me cowering and pliant. I shrugged. "Fine, I'll find a supply on my own."

"I can't wait to see how they write up those charges."

Much to her chagrin, her suggestion made me laugh. "Grand theft holy water? Baptismal burglary?"

"There is no way I am going to let you steal from a church."

"I'd rather not even step on church grounds, but Kenrith said the golems are powered by infernal magic, and Razcolm added they were being controlled by spirits. I've got nothing to hurt them, so—"

"You mean damage Thoth property, in violation of court order?"

"Okay, since I know of no spells to help me damage Thoth property in violation of court order, I was hoping dousing them in holy water would drive out the possessing spirits, restoring the automatons to Thoth control."

"What a good Samaritan you're becoming." Sunny's mocking smile grew into a warm, cheerful smile that scared me to death. "If that's the case, you don't need to burgle a church. You've got me."

"You're going to steal the holy water for me?"

She rolled her eyes. "You can't be this dense. I'm going to cast out the unclean spirits for you, problem solved."

My hands leapt up, stopping her headlong charge toward the door. "Whoa, I don't think so. I've already got one hospitalized...acquaintance."

"And he called to him his twelve disciples and gave them authority over unclean spirits, to cast them out, and to—"

"No, not happening," I said. "I've fought these things. You don't stand a chance."

"I was there, remember? You might as well just concede, you know you're going to lose this argument."

"*Please*, Sunny, just help me get the holy water and stay out of this fight. People's lives are depending on what we do."

She watched me for what felt like a half dozen eternities. "I really can cast out unclean spirits."

"Right." I couldn't help my chuckle. "You're some badass cleric." Her hands returned to her hips, and her glower intensified.

"Fine, you can. Whether you can manage it without getting your skull pulped like a melon in the elephant enclosure is what concerns me most."

That unsettling smile returned. "So. You're asking for my help, huh?"

A frustrated roar escaped my lips, greeted by her laughter as she picked up her phone. A moment later, she hung up, scribbled a note and extended it. "Pastor Grance will have two gallons waiting for you at this address."

I reached forward to take the note.

Sunny snapped it back. "In exchange for my help and my *not* accompanying you, you agree to attend Sunday night dinner and fellowship."

"You're *blackmailing* me for the supplies I need to help people?"

"Six o'clock. Don't be late."

I bit my tongue, snatched the note and exited before the snarl behind my clenched teeth worked its way free.

Pastor Grance asked no questions when a black, homeless man with a paper spider riding his shoulder like a parrot appeared at his door for two gallons of holy water. His casual acceptance made me question both Sunny's clout and the general intelligence of the clergy. Either way, I found a small park and went to work with a hand siphon pump, holy water and a bag of water balloons.

I'd assembled half of my second dozen when another man dressed much as I was approached. "You can't camp out on that bench."

"Do I look like I'm sleeping?"

"Camp out, sit there, eat there, nothing. Go away."

My scowl didn't faze him. "Exactly why can't I sit on a public bench?"

He pointed to a sign.

"Don't worry, if my dog craps, I'll bag it even though the crap is fertilizer and natural fertilizer is good for the environment."

"No, you moron." He jerked me roughly from the bench, spilling my open jug of holy water and bringing my nose around the back of the sign.

I decked him, hurriedly capping the bottle before he recovered. I met him with my fists up. He looked down and away like he'd given up, but my fist caught him when he ducked in. If I'd been in the Wasteland, he'd have stayed down a while but back, in reality, I had to make him go away the old-fashioned way. "Look, I can't read your scratches, but I can beat you bloody if you don't leave me alone to fill my balloons."

"Duval will hear about this."

The strange European head of the bum mafia leapt to mind. "Look, I just want to fill my balloons in peace and move on."

"You've squatted in my territory and assaulted me. You'll hear from Duval, I guarantee it."

<You know there are illness spells: pneumonia, smallpox, various short-duration plagues. No one could ever connect the deaths to you.>

Killing people is wrong.

<Who says? The God you don't believe in?>

I believe in God. I'm just not speaking to the bastard.

<Says the guy who intends to fight demons with God's power all the while robbing Him of the credit by calling it alchemy.>

There's a basis in science for all magical phenomenon.

<Even if you don't know said science? Put that way, sounds like faith.>

"You hear me?" the bum demanded.

Razcolm's spider unfolded and refolded becoming a pigeon. He shook out his feathers. *<You know, your world's severely overpopulated. Killing people like this leech eliminates waste and preserves oxygen for those that'll use it to do something worthwhile.>*

Shut up, Razcolm.

I stared down the other homeless man. "Unless Duval has demon-possessed rock monsters on his payroll, I've got bigger problems. Go away."

I re-engineered my slip-n-slide spell while I crossed the city toward the industrial zones. It probably would've been smarter to have a tracking spell up, but I figured I had a good idea where to find the golems. I wanted the slip-n-slide spell ready. It would drop the golems, I'd hit them with the holy water, and God—or more likely alchemy—would do the rest.

Raiding a dumpster just outside the city center provided components for a slip-n-slide or three. I tossed around puzzling out some kind of sonic attack on the hoof but decided to bring up a seeking spell instead.

Some thread, a magnetized needle, and some castoffs courtesy of Tunoh spun me around more than ninety degrees left of my intended course and away from the Columbia. *Shit, maybe I should stop making assumptions.*

·15·

SPELUNKING FOR GOLEMS

Following the taut elastic tug of the seeking spell brought me into quickly-deteriorating neighborhoods. Pervasive Edison blocks forced me to backtrack to a mananet pylon and draw in energy to sustain my seeking spell before returning to my search. Something about the magic still felt off, like the magic I'd used before my release had gone stale in comparison to the raw ley energy.

City works hadn't done a very good job keeping up the roads, making streets far too Mad Max for nicer cars. Stained, faded and cracked apartment complexes lined the street the spell led me along. Empty chairs sat outside almost all the ground floor front doors, the otherwise social neighbors driven inside by the cold. Small strip malls came and went between the complexes. Convenience stores and pawn shops, liquor stores and closed businesses clustered together like homeless in financial winter.

The cars parked around stores and apartments were old model hybrids held together by bumper stickers espousing a war of liberal and conservative candidates, socialist and capitalist ideologies, pagan coexist declarations and the occasional sports team logo. Only an occasional LUX drone wove its way through the poor streets.

Streetwalkers took note of me at first but quickly discounted me as worth their time.

<Prostitutes always seem to be capitalists.> Razcolm chuckled, the spider unfolded and refolded into a foil-wrapped bird. He let out a large squawk. "Booty ahoy." Razcolm squawked again. "Pieces of ass, pieces of ass."

Rather than be outraged, the ladies laughed at the bird's antics. I sped up my gait to escape lest the prostitutes take offense and take their outrage out on me as Razcolm probably intended. After six hundred miles of bad neighborhood, magic brought me to a small, dilapidated strip mall.

A gigantic sinkhole had eaten half the parking lot. Behind the veritable crater, a new age shop that should've known to pick another location displayed a holographic tarot reader. The hologram didn't include an auditory track, but the grim and mysterious reader presented omens to overly animated and deliriously happy customers. The few cars parked in front of a boarded-up VCR repair shop.

I circled the sinkhole warily, glancing into its depths while approaching the Mystic Menagerie. My hand drew the shop door open enough to ring its jingle bells a moment before the seeking spell yanked my attention sideways. I circled the joined buildings, attempting to triangulate. Half way around the building I stepped over rushing magical current that almost swept me away.

Every hair rose. Like with the power I'd felt below the Columbia, it seemed far away yet close—closer than that beneath the riverbed. Elation surged through me. Not only had I likely found my quarry, but a source of Ley I could almost touch. Hunger and need followed close behind exhilaration.

Chuckles bubbled from my lips.

They've found the perfect place for wizard mischief. Who'd have looked for the source of a magical plague in Seufert Fells' worst neighborhoods and biggest Edison blocks?

After the initial swooping sensation, headiness eased without stealing away the subtle tingle. I drew long, slow breaths in through my nose, inhaling magic with the winter air and feeling more confident with each lungful of air and power. I'd discovered them, found their hideout.

<It's lucky for the tracking spell it had you along.>

I ignored the little pest, drawing in even more of the sensual power until I'd filled every corner. The ley line had to be deep beneath the ground as I could just barely feel the warm press of it against my skin.

I backed up and wandered over the side lot trying to define the boundaries of the small but fast-moving stream of raw magic. Uneven concrete caused an occasional stutter step or a slight shift of balance.

Something about the earth-filtered power reminded me of something, but I couldn't seem to catch the fleeting thought.

Something about old pizza, guess I'm just hungry.

I hurried to circuit the building, cursing the uneven footing more than once. I found the downstream path of the ley line, verifying it went straight beneath the strip mall.

Kenrith has to be inside the repair shop.

My footing slipped as I whirled back to charge the shop and rescue my friend. "Come on, Razcolm. Let's rescue the rhet so I can go home."

<All right, if you say so.> Razcolm snickered. *<Maybe you should sit down first, maybe eat something?>*

My head shake seemed to wobble. "No need, I have all I need right here."

I took a deep breath, bolstering courage and drawing energy out of the ley line. More warmth filled me. My nose tingled. The next breath of ley energy overwhelmed my senses with rot. My stomach roiled. I bent over and vomited onto the broken concrete.

<Out with the old.>

When I finally caught my breath, I realized getting sick had cleared my head.

This is definitely the place.

<What now oh mighty wise guy?>

"Is the ley energy what's—"

<*Knocking you on your ass, drunk as a freshman after an initiation party?*>

"Yeah."

Razcolm chuckled. <*Your master should have introduced you to channeling the raw a little bit at a time as you were training.*> "I didn't have a master, well okay, I had Emlimn, but he wasn't my master in the same way as the old fantasy novels."

Razcolm cradled his face. <*Old buzzard has it in for me.*>

"We need to figure out how to get inside?"

<*They have these new inventions, they're called doors.*>

I snorted in spite of myself. "I imagine they're locked."

<*Well, you could bother to check, or you could knock on the door.*>

The back door of the out of business VCR repair shop was locked. In the Wasteland, there'd been no need to learn lock picking. Breaking and entering had been mostly breaking. Plywood boarding up the windows offered no easy access, and the rear door was a typical exterior security door.

<*You are utterly hopeless.*> Razcolm refolded into a spider. He leapt off of my shoulder inserting needles into the lock that moments before had been little fangs. The lock clicked open. Razcolm leapt back to my shoulder and bowed, foreleg extended toward the door.

I hesitated.

A girlish scream exited Razcolm's mandibles. He placed a foreleg on either side of his face. <*Oh, my, officer. I heard a damsel in distress. When I rushed to her rescue the door was unlocked.*>

"You're not as funny as you seem to think you are."

<*Did they kill your sense of humor in prison or were you born retarded?*>

Illegal activities hadn't been one of my electives in college. Anything I did without my identity hidden underneath glamour risked further incarceration. My instinct was to take cover behind the door jamb and push the door open slowly, but doing so meant looking suspicious in broad daylight. Instead, I slipped inside the building as if I belonged there, pushing the door closed behind me. The magic hit me once more as it had at the factory, but either I remembered it wrong, or the taint over this place was at least twofold. Blinking furiously, my eyes finally grew more accustomed to the dark, turning pitch black into black dotted with darker silhouettes. I lowered my voice to a whisper. "Kenrith?"

No one answered.

Can you search the place?

The origami spider shot me a dirty look complete with extended tongue, but jumped off of my shoulder and skittered into darkness. I slipped further into the repair shop. I moved with exaggerated slowness to compensate for my unsteady footing. I bumped into several of the heavily-laden racks and overflowing boxes making cacophonies that earned me Razcolm's dirtiest looks. An archway rather than a door separated the retail and repair sections of the shop. A small desk sat in one corner of the back room beside the door that led to a bathroom the size of a gym locker.

Tiny slivers of light filtered through the cracks in the boarded-up windows. The dust our movement through the neglected storefront raised glittered in the small shafts of sunlight leaking in.

<Nothing.>

"What about a basement, stairs, ladder, anything?"

Razcolm propped spider legs on his waist. *<I know how to search.>*

"They aren't here. If they aren't here, and they aren't next-door, then there has to be some way to get beneath this building."

Razcolm crawled up to my shoulder. *<You mean like a massive hole in the parking lot?>*

"There wasn't anything in it."

<And just how close did you get? Did you check for, oh, I don't know, an illusion?>

I hadn't. At the time, the whole area had seemed to be Edison-powered without any magic to power an illusion. I hadn't rechecked after discovering the ley line.

We exited through the back door and approached the sinkhole once more. The whole way I kept my thoughts on Kenrith and his matron as much as I could, allowing it to be a surprise when I snatched Razcolm from my shoulder and hurled him into the hole.

"What do you think? Illusion?"

<Yes, jackass. Get down here.>

I blinked down into the hole. Curses spilled from my lips as I eased myself down inclining concrete chunks. A dumpy little old lady exited Mystic Menagerie, sipping from a teacup held just below a tag that named her Maven. She smiled and lifted her teacup when she caught my eye then re-entered the shop.

Shaking my head proved a mistake. I took a dizzy step to regain my balance only to step on a concrete slab that was pure illusion. Absent footing tumbled me down the broken parking lot fragments like cheese against a gritty grater. I hit the ground almost two stories down in a rain of dust and debris.

Razcolm giggled. *<Oh, you should see your face.>*

I glowered up at the little asshole perched just beneath a shaft of sunlight that illusion had hidden. Half my body, including my face, stung. I picked gravel out of my hand and forearm, afraid of what my reflection might reveal.

He might have warned me.

<Might have, didn't.>

Ignoring Razcolm didn't cool my temper or sooth the pain in my face but kept me from shredding the little spider. Various forms of emission and reflection offer our eyes light, colored by light wave scattering and at least a quarter a semester's worth of additional physics technobabble. The concrete under Razcolm seemed light grey beneath the sun. It didn't emit much if anything, but I broke a piece from one edge. Magic and will connected the fractured orphan to the whole still basking in relatively rare winter sunlight. The chunk remained illuminated despite my taking it beneath the ground. An additional trickle of magic fed into the rock and excited the electrons along the sympathetically illuminated surface. Together, they provided sufficient light to navigate the section of old sewer at the foot of the hole.

The concrete tube led into the Earth over, around and on either side of a sludge that stank more than the ley-line's magic had. I turned right at the first junction, intent to find the space beneath the repair shop.

Razcolm cleared his throat.

I turned back to him. "What?"

<This way.>

"The repair shop is this way."

<Thank you, Captain Obvious, but I'm pretty sure you're not thinking three-dimensionally.>

"The seeking spell led me to the repair shop."

<Suit yourself.> Razcolm continued down the other tunnel.

I cursed and rushed to catch up with him. The spirit inhabiting my construct was a colossal pain in the ass, but he had a job to do. Until he completed that nebulous chore, he was stuck with me. As far as I was concerned, I wished him speedy success with whatever he'd been tasked.

A break in the sewer wall offered a massive tunnel descending deeper into the ground along a slow downward curve. Not far into the rough passage, the slope pitched sharply downward. Occasional ridges that might've been meant as stairs slowed descent into short headlong slides broken up by brief gasping pauses.

The up and down, side to side descent into the Earth quickly foiled any sense of depth or direction I might've had. The passage leveled out, opening up right and left to a precipice over a vast natural cavern.

No longer focused on not doing a Jack and Jill, the progressive rise in magical energy surprised me as I stepped out from behind solid stone into a deluge of power.

Ley energy tumbled out of the far rock face in a short waterfall. The pearly white stream of floating magic plummeted into a sunken riverbed without ever touching down. Undulations swept the cavern interior with a kaleidoscope of rainbow light. An occasional touch of ley energy against the bank left molten rock dribbling into a sunken riverbank wider than the ley line's girth. Another touch blossomed amazing but bizarre flowering plants that wilted and crisped a moment later. The airborne river split around a small island bearing a cage formed of tight iron pentagons. The ley line's glow seemed drawn into the prison's interior only to escape even brighter.

Both outer banks teemed with smaller creatures that resembled the handful of demi-goblins at the horde's outer edges.

<I hate goblins. Disgusting, infernal things.>

What were apparently goblins cackled and snarled, screamed and savaged one another armed with iron, serrated-edged swords and vicious knives. Their dark blood dribbled from the banks, staining the ley line where they connected and turning white to vomit yellow.

Goblins hurled themselves at the cage in groups or solo kamikaze charges. The river caught some, either perverting their shapes into shriek-inducing Picassos or incinerating them outright. Those that overcame the ley line met a tiny shape racing back and forth around the cage's perimeter. Kenrith's curved blades and pure nerve repelled goblins from the isle.

Glowing green-eyed golems wove through the writhing, ravening crowd. They scooped up the fallen, wringing out recently dead goblins over a bronze vat of almost black blood.

Razcolm? What are we looking at?

<A killing floor.>

For what purpose?

<Have you no eyes? Where the rhet originate goblins keep their numbers in check. The scent of rhet drives them into a frenzy.>

What has that to do with the golems? Why do golems want goblin blood?

<Time to leave, human.>

"Leave?" I demanded in a harsh whisper. "We just got here."

<Quiet. If you're heard or scented they'll shred you for taco night. Goblins are quite partial to dark meat.>

Kenrith is down there, and I'm betting that light is at least one rhet matron.

<So what? Do you see any good hiding places? If you go down there the golems will see you and stop you. If you make it past them, shredded human. So unless you have a real whizzbang of a fireball hidden in your ass, we're done here.>

Razcolm knew full well that I didn't. I had holy water balloons and components for a few slip-n-slide spells. What I really needed was a SEAL team or at least an 80's action hero.

How did goblins get into Seufert Fells? I thought all fey were extinct.

<Can humans be any more pathetically naïve?>

Probably.

At that, Razcolm snorted loudly despite possessing no nose. A nearby golem raised acid green eyes, dropped the corpse from his blood-blackened, clay fingers and marched toward us. A quick peek over the precipice offered a view of the stairs carved into its face.

Shit. Yup, time to go.

Kenrith's voice rose triumphant over the horde. "Magus, at last! Lay waste to our enemies!"

Goblins and golems turned our way. A one-count later, goblins and demi-goblins charged us with roaring battle cries. The golems followed, sedately chasing juggernauts.

<Dig deep, human, find that fireball.>

I stepped to the edge of the precipice and incanted slip-n-slide. I drew magic as part of the casting, not considering the effect of drawing on the rushing ley line as part of an active spell. Magic burned through me. Heady, drunken euphoria proceeded searing pain behind my eyes. I threw myself backward as goop smelling like rancid french-fry oil rained from the cavern roof. Thick slime covered the rough stairs and surrounding ground. My design improvements on the slip-n-slide spell had been meant to employ inert goo similar to that used by my flame extinguisher spell. The scent worried me, suggesting the resultant ooze should be kept away from matches.

"Give them what for, Magus!"

Yeah! I pushed up my sleeves and balled my fists.

I can take these things.

Razcolm yanked my ear. When I turned to him, he slapped me across the face—his tile leg-tip drawing blood. *<No, you can't. You certainly can't beat a goblin horde and half a dozen golems with your fists. If you're going to commit suicide, at least stick to your plan. You're halfway decent with those.>*

The pain in my face helped me think.

The water balloons.

I strode to the precipice's edge, picked out my target and curled one corner of my lip. I withdrew a yellow balloon, hefted the bulbous weapon a few times to learn its weight and threw. Rubber-encased holy water wobbled along a clean, high arc and then into a slow fall.

My breath froze.

The balloon hit a golem square in the face, compressing and distending to fall unbroken to the cavern floor.

Shit. The next one I threw broke against a golem arm with only dampening effect. Below me, goblins climbed over top of their slipping and slippery brethren. I didn't even spare time for another curse before I hurled a third.

The orange balloon hit an asphalt golem directly between the eyes. Holy water exploded over its face. The glowing eyes vanished.

"Yes! Score one for—"

The golem wiped his face and opened his eyes once more.

<Score one for the big rock monster about to kill you.>

My gut knotted, but hopefully Kenrith would respect my knightly efforts to haul ass back up the passage. The steep descent-become-impossible climb quickly exhausted my energy reserves. I wanted to climb higher before releasing my second slip-n-slide or at least reach stable footing to minimize the chance of falling down into the spell's area of effect.

There wasn't time.

I unleashed the spell just as the slippery goblin horde swarmed into view. The sudden slug of descending slime carried the goblins back down the hole, but the goblins and demi-goblins didn't stop. Long nails dug into rock but offered insufficient traction to narrow my lead. I reached the upper landing unscathed and unchallenged with enough time to cast my last slip-n-slide.

I afforded myself a few deep breaths before fleeing toward the sinkhole. Razcolm and I hadn't quite reached the junction where we'd argued when the boss golem slid out of the concrete wall opposite the passage to the surface. He turned, intricately carved face furious.

I hit him with a water balloon, ducked under his arm, hit him with another for good measure and ran hell for leather for open sky.

Razcolm disappeared shortly after we reached the surface. I rushed away, my mind moving even faster than my feet. Razcolm caught up moments later on a stolen moped he claimed had been left there for us.

I made a note of the cross streets so I could return it later and scootered to safety.

.16.

STUDENT WISDOM

Truth be told, I wasn't sure where to go.

I'd found the matrons, but my plan to help Kenrith hadn't worked. Holy water didn't clean out the spirits possessing the golems. At best, I'd cleaned the walking petroglyphs.

Maybe I should've let Sunny come after all.

<Good plan. You can sacrifice her while you...what was the new plan?>

It isn't to sacrifice anyone.

<Not even the jerk from the park?>

No.

<How about Adam?>

I considered his suggestion a moment.

Razcolm snickered in my mind.

Couldn't get him out here anyway.

<You sure? Isn't SMLE tracking the golems? One anonymous tip could bring him out here and splat! You reclaim your sex toy, take over the company, and we live it up.>

We?

<You're going to need an advisor. You're way too naive.>

No.

Discarding Razcolm's Machiavellian plot left me with limited options. The golems had attacked me in my alley once already, and I still hadn't come up with a way to defeat them or even stand them off outside a fifth rez barrier. If they didn't pursue me right away, I'd have time to prepare defensive circles near my alcove. Unfortunately, a defensive attitude didn't offer much to recommend

173

itself. Kenrith fought a defensive battle to protect Biuntcha and any other matrons in that cage. He couldn't keep it up forever.

He needed help, and I was all he had.

<Humans—insufferable, arrogant, self-important monkeys, the whole lot.> Razcolm cursed in a language I didn't know, but his tone required no translation. *<You're all he's got. There's no way a whole warren of rhet could help?>*

"You're right. Go to Tunoh, tell him to meet me at Gateway Park with as many adult rhets as he can get."

<And if he asks why he should do anything you say?>

"I need their help saving Kenrith and his matron."

Every one of Razcolm's foil surfaces rippled, coming to a stop in a new shape that resembled a particularly shiny pigeon. He flew off, leaving something behind on my shoulder that couldn't possibly be what it resembled but probably was anyway.

I continued up the street and turned toward the hospital. Spaces marked for motorcycles near the entrance made parking the small scooter easier and kept it close at hand in case I needed to make a hasty escape.

As with most hospitals, this one smelled like sickness and chemicals. I'm not a big fan overall, but that was more about history than about the hospital's ability to take care of the sick. A receptionist looked me up and down several times with disgust but gave me a room number when I inquired after Darrin. The security guard paced me down the hall. He rode the elevator up to the third floor. I stopped short just outside the elevator as security sidled up to the nurse's station.

Two large Thoth goons guarded a door that had to contain Darrin.

Shit, what now?

The security guard watched my reaction and tensed. I wasn't really dressed for blending, but I didn't have any illusion magic.

Besides I have every right to visit Darrin.

I strode up the door. "Excuse me, gentlemen."

"I am sorry, Mister Graham, but you are prohibited from entry."

I looked at the shorter of the two guards. It took a moment to recognize the man. His buzz cut was barely long enough to see the strawberry blonde of his hair, but it clued me in. "Francis?"

The other goon, Clayton, shoved me backward. "Buzz off."

I glanced back to see if the security guard was going to do anything. Since he didn't look interested in intervening, I turned back to the door. "Francis, I need to talk to Darrin."

Clayton shoved me harder. "I said to get. You're not allowed within a thousand feet of Mister Silus."

"On whose authority?" I demanded.

"Restraining order." Clayton licked his lips. "If you persist I get to beat you and return you to prison."

My brows rose. "Are you calling Darrin property? Francis?"

Francis frowned.

The security guard stepped forward. "I'll escort him out. We don't want any trouble."

I jerked out of the guard's grip. "The restraining order prevents me from closing to within one thousand feet of Thoth *property*."

Clayton grinned and balled his fists.

I dropped my head dejectedly. "Don't bother, I'll go—" *past you.*

I focused on the cracks along enough tiles to encircle the three of them and threw up a fifth rez circle. I squeezed past the sudden cage, pushed open Darrin's door and stepped inside halfway expecting Adam to be there.

He wasn't.

I threw another fifth rez behind the closed door to keep it from opening and released the guards outside. I rushed forward.

My former protégé lay strapped to the bed in a mishmash of struts, slings, and plaster. His eyes met me at the door, brightening as bandaged lips curled up a heavily bruised face.

His voice was a rasp. "Eli, you're okay."

"Which is more than I can say for you. I told you to run."

"I had a sentinel, I thought I could help you."

The guards pounded on the door.

"Darren, you might be all grown up now, but give me a little credit. I wasn't going to go toe to toe with those things. I was right on your heels."

"You—" Choking cut off Darrin's words. "You looked like you were trying to cast something, not run."

I sighed. "Yes, to slow them down so we could all *run*."

Clayton shouted through the door. "Mister Graham, you have to come out of there this moment."

"What's going on?" Darrin asked.

"Adam doesn't want me talking to you."

"Clayton," Raising his voice sent Darrin coughing, but he tried a second time. "Clayton. I asked Eli to visit. I'm fine."

The pounding stopped. A moment later Clayton's voice returned. "Are you sure, sir? He hasn't ensorcelled you or anything?"

I rolled my eyes. Whether or not I'd bespelled Darrin, his answer would've been the same.

"No. I'm fine. Please stop pounding on the door."

The security guard shouted next. "Mister Graham, you need to drop your spell. Blocking Hospital doorways is unsafe and violates...no, you're staying out here. I don't care what your boss told you."

"Seems it's equally unsafe to unlock the door. We'll stick with the privacy lock I've installed."

Darrin and I looked at each other a long time. The gears turning behind his eyes gave no indication of the equations grinding between them. My own gears weighed how much I could tell him. In the end, I chose to inform him of everything but the rhets.

"Glamour, when casting the spell with tainted components works perfectly, changes the target into a Demi-goblin."

The color drained from behind Darren's bruises, making him look like an oddly splotched Dalmatian. "That's not possible."

"Why? Because fey are extinct? What if I told you they weren't?" I held up a hand to stop his questions. "I can't tell you everything, but I can promise you the fey are not extinct. You already know about the golems tainting the component somehow. They've also taken... prisoners."

"This is all impossible, Eli. Golems do what they're supposed to do."

"Not if they're possessed by some kind of controlling spirit." I took another deep breath. Even with as serious as the situation was, I couldn't keep the awe out of my next sentence. "I *saw* a ley line, a floating, swirling stream of wild magic."

His awe joined mine. "What was it like?"

"First time I got close, the Ottiren warned me off. The second time I couldn't get close because of the goblin hordes that swarmed all around killing one another trying to get at and eat the prisoners."

"Ottiren? Goblins? Wait, *real* goblins? How could you even know what they are?"

"I *know*, that's enough. Somehow the golems lured goblins from where they hide and tricked them into a killing frenzy so whoever is controlling them could wring the blood out of dead bodies into vats."

"I don't understand. Why would they want to do something like that?"

In some ways, I really didn't want to answer because what answers I had didn't complete the puzzle's whole picture. Of those that might talk to me, only Emlimn and Darrin knew enough about magic to help me think this out. Emlimn was—I shuddered—not easily accessible.

Hard as it was, I chose to surrender the superior mystique of being his teacher. "I don't know, Darrin. I can't figure this out. I need your help."

Darrin laughed. "You say that like you expect that I think of you as some all-knowing Superman. I know that you're human, a particularly prideful human in fact."

I laughed too. "Me? Prideful?"

Darren squeezed thumb and forefinger closer around the plaster between them. "Maybe just a little."

The color drained from Darrin's face.

"What is it? Are you all right?"

"This is all my fault," Darrin said.

"You did something to the golems?"

"No, not that part. You said the spell is creating demi-goblins. None of the test subjects in Thoth's care that experienced a full transfiguration into a monster have changed back. They won't either. God, how could I have been such an *idiot?*"

"Help your old teacher out here, Darrin. What have you figured out?"

"The blood."

While the golems and their motives remained a mystery, pieces of Darrin's puzzle clicked into place, and with the picture completed, a possible solution arose. "Goblin blood plus Glamour and vain human equals demi-goblin."

"Yes," Darrin said. "I left the DNA component out. The golems added it back in somehow. Shit, this explains the product delays, even the lost temporal component despite a huge power cost. Magic tries to accommodate the story *and* the DNA, but runs out of juice before it powers the stopwatch."

"Magic doesn't accommodate, Darrin. It's not alive." But all this does mean Tunoh's transfiguration is temporary.

Darrin bristled. "Explain how that elf dog happened then."

"I can't, but I can guarantee you that Glamour is adhering to rules we might not understand yet. Magic is not alive."

"Fine. You've got to stop the golems from using that blood before they irrevocably change too many people."

"I'm open to suggestions." The further along my brain got assembling a reversal spell, the more likely I thought it possible. I didn't tell Darrin, if only to keep him focused on recovery rather than false hope.

"What did the ley line do when a golem neared it?"

I shrugged. "Didn't see that happen."

"What do you think would happen if they did?"

"It melted itself a riverbed—or changed what it touched. No real way to tell, but something tells me I'm not getting golems to voluntarily walk in for a soak."

"Then trick them into it."

I opened my mouth to object when a thought occurred. "Third rez."

Darrin beamed. "Exactly."

Third resonance circles could be used to connect magical constructs and spells. Combined with sixth and second resonance barriers, they'd been used to connect pylons and make the mananet possible. PGE's tap room flashed into memory.

Employing magnitude five rune sets perpendicular to the ley line—like tapping an irrigation hose to add a sprinkler head—could redirect some of the flow.

Giving me a weapon in and of itself.

I'd have to splice my new mana path in a place where none could tamper with the circle—preferably where they couldn't even see it. The goblins crashing into the ley line flashed before my mind's eye, seeding my gut with nauseating twists.

Invoking a fifth-sixth-third-second resonance construct won't be easy, and I've got to lay it out in the bedrock beneath the line...without letting it touch me.

The derisive snort escaped under its own power.

No problem, just a minor issue after you've gotten by the golems you don't know how to hurt and the army of the goblins not to mention the demi...oh, shit.

"Darrin, any ideas on how I can deal with demi-goblins without hurting them?"

"Trap them in a fifth-first rez?"

The idea had merit, but I had no idea how I would draw that big a circle before I got clobbered. Moreover, such a large circle would catch goblins too.

Probably feel bad if I caged the demi-goblins with goblins that ate them. I need smaller circles, but I won't have time to draw them.

A solution sprang from the depths of my mind. "Darrin, could you get me more spell boards?"

"Kind of laid up here, Eli."

"Didn't you call yourself Thoth's chief spell architect? Can't you just make a call?"

"I was joking. Adam's not giving anyone the chief spot. He'd rather dangle it so we'll try to outperform each other for the promotion."

"Sounds like Adam. Please tell me you can get them. I'd *really* rather not have to ask Sunny for materials."

Darrin blushed. "Could you, um, hold the phone to my ear?"

From my side of the conversation, whoever Darrin called for a dozen spell boards and cases didn't seem like the cooperative type. Darrin stopped mid-wheedle, staring up at the television.

"Just have them delivered," Darrin said. "I've got to go."

I hung up the phone as hard as you can by touching a crystal. I took the hint, picking up the remote locked in Darrin's gaze and turned up the television.

A man's voice overlaid the video feed. "Reports are sketchy, but it seems several groups of stone men are abducting people at random. Despite the amazingly quick response, SMLE has been unable to stop the abductions; several officers taken with the other victims."

Shit.

"An anonymous tip places the blame on notorious criminal and former chief architect for Thoth Corp, Elias Balthazar Graham."

Fucking Adam.

I spun back to Darrin.

"Haul ass, Eli."

Mopeds don't make loud revving noises, squeal tires or screech to a halt. Nonetheless, I took the borrowed bike from best speed to least as rapidly as I could manage. I didn't want to risk not finding the right kind of dumpster on my way from Gateway Park back to the ley line cavern, so I stopped at a dumpster I knew would have slimy food fit for the slip-n-slide tweak I had rearranged in my head.

The dumpster lid rewarded me with a world of slimy stink, some of the waste still warm from recent dumping. Food oozed from each fistful. I grabbed deeper than I should have in my rush, getting to-go containers and paper I had to pick out. I was about to close the dumpster once more when something shiny caught my eye. Shoving a box aside, I uncovered the head of an industrial kitchen sprayer. The handle and trigger assembly had been dented, and a raggedly-cut section of flex conduit trailed off of it. I snatched it up, shoved the chow mein covered treasure into a pocket, and raced back to the moped.

I stopped a once more at the foot of Gateway Park's guardian statue. The broad, overlapped mananet crossed my eyes. I reached out to let the mana seep in only to feel fierce, wild magic deep beneath the somehow lesser mananet. An intern with a Thoth Corp security badge shifted his weight from leg to leg, guarding several portfolio cases stacked atop a park bench.

I strode over to him. "Thanks. I'll take those so you can go."

"The hell you will, Mister, bug off."

"Those spell boards are for me...from Darrin Silus."

He narrowed his eyes. He activated a holographic chip and poised a finger over the screen close enough to summon the keyboard. "All right. I need your name for delivery tracking."

"Elias Graham."

The poor white kid didn't have much color to spare, but it ran away so fast, in other circumstances it might've left behind a wet, yellow trail. He squeaked a response. "I can't give these to *you*."

Tunoh's rhets whisked the stacked boards away behind him.

I smirked. "Too late."

He whirled about too slow and mouthed at the empty bench and me in seemingly random intervals.

"Might as well head back to the tower."

Kid narrowed his eyes. "How did you do that?"

"Enchanted rats."

"Fine, be that way." He scowled further and stomped off.

Moments later the stack returned.

Guess Tunoh didn't want to risk him being able to see through glamour.

I grabbed the top portfolio bag, unfolded the board onto the bench and knelt beside it adding rune markings with a silver sharpie. I had the second one done and inserted into a case with the first and room for a third when Tunoh spoke.

"Pardon, Magus, but your creature said we were needed. How may we serve you?"

My head popped up. "Where is the little terror?"

Tunoh flipped long, beautiful hair over his shoulder and off his face. I followed his gesture to find a shiny pigeon perched with the other grey birds atop the griffon statue.

"Get down here, Razcolm. I need something cleaned."

"I am not that kind of servant."

"Don't really strike me as much of a servant at all, but I can't start inscribing it until it's clean and dry."

"We can do it, Magus," Tunoh said. "We are also excellent multitaskers, fully capable of doing what you need while you fill us in on the plan."

A chuckle bubbled from my lips. I was in a hurry too. I had no idea what plans the golems had for the matrons nor any idea how long Kenrith could hold out. Add to that golem abductions; the need to return to the cavern mounted. I poked fun anyway while I inlaid more marks upon the spell boards. "Is patience not covered in the Rhet Knight Code of Chivalry?"

"I'm a squire," Tunoh said.

"Ah."

"Speaking of patience reminds me to warn you. Golems lurk near your place of rest."

I stiffened. "How many? Is there one with a detailed face?"

"Five including the leader with intricately-worked stone," Tunoh said.

Glad I didn't go home.

I hurried my strokes, marking the third board with the necessary runes. The pen caught between strokes leaving a slight tail.

Probably won't matter, but we'll use that one last.

I folded the board up, exchanging it in the portfolio bag for another and laid the new board out atop the silver X I'd marked on the mismarked board's case. "Tunoh, can your people write runes—these runes—in tight places where they might not be able to see what they're drawing?"

"I can try," Tunoh said.

Considering his answer was probably the best I was going to get, I nodded. "Your matrons and Kenrith are surrounded by many goblins and demi-goblins."

A murmur drew my eye to the rhet lurking beneath the foliage just behind the bench. I ran my eyes throughout the nearby plants, seeing rhet hidden in large numbers. "These rhet are all adults?"

"Yes, Magus."

"*All* your father's and Biuntcha's offspring?"

Tunoh's expression soured. "A matron may not mate, and my father would *never* rob a warren of their matron for mere pleasures. Besides, my mothers would never tolerate him taking a third wife."

Third?

"I apologize for my mistake. Just haven't seen any female rhet other than Biuntcha."

"Are you certain, Magus?" Tunoh placed one finger to his lips then opened his cloak more fully. A sheen of magic shimmered into view atop Tunoh's skin, sparkles fading away to reveal a young woman more beautiful than Biuntcha in the same if slightly differently shaped armor. By the time I blinked a third time, Tunoh's glamour had turned her male once more. "Females are rare, though not so rare as matrons born. Our warren has many fathers, but my father, Knight Kenrith, fathered them all."

"Does anyone else know?"

"My father, my mothers, our matron and you."

I lowered my voice. "How do you, I mean, how do rhet find a spouse if they never know they're seeing a female?"

Tunoh smirked. "When I choose a male, he will know."

"Why the disguise?" I whispered.

"Not all females disguise their gender." A sad smile touched Tunoh's face. "Unfortunately, your people aren't the only ones possessed of wrong thinking."

"Did your mothers tell Kenrith, that is, does he know—"

Tunoh smiled. "My father knows you tested your spell on his singular, infirmed offspring."

Oh yeah, when the spell wears off, I'm in deep shit.

Razcolm returned with the sprayer. Water dripped out of the broken hose. <*What?*>

"It's still wet."

<*Only on the inside, what's that matter?*>

I handed the sprayer to Tunoh. "Can you get the hose off of this and dry its interior?"

Tunoh bowed. "At once, Magus."

I finished modifying the spell boards and worked out the latest changes to my slip-n-slide spell while I waited.

When the sprayer returned, I checked the trigger laid along its handle. It levered out a screw that hypothetically opened the valve. I set to work with my sharpie, drawing a circle around the open end where the hose had connected. When I finished, I passed the handle and pen to Tunoh. "Much as I hate to waste, you can break the pen to fit the tip inside for drawing."

Tunoh shrank—pen and all, entered the handle, stepped over the circle I'd drawn at the sprayer's butt and set about drawing. "All the way to the other end, Magus?"

"Yes. Please."

They can slow time, why couldn't they get smaller. How much bigger can they get?

Tunoh finished the task, stepping gingerly through the marks before handing me my pen. I thanked her then explained what I needed of her warren. Tunoh found me volunteers among my reluctant helpers willing to shed their own blood to save their matron.

·17·

ASSAULT ON GOBLIN CAVERN

I returned the moped on the way back to the cavern. The modified spell boards added to my already heavy load. Razcolm sat atop my shoulder not lessening my burden with his endless litany of things he expected to go wrong. Tunoh and her young warriors moved from cover to cover in the periphery. I imagine they could've used a group glamour, but they seemed to be saving their energy for the fight ahead.

We descended the sinkhole into the sewers. Before I could illuminate another chunk of sunken concrete, a soft nimbus surrounded several rhet. The air, the stink, the feel of magic—none of it felt different, but tension knotted my shoulders. It manifested in the slumped stance of the rhet around me. Even Razcolm withheld his ordinarily abrasive commentary.

We reached the section that descended into the cavern. I turned to Tunoh, unpacking the spell boards from their portfolio cases. "Have the others remain up here and wait until summoned."

"Yes, Magus."

I lurched toward the descending tunnel eager to do what must be done only to pause. "Razcolm, scout ahead."

If I had thought Razcolm's comments projected into my head felt strange, they were nothing compared to his wordless grumbles. Tunoh and I waited for the construct to return.

Razcolm invaded my thoughts before he came into view. <*Two golems guard the precipice.*>

I extended a hand. Razcolm leapt into it, bouncing up and down on his spider legs. Tunoh provided the three small swollen balloons. I cautiously affixed the straining, red balloons to Razcolm's back by pulling their knots through the tight pockets in his torso then anchoring them with small rusted paperclips beneath his stomach.

"Are you two ready?"

Razcolm's mandibles rubbed one another across smiling needle teeth.

Tunoh merely inclined her head.

I took a deep breath and took great care stepping sideways down the natural tunnel's steep descent. I stopped part way down, scratching a back and forth "circle" reminiscent of coils on the back of a refrigerator and the accompanying runes in the cavern side with a spoon worn down to a sharp point. I hadn't asked where Tunoh had acquired the makeshift stylus. Razcolm paced the ceiling above us while I drew, balloons straining each time he switched directions.

We descended further, and I drew another switchback circle. The third time I almost lost my footing, sending pebbles skittering down the tunnel. I held my breath and strained to hear the approach of golem footfalls.

When none approached, I released my pent-up breath and hurriedly carved another circle. My three landmines in place we followed Razcolm until we were forced to stop or reveal ourselves to the guards. I looked up at the origami spider and mouthed, "go."

Razcolm stuck out his tongue then scurried across the rock ceiling out of sight. Tunoh pressed her face close, whiskers tickling my ear as she sniffed a few times. "He is not a very respectful servant."

"Tell me about it." I reviewed the plan once more sneaking peeks around the corner to check Razcolm's progress. He scuttled along the cavern ceiling beyond and between two still golems—neither with glowing eyes.

This is going to work. It has to.

Razcolm crawled two-thirds of the way across the cavern before he stopped. He hooked a leg into one of the paperclips, pulling it away like the pin of a grenade. The red balloon already straining to accept gravity's pull dropped away.

Our vantage prevented seeing the actual impact, but a sudden uptick in snarls, growls, and screams proclaimed the payload of rhet blood had intensified the goblins' frenzy. If Razcolm had stuck to the plan, then the balloon had splattered pure goblins with the fresh blood of their enemies.

A second balloon dropped from Razcolm as he rushed to his next position. The tumult of frenzied bloodlust redoubled. Green light burned to life in the guards' eye depressions. They turned toward the precipice and descended into the cavern.

I flashed Tunoh a smile and crept forward. When I neared the edge, I dropped to hands and knees. The goblins writhed in a berserker melee half a cavern away from the stairs. Golems waded into the battle, snatching up the dead and dying to wring their blood into the waiting vat. On the island, Kenrith bent over and rested against his knees, watching the mayhem in the momentary respite. "Now, Tunoh."

Tunoh had barely vanished back up the passage when Razcolm's sudden exclamation in my head yanked my attention.

<Oh, shit.>

The origami spider plummeted from the high cavern ceiling, his previous slow descent sped by the weight of exploded rhet blood and balloon fragments.

My heart rose to block my throat. I found myself already on my feet and headed to Razcolm's rescue when I realized I might never get another chance to enact the plan.

The construct's just paper. Razcolm can always hijack another body.

I raced down the stairs and across the cavern with one eye on the fight and the other on the undulating stream of power. A savage cry seized all of my attention just in time. I ducked a demi-goblin's sharp, bloody claws. He leapt at me once more. A claw caught me across the chest, ripping fabric and tearing flesh. Pain followed a moment later. I snatched the sprayer handle from a pocket, raising it to parry the next blow.

Two rhet careening into my calves, ripping away my footing. I hit my back and tensed for an attack. A demi-goblin claw slashed through the place my face had just vacated. The perverted human froze all except his frantically sniffing nose. My saviors smiled at me from behind his legs and pantomimed a shoving motion.

I kicked out with both legs.

He tumbled backward, tripping on the two rhet. An instant before the demi-goblin hit the ground, four more rhet positioned a spell board beneath him. A fully opaque fifth rez circle sprang up around the demi-goblin in an instant, made possible less by the added runes or my will than the massive amount of energy coursing down the ley line.

Unfortunately, our little altercation and the appearance of live flesh and blood rhet drew the horde's attention. I scrambled back to my feet, dodging left and right around golems in an all-out sprint toward the energy river.

"Magus, no!" Kenrith said.

I threw a slip-n-slide spell ahead of me in a swath ten feet wide. My heart hammered against my rib cage, trying to batter me away from rapidly-approaching peril. Over the span of four full-speed strides, I guessed where the floating ribbon of energy might rise, sidestepped into line and dove headlong into the slip-n-slide spell.

The ley line dipped lower than I'd ever seen it go. A pearly white wall of death and rainbows filled my vision. I close my eyes, oddly wondering what Sunny would've said were she in the situation.

Jammed fingers and wrists offered a moment's warning before I slammed face first into rock. They cushioned the impact, though the speed I'd picked up careening through slime still slammed my head into stone and rang my unintended battering ram.

Groaning and disoriented, I opened an eye and massaged my neck. Every hair on my body stood straight up, straining to escape the rioting mob of goose pimples. My stiff neck punished me for the slow turn which allowed me a view of the wild magical lifeblood pumping into my world. At that moment, I might've been willing to attribute anthropomorphic qualities to magic, but I had no time.

Crawling a slow turn and staying as low as possible, I positioned myself in the center of the riverbed and started to carve. Beyond the riverbanks the sounds of pain and battle reached me. I only hoped Tunoh and the other rhet remained alive long enough for me to finish my task, free the matrons and make our escape.

When every carved line was perfect, I traced the grooves with a black sharpie. I'd intended to leave off the fifth rez circle in case it hampered my siphon, but it occurred to me that absenting the physical barrier to guide the magic might bring about disaster. At best, the redirected energy would change the stone where the runes were carved, eliminating the circle. At worst, I was about to bath myself and the riverbed with pure ley energy.

The runes shaped the combined fifth-sixth-third-second rez into a cylinder. The inscribed geometry canted the upper facing to form a kind of scoop. I readied myself to energize the circle, about to congratulate myself for a job well done when the next flaw in my plan nearly took off my head.

I'd carefully planned how to slip beneath the ley line, how to tap the energies, how to distract the goblins, how to destroy the golems, and even how to trap the demi-goblins until I could attempt to correct their condition. I just hadn't given any thought as to how I'd escape the riverbed without burning my fool head off.

"Magus, this way." Kenrith waved me upstream to where he crouched. He leapt upward a moment later, disappearing back onto the island between parted magic.

There are plenty of movies where an angry drill sergeant kicks the hero's ass when he sticks it up too high crawling through mud beneath barbed wire. The death above me might've had nothing to do with bullets, but it was real enough to be my end. I wanted to take my time. Agonized screaming didn't allow me such luxury. I reached the lee of the island, and its slightly less imperiled assent.

I watched the ley line, once more trying to get a feel for its rise and fall. I took a deep breath and jumped.

The magical energy in the cavern far outstripped the mananet covering Gateway Park. When I first experienced the wild magic, the intoxicating power had been almost blinding. Casting that first slip-n-slide in the cavern had seemed to sear my every nerve. None of those experiences prepared me for merely wetting the tips of my curls in raw ley energy.

Lightning seeks the closest path to ground. Fire reaches upward from its fuel, consuming all within its reach. Raw, wild ley energy grabs you like direct-current and shakes you like you're a rat in a terrier's teeth.

Whether the bare handful of my short curls wasn't enough to keep hold or momentum stole me from its grasp, I landed on the island wrapped in agony around euphoria around need.

I reached a hand for the power.

Kenrith's sword sliced a line across one cheek.

Fingertips strained to touch magic's blood.

He sliced the other.

I rose onto hands and knees that shook so violently I could barely keep upright. I wove drunkenly as I leaned toward the ley line with a hand extended. Kenrith yanked me backward, screaming incoherent sentences at the top of his lungs. A flash of steel near my eye reflexively brought up hands in defense. His blade sliced across the dense nerves in my palm.

When I first returned within reach of the mananet after my century of imprisonment, I compared the feeling of that moment to one of an addict sighting a fix. I'd never actually taken drugs. Drugs threatened to steal my mind, and my mind was my most precious possession. In that moment, having only barely touched the raw, wild magic, I suddenly knew true addiction.

Plunging into the ley line would probably destroy me, but part of me didn't care about the arguments pummeling the insides of my skull. People needed my help, but I was willing to let them die if I could just touch the magic a few moments more.

All at once the power vanished but not the need.

Kenrith stood before me within a glowing circle traced around us. "Breathe, Magus. Long slow breaths and all will be well."

The sudden lack of all magic wracked me with physical torment. I drew up my knees, wrapped my arms to pull them tighter, shuddered and sobbed.

"Your kind are not meant to touch the Ley." Kenrith peered up into my eyes, deep sadness in his gaze. "I wish there were time for you to grieve and heal, but it is not so. You must rise, Magus, and fight the enemy that has done this to you."

Maybe Kenrith knew me better than I knew myself. Maybe his age granted him a better understanding of our race. Anger was something I knew well. The idea of vengeance had driven me to stay alive in those first years of the Wasteland. I pushed away the pain and the need and met Kenrith's glowing eyes.

He nodded. The first rez circle vanished, taking with it the soft blue-white haze coloring the world.

Plunging back into the magic-heady cavern dampened my anger but didn't douse it. I yanked the sprayer from my pocket, raised it in my fist and invoked the third rez circle that capped its end in swirling creamsicle magic. I reached beneath the ley line and opened up the conduit.

Ley energy sprayed the goblins on the opposite bank the moment I squeezed the trigger. Streams of ley incinerated goblins or warped them through agonizing transformations.

The euphoric power in my hand wrapped me. Goblin screams filled me not with guilt but more fury. Their deaths delighted me.

And they're only the start. These creatures forced me from my quiet return. They attacked my city. They'll pay for every injury. They'll—

Tunoh's voice rose above the din. "Magus, the demi goblins, please help us!"

I froze, loosening my grip so that the spray ceased.

Demi-goblins ripped open rhet bodies with their teeth, spun atop spell boards trying to catch more of the circling little creatures. Disemboweled carcasses littered their feet.

In my moments of distraction, countless rhet had been eaten alive following my instructions. I reached out to the magic around me and hurled it at the spell boards. Mag five fifth rez fields sprang from every board. Demi-human limbs caught in the overpowered circles were knocked away so hard the impact broke limbs and wrenched them from joints. Their owners howled in torment behind opaque milky white power. I invoked first rez circles just within the fifth.

"Tunoh, now!" I yelled.

Demi-humans protected from physical and magical harm and rhet in rapid retreat, I cut loose with the sprayer. A typical industrial kitchen sprayer couldn't possibly have reached the edges of the cavern, but the back pressure behind my weapon stretched its ability to lay waste to the farthest walls. Rock melted in glowing dribbling lines like mere tallow.

Rhet bodies littered the ground, bloody, disemboweled and half eaten.

Raging fury stilled, icing over. The steady stream of ley melting goblins and stone heated the already warm cavern.

Mere goblin deaths were not enough for me. Adam's golems had brought death to my little friends, and they had to pay. Sandblasting beams of wild magic drilled steadily into golem stone. Their doom must've been apparent to even them, because several lined up as a wall of rock, using their bulk to shield a hasty retreat with the goblin blood.

The river kept me from pursuit as much as it had thwarted the goblins' attempts to reach the matrons, but I was a Magus.

I have all the magic in the world. I can do anything, be anything.

"Magus, help me free them."

I didn't have time to help the little rhet Knight. I had to chase the golems. I had to stop them. I remembered the plan in a rush. Despite maintaining more than a dozen hybrid magical circles, I invoked the three fifth rez switchbacks prepared in the tunnel.

There was no way for me to tell if I had cut them off from escape or at the waist with what would have been two-foot-wide zigzags of magical energy. I sucked in power. The cavern's temperature rose and my temper with it. Thoughts flickered of growing wings— angelic or draconic—to carry me to deliver my foe's destruction. Not knowing how to fly, I settled for empowering my legs in preparation to leap over the ley line.

"Magus?"

An incoherent snarl escaped me, but I turned to direct the sprayer's beam across the top of the iron cage. I'd expected the metal to melt away like the stone.

It didn't.

The iron cage warmed slowly, glowing heat coming to life with agonizing slowness. Heat buffeted me as raw ley turned the cage into a heating element.

"Magus, stop!" Kenrith demanded. "You'll kill them."

I cut off the sprayer, spitting impatient snarls at the knight. "What the hell do you want? I'm trying to cut them free."

"Iron and fey magic are antagonistic. You'll cook them before you melt the bars."

Blood vat and golems disappeared atop the precipice.

"I don't have time for this."

I threw a slip-n-slide over the cage to quench the heat without considering the possibility of it igniting and leapt away over the ley line, landing harder than I expected. Bodies and bizarreness littered the cavern floor. No clear path allowed pursuit without wading through blood and guts. I climbed the stairs in a hurry. Heat pressed against me. I forged on and upward toward the first of my landmines. I could barely breathe in the narrow, stone stovepipe trying to vent the veritable oven I'd created below.

There'd been no time to properly measure the dimensions of the passage. As such, runes drawn to define the trap set in the hastily estimated space had been infuriatingly inaccurate. The end result blocked the passage with cut rock, fallen stone, and scattered golem chunks. I willed the trap circles further up inert and returned to the cavern for help clearing the rubble.

Maintaining so many circles represented a significant drain even with the ready power nearby. Neither the circles nor the trip back to the precipice should have left me gasping. By the time I reached the cavern floor, dizziness threatened my footing.

My captives snarled as I approached, throwing themselves against the fifth rez barriers. Not one seemed improved by the blue-white energy cutting them off from magic.

The transformation is permanent then like Darrin said.

I adjusted the circles imprisoning the demi-goblins spell board by spell board, activating runes that tapped directly into the ley lines to maintain the combined fifth-first resonance cages.

I managed the last one before darkness threw me to the floor.

·18·

GIVING UP, GOING HOME

I awoke in a psychedelic, hell-tainted paradise. Exotic foliage sprouted at random intervals on walls and between illuminated columns caging demi-goblin victims of their own vanity. Cooled, melted stone ran down walls with just as little logic in their placement.

Razcolm studied me from a foreshortened stalagmite. *<You're crazy, human, but I admire your sense of style.>*

Something in his tone left me feeling the butt of the joke, but his opinion meant less than nothing until our crisis had been defused. I struggled to my feet. The cavern swam. The stalagmite proved too short to steady my balance, allowing me to tumble back to the ground.

"Steady, Magus," Tunoh hurried up to us. "Rest. Trust us to handle cleaning up."

The cavern had been partially cleared of goblin corpses. A team of rhet collected whole and severed bodies, carrying them to the ley line for incineration. Kenrith's back was to me and stiff with anger. A knot of glowing, slimed-fouled matron scowled down at him. Biuntcha seemed the only matron defending the little knight.

"What's going on there?"

"They want to slay the demi-goblins," Tunoh said.

"No." My voice carried farther than I expected. I fought my way upright and stumbled over to them. "These demi-goblins are my prisoners, and you will not harm them."

"Magus, this is rhet business," Kenrith said.

"The hell it is. They're humans perverted by whatever force empowers the golems."

A matron at least twice as old as Biuntcha glowered up at me over folded arms. "These humans owe us blood debt for slaying our kin."

I drew on the ley line without thought. Pain sweetened the rush of euphoria. My body shuddered with pleasure. "If you harm them, you will answer to me."

Every rhet in the cavern froze. All attention riveted to me.

<Woohoo! Threatening a rhet matron. Way to make friends and declare war.>

"You will show respect, Magus," Kenrith growled. "I do not wish my hand forced to slay you."

My conduit sprang open as the sprayer catapulted across the cavern into my hand without being consciously called. "I have no idea how Knight Kenrith kept you safe as long as he did, but you owe me for your freedom and ultimately your lives. All of you."

Another matron spoke with undisguised disdain. "No, human. You soiled and insulted us. It was Matron Biuntcha's warren who rescued us. Shed their blood to—"

"Distract your captors long enough for me to engineer your rescue." I'm not sure whether I was drunk on ley power or just so pissed off I didn't care anymore. "Matron Biuntcha's generosity leads me to ask her forbearance to restore my people. You, I'm ordering. Leave them be."

The first matron hissed. "We could reduce you to a gibbering monkey."

A squeeze of the sprayer shot ley energy high over their heads. "Shut up, I'm talking."

<Oh, shit. I might have to thank the old buzzard after all.>

"I didn't want any part of this. I just wanted to be left alone, but Matron Biuntcha convinced me to help." I pointed at the nearest demi-human. "They're the price for my help."

The three matron joined hands. Power gravitated from around me to the glowing trio at my feet.

"Go ahead. Kill me. I'll laugh at you from the afterlife as demi-goblins overrun the city and eat your warrens."

"We control this cavern." The second matron said. "They won't draw any more goblins through to this world."

I laughed. I couldn't help it. "Here, maybe, but the golems are using so little blood to create each demi-goblin that I couldn't even sense it. They took gallons away with them. Enough to transform half of Seufert Fells."

Even as I said it, the weight of the realization pressed down on me. I turned toward my closest prisoner. I'd have to determine her identity and track down where she lived for any chance of transforming her back. My gaze swept over the others. Thoth caged dozens beyond the eight in my circles.

How can I ever cage and restore so many?

Icy claws gutted me as my eyes fell upon a crumpled body just beyond a caged demi-goblin cradling his arm. Large toadstools grew out of her burnt flesh, complete with door, windows, and a little welcome mat.

The sprayer tumbled from my fingers. The light metal hit the ground with a crash like a locomotive. I ran to her, matrons forgotten. The demi-goblin in the cage that had obstructed my full view threw himself at the circle when I stopped short. A half-demolished mushroom house stuck out of her head where she'd tried to claw it off her ravaged face.

I killed her.

True, I'd killed I didn't even know how many goblins. They were goblins. Whether they were living, breathing, sentient creatures or not, goblins weren't real to me. The horrify corpse couldn't have been older than twenty.

Young, vain and very, very dead because of me.

<Magus? Beware. They're debating your death.>

Did you just call me magus, Razcolm?

<You're obviously delirious from trying to suffocate yourself.>

198 | MICHAEL J. ALLEN

The sound of metal hitting stone turned me around. Kenrith glowered at the matrons, arms folded and swords discarded on the floor. The three matrons stalked toward me like a tiny version of the Sanderson sisters.

Tunoh stepped in front of them. "I will not permit you to harm the magus."

They stared at her. The third matron who'd not yet spoken in my presence let out a disbelieving songbird's voice. "You're Kenrith's cripple."

"Not anymore," Tunoh said. "If the magus says he can restore his people, then he can."

Guilt strangled my already torment-twisted guts.

The first matron pushed Tunoh aside and continued her charge. Tunoh raced around to interpose herself once more, arms outstretched. "I won't let you harm him."

She pushed Tunoh aside again. "This isn't any of your business, boy."

"It is." Tunoh cut them off again. "I've chosen Eli to husband."

A quiet surpassing all of its predecessors fell, seemingly sucking air from the cavern. The silence reigned six eternities only to be shattered by Razcolm's laughter.

I rushed forward and scooped Tunoh from the ground. "I need to talk to you."

Razcolm addressed the cavern, front legs in the air. "Everyone go about your business. The two lovebirds need a little *alone* time."

Read what I'm thinking, Razcolm.

He laughed harder, and I shot him a dirty look before turning it on the rhet in my palm. "What're you doing?"

"Saving your life," Tunoh said.

"By claiming me as your husband?"

She folded her arms. "I didn't imagine you'd find me so distasteful."

"We're not even the same species."

"I would have a word, Magus," Kenrith all but snarled.

"Not now."

Metal rang as reclaimed blades slipped from his sheaths. "This instant, *Magus*."

I glowered down at him. "So talk."

"Alone," Kenrith said.

When I looked, Tunoh shrugged. I set her down and stepped to one side. In an instant, Kenrith was atop my shoulder with a blade to my throat. "I would know your intentions with my...Tunoh."

"Think the word you're looking for is daughter, and as for me, I'm as shocked as you are."

"So you trifled with her emotions? Led her astray speaking like a deceitful knave? Seduced her with words too large?"

"Jesus, Kenrith, when exactly have I had time to trifle? You've been with me or had me watched since I set foot in the alley. As for the rest, I really don't understand what you asked."

His eyes narrowed, a glint of magic squeezed between their lids. "I like you, Magus, but not so much to leave your throat intact should you do something that hurts Tunoh."

"I don't have time for this. Those golems are getting away with a crap ton of goblin blood. They've been taking hostages all over the city. If they do what I fear, then we may soon be facing an army of demi-goblins." I raised my voice so that everyone could hear. "If the matrons want to try their luck against tenfold the number of demi-goblins that abducted them before, by all means, force me to stay here and protect these."

"My *daughter*," Kenrith hissed.

"Hasn't been tempted, touched, or otherwise treated in any inappropriate way. I only just learned he was a she on our way to rescue you."

Razcolm dropped onto my other shoulder. "I've been ordained to perform handfastings if the lovebirds are in a hurry to get bus—"

"Shut up." Kenrith and I said in unison.

Spiders shouldn't shrug. "Live in sin, see if I care."

I closed my eyes and counted six eternities until my blood eased off the boil. I felt their eyes on me as sweat beaded down my face. I needed to get out of there, chase down the blood and stop the golems before they unleashed a horde of transformed monsters into the streets.

Regular people who'll be killed because I let the golems escape with the blood. Like her.

The mutilated corpse drew my gaze, wringing my heart into tighter and tighter knots the longer I looked. I hadn't just let the golems escape, I helped them. I'd seen the riverbed, the melted stone around the waterfall's splashdown area. I knew the Ley had melted rock, but I'd used it as a weapon without considering the full ramifications around melting rock in a confined space.

What was I thinking?

<*You were trying to save the matrons and destroy any golem that pursued. Look around, human. Do you see any captive matrons? Any golems to stop them leaving?*>

"No."

<*You win. Go back to your alley, and I don't know, fold something.*>

I won?

The demi-goblins' imprisonment prevented them from assaulting their warrens. The golems could make more, but the rhet knew what they were dealing with now. SMLE would figure it out sooner later. Even Darrin had his answer.

<*You did your job. Everything else falls to we fey.*>

Even though the golems are still out there?

<*Not your problem.*>

Killing humans.

<*They turned against you, imprisoned you and for what?*> Razcolm sighed. <*Why would you help them escape their, what did you call it? Terminal vanity?*>

Why would I? I'd been so focused on solving the problem before me that I'd blinded myself to the simple truths Razcolm offered.

I didn't craft Glamour. Darrin knows the source of the problem. He has the resources to solve it and restore the demi-goblins to their humanity. Why do I have to do anything? I'm done. I win.

My heavy footfalls echoed off the cavern walls until I towered over Matron Biuntcha, folded my arms and waited for a break in the matrons' conversation. They stopped speaking one by one.

"Yes?" Biuntcha asked.

"Have I accomplished the task you willed of me?"

"Technically, but the threat remains."

"Forewarned is forearmed."

"Yes, Magus. You have saved the matrons, found the source of the magical corruption and freed many of us."

"Great. Then I'm leaving."

"What about your prisoners?" the first matron asked.

I'd captured them to protect them from the sprayer, ultimately saving them so they could be restored. I hadn't thought it through, hell, I'd barely thought about the costs in time and energy. There was no reward waiting in the wings for me should I succeed, but I'd made enemies of the matrons. Why? So I could chase down Adam's golems, fight off a nearly invulnerable fighting force and eventually return so I could run all over the city on some quixotic crusade to restore these demi-goblins to their horrible, vain selves.

God! Will I never learn? This is precisely how I ended up in prison—trusting in the good that could come from helping people.

Someone replaced my stomach with buckets of writhing maggots, but I pushed the words through my lips. "Not my problem. Would someone please help me leave?"

Biuntcha gestured, and rhet swarmed up the stairs.

I'd made it halfway across the cavern when Tunoh whispered in my ear. "Don't do this to yourself, Eli. Don't walk away and regret it your whole life."

"What's there to regret?" I snapped.

"Surrendering to the selfishness inherent in the wild blood."

"I'm not being selfish, I'm just not getting involved. None of this is my fault. None of it."

"You're a hero, Eli," Tunoh said. "Trying to defy your nature will only destroy you."

My hand whipped up so fast and grabbed her that it might've had a mind of its own. Despite the instinct, I held her softly and set her down gently. My fists squeezed so tight my knuckles ached.

The selfishness of the wild blood? Is she right?

I stopped on the precipice, looking once more on the undulating ley line.

Is there something about the ley magic that accounts for the amoral, capricious reputation lent to the fey in folklore?

<*You caused none of this. You only wished to live in peaceful squalor.*>

Razcolm was right. I marched up the cleared passageway, leaving rhet and demi-goblin problems behind me.

A soft drizzle met me outside. I don't think I ever realized just how wet our winters tend to be, or maybe the weather was unseasonable. Either way, the world just loved to rain on my day. I ignored the knowing smirk of Maven as she smoked on the sidewalk before her shop.

Tunoh's words haunted my steps.

I stopped.

Anger and heat flowed through me over, again and roundabout in a seemingly unending cycle. The slow drizzle had soaked me in icy water and yet my skin burned under my collar. "What does she know about anything? She's a little girl in her father's house. How dare she presume to know me?"

"Bitches, what you gonna do? What you got in the pack, Mister Hair?" I'd never met the young gangbanger before, but I'd seen him countless times. The faces changed, but the attitude, the thin cigar stinking from things other than tobacco and the nickel-plated gun hidden low out of sight didn't. "Come on, man. Let's see."

I shrugged out of the pack and extended it to him. Angry as I was, there wasn't anything of value to fight over. He tucked the gun into his belt and rifled through my things, dumping some haphazardly to the wet pavement. He cursed and shoved it at me. I reached out to catch the bag before everything got soaked. He grabbed my wrist. His sudden yank forced me off balance as his other hand flipped open a red-handled butterfly knife.

"What are you doing?" I asked

"These are gold, pops. You've been holding out on me."

The meaning of his words horrified me so much that it took a few moments for them to truly sink in. In an instant, I was back in the Wasteland being robbed for the umpteenth time. The flash of memory lasted barely more time than a blink. A growl rumbled out of my throat ahead of my words. "Back off, kid, or bad things will happen."

"Shut up, clown. Either you're losing a couple chunks of arm, or I'm blowing your brains through the rainbow."

I didn't understand all of that last statement, but the knife sinking into my forearm was self-explanatory. The blade's tip levered up almost immediately to rip one of the jack-in sockets from my flesh. Pain exploded up my arm and set my temper ablaze.

Picked the wrong day, junior.

I'd gone out of my way to avoid others in the Wasteland, but sooner or later you got caught no matter how careful you were. Truth be told, it happened too often, especially early on. I hadn't avoided others to protect my avatar or its belongings.

I avoided the others to protect my soul.

I'd kept to myself in the real world for the same reasons. People let you down. People took and took. People betrayed you. Sooner or later, people forced you to do things no one should have to live with.

Like killing that young woman. No matter how vain she was, she never asked to become a demi-goblin.

He dug the knife tip in for better leverage and inhaled on his cigar.

Ley energy I hadn't realized I was still carrying lashed out. The embers in the cigar's tip exploded in a backwash of flame that shot down his throat into his lungs. I grabbed the knife, riding him down to the ground. The blade rose in my hand, poised to slash open his neck. He tried to scream or shout, but his throat wouldn't cooperate.

My hand shook, blood running down the arm. The knife fought to deliver the blow while a tiny screaming voice held it back in an attempt to preserve my soul.

The knife slashed downward. Its edge cut open his T-shirt not taking care to spare his skin. My second cut drew less blood as it finished cutting away a strip of cloth.

He struggled to get his gun. The hammer caught in his belt. I drove the knife into his shooting shoulder and yanked the gun free. If the knife had wanted to kill him, the gun really *needed* to put bullets into him over and over. The barrel pressed into his uncut throat. Fear-filled eyes met my own in a sudden wash of déjà vu.

I don't know what genius thought giving prisoners the ability to vent their frustrations by killing each other would help reform criminals into citizens. One of the most significant problems with the Wasteland was that killing your enemy only pissed him off for round two.

Even so, sometimes they'd hurt me badly enough that I'd put them down just to be rid of them for a short breathing space. Killing another prisoner meant more than just having to pack up your things and find a new home.

I wrapped my arm tightly in the rag and tied it into place with my teeth. I stuffed my things away and rose, never letting go of the gun. I pointed the pistol at the gangbangers face. "You're going to stay down until I'm gone. I'd better never see you again."

I know nothing about guns beyond the obvious point one direction and pull the trigger. I managed to unload all the bullets including the one in the chamber before dropping the pistol in a particularly nasty restaurant dumpster. The bullets clinked in my pocket—a wind chime of hate fanning my fury all the way out of his neighborhood.

·19·

TEMPTATION'S MERIT

Winter wind and icy rain failed to douse my temper as the afternoon waned. The closer to my alley I got, the more I anticipated facing down the boss golem. I didn't have a lot of weapons at my disposal, but I knew a fifth rez wall could chop them up into little pieces.

Tinkling bells offered the only warning I received to a very different kind of ambush. Sunny snatched me off the street and into the Manger. "Thank God. Eli. You're sa—what the heck happened to your hair?"

I jerked out of her grip, snarling in her face. "What you think you're doing?"

"Getting you off the street. Golems are out snatching people. There are some lurking in your alley."

The rich aroma of fresh coffee performed a follow-up ambush, seizing my nose and attention. I shook it off. "How would you know that?"

"When I saw the news I went by to check on you," Sunny said.

"Why won't you leave me alone?"

Sunny was an ugly crier, and I can't say anger made her much more attractive. She shoved a finger into my chest. "No one should be alone. Human beings are social creatures. You won't tell me what happened in the Wasteland, but I know enough to know that above everything else right now you need people around you. People who

205

care. People who give without wanting anything back. People you can trust."

I snorted.

"You died in there, ri—no, you were forced to kill, weren't you?"

I folded my arms.

"Probably told yourself that those deaths didn't matter, that they weren't real, but the act of killing, deciding to take a life indistinguishable from a living breathing person...." Sunny closed her eyes and shuddered. She opened them once more. "There's a cost, Eli."

"You don't think I know that?" I stormed out of the Manger. I couldn't have said if I was angrier at her in that moment than I was at humanity, Adam or the rhet matrons. I caught my reflection in a storefront and stopped. My curls had been colored a bright rainbow. *Razcolm. That little shit. I'll kill him.*

I turned into my alley ready for a fight.

There wasn't one waiting.

Instead of the golem ambush I had been expecting, a single drone sat on the ground in front of my alcove. I approached it with caution. When I managed to close to within a few feet, it hovered into the air. Cameras along its base projected a holographic figure hidden in the folds of a voluminous cloak.

The figure spoke in a hard tone but an airy voice. "Good afternoon, Magus."

"Should I take from your presence that you are allied with the golems?" I asked.

He chuckled. "Such things could be said."

"I've had a really bad day. I suggest you and your drone just fly away."

The drone hovered a slow circle allowing him to pace around me slowly. "*You* have had a bad day? You haven't had your sanctum invaded. You haven't had your servants slain. You haven't been forced—"

"Yes, I *have*. I don't know what it is that you are trying to accomplish, but your actions have forced this situation. You didn't have to take over Thoth's golems and attack our city."

He stopped. I could feel his eyes on me from the deep shadows of his cowl. "I am defending my people. Your kind are the aggressors."

I bit off the rejoinder before it escaped my lips. My instinct had been to demand how it was that we were attacking his people, but I took a slow, protracted breath and considered his words.

Ever since I'd set foot back in Seufert Fells, I'd been pulled this way and that until I'd been reduced to just reacting with only the barest semblance of the plan. My plan to live anonymously on the streets had been interrupted by the demi-goblin attacks on the rhet.

"I don't know who you are. I don't know who's wronged you—"

"You have."

"How have I wronged you? I just got back to Seufert Fells, and all I wanted was to settle into a quiet life of being left alone."

"To study magic and craft spells further pampering lazy people and their selfish whims?"

"No." I seethed. "I went without magic a century before this mess thrust it back into my life."

The figure stopped pacing, and its cloak's hood tilted ever so slightly. "So you no longer wish to dabble in magic? You merely wish to be left alone to live in squalor?"

"I don't know about squalor, but otherwise those were my plans."

"This has changed?"

"I've been forced to accept that magic is part of who I am. I feel whole when working with it. I no longer wish to give it up."

"Under any circumstances? No matter what I could tell you, you will still trade magical contrivances for mere riches?"

"Look whoever you are, you obviously don't know anything about me. The only thing I've ever wanted to do with magic is to help people with a genuine need. What's happened while I was away sickens me, but I'm only one man branded a criminal. No one will listen to me."

"Were you not a member of the triumvirate that daily hands magic around more freely than bathroom tissue paper?" He gestured toward Thoth's eye.

"Thoth Corp? I was. I stood against the other two, insisting magic be reserved to help people where technology hasn't yet evolved to perform the task."

The figure paced around me once more in silence. A light tingle like fingertips barely brushing arm hair washed up and down my body. I drew in from the mananet, preparing to defend myself.

He stopped and the magic faded with the cessation of his motion. "Why do you choose to live here, Magus? You have the forces of the universe at your disposal. No matter your setbacks, surely you could return to affluence."

"No, I can't ever have a home—not without claiming guilt that isn't mine."

"If I were to offer you a place where magic lived at your disposal and you could live as you pleased, would you agree to leave this field?"

My gaze slid up and down the alley. I'd never have referred to rain-soaked concrete and brick buildings as a field, but I wasn't so enamored of it that I was unwilling to give it up. My eyes shifted to the drone. Everything about the flying device and the hooded figure that it projected seemed perfectly reasonable.

Still, he had said things that fell awkwardly on my ears. If I were to believe my eyes, rather than my ears, I'd be forced to wonder how it was this strange man was involved with possessing Adam's golems. I reached outward my magical senses and was rewarded with the vindication of my suspicions.

The drone and the apparent hologram were nothing more than a highly advanced illusion—glamour. To be so interactive, the caster had to be nearby pulling the strings so its puppet responded to me in real time.

How far does this deception go? Is the caster even male?

"The drone's a nice touch—for a fey."

The hooded figure inclined his head. "Nonetheless, my offer stands. If you wish to be free of all of this, you merely need say so."

"The place you offer, where is it?"

"For the sake of expediency, let's call it fairyland."

He's going to take me to fairyland? Beyond the Silver, where the goblins must've originated.

The thrilling idea quickened my pulse. I opened my mouth to accept his offer only to have a twinge of guilt stop my tongue.

"What would happen to the rhet if I accepted?"

Laughter escaped his hood. "You are a peculiar creature, Magus. You asked after the little fey rather than your own species."

I extended my senses into his illusion, searching out the strings without success. "The rhet have been kind to me, humanity has not."

"Fair enough. Your rhet friends are rebels in exile."

"What did they do?"

"They abandoned us."

It sounded to me like there was a lot more to tell than what he said. The rhet might control the one cavern, but I'd seen at least one other portal through the Silver into our world.

Our world.

I hadn't had time to think about the ramifications of the Silver and another world beyond.

Agree to peace and quiet and he'd escort me to the other side, no more stigma, no more guilt.

"If you bring more goblins through the Silver, they'll attack the rhet."

"You're right about my intentions as well as...did you just speak of the Silver?"

I smiled.

"I see. Yes, the rhet will have to relearn their survival skills once their natural enemies are reintroduced to this world. That is the natural order, nothing to concern yourself with."

"The fate of my friends does concern me."

"Your friends?" He laughed. "I think not. The rhet are pipers that have convinced you to dance to their tune. They've manipulated you to their ends, nothing more."

"A very *fey* thing to do."

His words became more clipped. "Delightful as this has been, I do have other things on my agenda. I can free you, see you safe, but it must be now."

"Right now?"

"I haven't any more time to spare."

What's up with the hard sell?

In whatever this other world was, I'd be free to live without the stigma of my conviction. I wanted to go, but his pushing made my back stiffen. On a hunch, I decided to push back. "No problem. I'll think it over. You can get back to me when you've got a minute. The extra time will let me talk it over with His Majesty."

The illusion flickered, and its subject stiffened. "I'm afraid that will not be possible."

"Which?"

"Coming back later. I must have your decision now. I can only transport you through the Silver before sunset."

I glanced up the alley at the horizon. Impending twilight hung beyond the Eye. Thoth had originally been attributed as the god of the moon and its phases.

Like a full moon, the most magical time of her phases.

"Razcolm said the Silver was hardest to penetrate during the full moon."

"What does an imp know of greater workings?" Contempt laced his reply. "I've offered you help and safety. Would you trust an imp's so-called wisdom over my own?"

Trust. He wants me to trust him, a fey that I don't know, and he wants me to do so in a hurry.

My head was shaking before I realized I'd made my decision. "Well, my financial advisor always advised sleeping on a big decision, so I guess I'll have to pass."

"If that is your wish." The hooded fey strolled up the alley beneath the illusionary drone. A moment later all the hair on my body tingled.

<*Magus, duck!*>

A loud buzzing whirled me around in time to see Razcolm hurdling toward me in the air trailing silvery thread. Electricity arched out of the nearest Edison node. I hit the ground. The bolt disintegrated the little automaton's body in a flash, coursing down the thread to ground. I dove into the alcove as another lance carved a black line along the building's corner.

"I *really* need to work out some combat magic!"

I ducked my head out to find the cowled figure. The nearby Edison node allowed me an instant to ascertain the illusion had vanished before filling the air with brick fragments and ozone. Another hasty glance confirmed nothing remained of the origami spider beyond burning confetti and a small puddle of melted, black plastic.

I cursed again.

There was no way to know if the annoying little fey had survived. The little bastard had turned my hair rainbow, but he had also saved my life. I pressed myself against the brick, careful not to touch the chain-link in case my attacker got creative.

The offer to live in a fey world had been supremely tempting. Part of me regretted turning it down, but ultimately all I'd wanted was left alone. Had the strange visitor just walked away, I'd have licked my wounds and settled in for a little peace and quiet.

Instead, he'd attacked me, tried to kill me. My temper, still lingering from earlier, returned to the killing rage I'd barely restrained. "You screwed up, pal! You could've just walked away, no harm, no foul. Now, it's personal!"

Using my off hand to shave my head without a mirror cost me more blood, but there was no way I was going into battle looking like a hobo clown. Like it or not, I had to get back to the cavern. I needed goblin blood to track where the golems had taken the rest. Shaving my head had used up an already short supply of time. It'd been a matter of pride, but, truth be told, it meant swallowing some crow.

Maybe I'm vainer than I thought.

212 | MICHAEL J. ALLEN

Going to the Manger for help ranked up there with my least favorite ideas of all time. Without an online bank account or credit card, I couldn't hire a LUX. I couldn't afford what taxicabs survived either, both monetarily and having a record of a trip that would likely deliver me into a restraining order violation. The front door bell rang. Sunny's smile over the Bible she was reading aloud became a supernova of delight.

"I'm not here for fellowship," I said. "I...I need your help. It's time-sensitive."

Shoulders relaxed around the room as she set the Bible to one side. "What can I do?"

"I need a ride."

Her grin widened. "You're going after them, aren't you? Going to rescue the people that were taken?"

"More or less."

"And if I'm driving, you can't stop me from coming along."

I groaned. I hadn't thought it out that far. "Fine, but you're staying outside away from the fight."

She patted my shoulder, gesturing toward a rear door. "Sure I am. Car's parked out back. Bald looks very good on you by the way."

I cradled my face in one hand, fingers parted enough to follow without running into any door frames. We were in traffic and headed toward the cavern when I remembered both the rough roads and rougher neighborhood.

"Um, maybe this isn't such a good idea."

"Oh, no. We're riding to the rescue, and you're not backing out now," she said.

"It's not th—"

The car hit a deep divot, jogging right and nearly hitting a parked derelict. She recovered well, but I couldn't help but wince at the thought of her repair costs.

"Sorry," I mumbled.

"My fault. I should've been watching more carefully."

Sunny's driving became increasingly erratic as she wove through what felt like war-ravaged roads. We parked in front of the VCR repair shop. My hand hesitated at the door handle. If I brought her down with me, there was no telling what might happen. If I left her up on the surface in that neighborhood, even worse could happen.

She got out of the car before I could decide.

That she insisted on going with me made telling her to stay in the car all the more tempting. I turned toward her, mouth opening to do just that when her hard gaze stopped me.

"I'm coming with you, Elias."

"Got a flashlight?"

She offered one. I led the way cautiously into the sinkhole. Sunny slipped half way down, arms windmilling as she fell. I sidestepped in a rush to catch her. Her weight impacted me and sent us both down the hole.

She groaned, shifting off of me in a very uncomfortable manner which necessitated several grunts. "You all right?"

"Thanks to God and my hero."

Flashlight scooped from the ground as I rose, we headed into the sewer.

"Wonder if these run all throughout Seufert Fells," she said.

"I imagine, why?"

"Make a great shelter from winter." She wrinkled her nose. "If you could get used to the smell. Probably be cool down here in summer."

"I'd rather not think about what this place would smell like in the heat." We turned off the sewer into the downward passage. "Watch your step. This is even steeper than the hole."

"Don't want to have to heroically catch me again?" Sunny asked.

I rolled my eyes, more worried about who might lurk in the cavern.

Miss having Razcolm to scout ahead. Wonder if he survived to haunt someone else.

I stopped at the corner, waving at her to wait so I could check what waited ahead.

Sunny stepped around me onto the precipice. She gasped. A reverent whisper escaped her lips. "Praise God and His miracles."

A blur of pixie dust rocketed toward us. I grabbed her and jerked her backward.

"Hands, Mister Graham," Sunny scolded. She pried my hands from around her. "Oh look, your rat friends."

The dozen rhet threatening us with spears didn't look familiar and really didn't look happy. I only just caught a glimpse of another group somehow scurrying across the ceiling to flank us.

Simultaneously raising my voice and lowering the tone amplified my words, echoing in the confined stone. "Knight Kenrith?"

Tunoh appeared. Her smile slid away. She folded her arms. "What's *she* doing here?"

"Magus," Kenrith said. "Why have you returned?"

"Elias? Are you going to introduce me to your friends?" Sunny asked.

"Kenrith, call off your dogs," I said without preamble. "I need goblin blood."

"I thought you divested yourself of responsibility in this matter." Kenrith gestured to the encircling rhet. They returned to whence they'd come. He raised his nose and sniffed. "Are you bleeding?"

"Yes and yes, but the golems' ringleader made this personal."

"All of the bodies were fed to Mother's blood," Kenrith said.

"I'm going after them. I need goblin blood to track them down." I cursed. "Any blood stains left? I don't need much."

Kenrith shook his head. "Goblin blood offends our noses."

Shit. Now what?

"I know where they took the blood," Tunoh said. "I can lead you."

My attention shifted to Kenrith, waiting for his objection or some other kind of veto. Our gazes met, and once more I saw Dad. My sister Zahda had been a particularly headstrong young woman. In some ways, she'd gone out of her way to flaunt her independence while Dad struggled to change how he treated her. All Dad wanted was to protect his baby girl, but Zahda had become an independent adult free to make her own choices and, hardest for Dad to accept, her own mistakes.

"Squire Tunoh will lead you where they've taken the blood." Kenrith's tone hardened. "Tunoh, you will not enter under any circumstances."

Tunoh inclined her head and headed up the passage.

"Wait, we're going?" Sunny asked. "I wanted to get a closer look at whatever that river thing is."

Tunoh rolled her eyes.

"Ley line," I said. "Maybe later, when we're not trying to save all of Seufert Fells."

∘20∘

BLOOD TRAIL

I braced myself for another mugging or some other obstacle, insisting on being first up the sinkhole. Nothing awaited. I imagine Sunny would've taken our unhindered departure with optimism, but good luck with everything else going on made me suspicious.

Tunoh did her best to dislike Sunny, but it would've been a doomed effort even if riding in Sunny's car hadn't delighted the little rhet. Early evening traffic seemed unusually sparse even in the industrial areas, and we made good time weaving through the city. We'd have made better time if Sunny hadn't insisted on driving under the speed limit. She tried to explain why speeding was a sin— even when peoples' lives were at stake, but I tuned her out.

There were much more important things on my mind, like figuring out how to deal with golems without a ready ley line.

Tunoh's directions brought us into sight of a wholly different factory. I knew something wasn't right the moment Sunny stopped us in front of a sign warning off trespassers on behalf of Thoth Corp.

"Eli, you can't go in there."

"Be nice if it worked that way, wouldn't it?" I got out of her car, Tunoh leaping onto my shoulder.

Sunny got out behind me. "Seriously, as your lawyer, I'm telling you. You cannot even be standing where you are."

"Let's go," Tunoh said.

"And you were forbidden from going in too," Sunny added.

"She for real?" Tunoh asked.

"Probably," I said.

Sunny's eyes reminded me of a puppy worried that it was in trouble.

"For the sake of plausible deniability, Sunny, how about you find a convenience store and buy me a doll with removable glasses."

"What?"

"My scout got fried. If you don't want Tunoh or me checking this place out, I need some doll glasses."

"You won't go in while I'm gone?" Sunny asked.

"Would I do that?"

Her eyes narrowed. "We likely both know the answer to that."

I pointed across the street. "I'm headed over to that construction site to see if I can find something to stop the golems."

Sunny turned toward the half-demolished building. She gave me a flat expression. "That's trespassing too."

"Urban exploration. There's a difference."

"Not with your record, there isn't."

Tunoh and I turned our back to her and crossed the street. Sunny's gaze lingered, making that spot you can never reach between your shoulder blades itch. I lowered my voice so it wouldn't carry. "You sure this is the place?"

"Yes. This is where they brought the blood." Tunoh sniffed the air. "Even now the stench lingers on the wind."

"Doesn't make sense."

"What doesn't?"

"This is an Edison block with an even weaker mananet then my alley. Their ringleader insisted he had to transport me to fairyland before sunset—I'm pretty sure because they need the full moon for whatever they're planning."

"When did you learn this?" Tunoh asked.

"Right before he tried to kill me."

"What?!"

I couldn't help but laugh. "I thought your warren was keeping tabs on me. Guards sleeping on the job?"

"I was busy."

"You?"

"What other use is a crippled squire?"

My guts wrenched into Bavarian pretzels. I stopped just inside the construction site's open gate, turning my head to look into eyes glowing without magic. "Tunoh..."

"Yes, Eli?"

I have to tell her. She needs to know.

I swallowed. "The spell I used on you...Glamour. Adam designed it to...expire."

Her voice came out quiet as a church mouse. "Expire?"

"End. The effects will go away." Her stricken, horrified expression forced my tongue into overdrive. "I think I can fix it with enough time."

"But I'm going to go back to being...broken?"

"I'm afraid so, but just temporarily. I'm really sorry."

She sniffed several times, and she wasn't scenting the air. "That's why you don't want me to wife. You're unsure you can fix me, and you can't stand the thought of being married to...," tears ran her cheeks. "To a broken freak."

"What? No, that has noth—"

"Don't lie! I saw your eyes when you first saw me. I repulse you."

Before I could plead my honesty, Tunoh vanished in a trail of fairy dust. I massaged the bridge of my nose.

Great, just great.

A search of the construction site turned up demolished building materials, ripped bags of instant concrete, a few sledgehammers and last but certainly not least a rotary hammer drill with inch-and-a-half masonry bits hooked to an Edison node conversion pack.

"Sorry, no doll glasses," Sunny said. "What happened to your friend?"

I laughed. "She ran off. I'm apparently unwilling to marry her because I think she's a repulsive, broken cripple, and—"

Sunny slapped me. "You *asshole.*"

I stared, pain throbbing against my face.

"Forgive my language, Lord." She mumbled through a clenched jaw. She hit me again. "Asshole."

I backed out of range and rubbed my cheek. "Don't you have to ask forgiveness for that one too—not to mention striking your neighbor after I don't know, judging him without all the facts?"

She glowered. "He knows I was asking for both curses."

"And the rest?"

She folded her arms and tapped one foot.

"I see, well, as I was saying before I was violently interrupted, and despite neither saying nor even thinking any of the words she put in my mouth, she ran off before I could properly defend myself."

Sunny dropped her eyes and sucked on her upper lip. "Oh."

"Yeah, oh." I turned my attention to my supplies. I knew what to do with the drill, especially if I could find a jackhammer to thaumaturgically upgrade its kick, but the rest?

No idea.

Whether or not I thought we'd come to the right place, this was the only lead I had. Whatever the golems were about, the goblin blood figured prominently. Until I proved otherwise, they'd brought the blood to the factory waiting across the street.

"What's the plan?" Sunny asked.

"Working on it."

"Aren't we in a hurry?"

"Yeah, but I'm having a hard time thinking through my aching arm and the pain in my face."

Sunny stood a little straighter, hands balled at her sides. "Elias. I owe you an apology."

"I'm waiting."

"That's it."

"You realize you didn't actually apologize."

"Yes, I did."

"No, Sunny, you said you owed me an apology, but you didn't actually apologize." I held up a hand to forestall her. "It's fine. You can make it up to me by going home where you won't get hurt."

"You can't go in there alone," Sunny said.

"I thought you said I couldn't go in there at all, now you want to join my felonious activities? What kind of help do you think you can be against stone monsters?"

"As if you and your KY Calamity spell can prevent those golems fusing a brick fist with the inside of your skull."

I stared at her.

"Well, you can't."

I shifted my gaze to my finds. Without warning her, I kissed her forehead and bolted deeper into the construction site.

"Where are you going?"

"I need a cement mixer. Hell, I'll take a wheelbarrow."

She found a portable cement mixer almost immediately after joining the search. Truth be told, she'd gone the opposite direction I had, and I would've seen it eventually. I collected instant concrete bags until I could piece together the instructions.

"Big strong guy like you has never mixed concrete?" She asked.

"And you have?"

She smiled and held up nine fingers. "Nine, count them, nine churches built on missions trips."

"Of course." I took a deep breath. "So, I can leave this to you? You can mix this stuff up so it hardens fast?"

She folded her arms and glared.

"Great." I bent a piece of copper wire back and forth against the blade of a mason's trowel until it broke apart. I wrapped half the wire around a jackhammer and the other around the drill.

The trowel helped cut apart a short rubber hose so that I could knot the shorter half around the trowel. The other length went into Sunny's concrete.

I turned to the demolished building materials and started dragging bent aluminum framing beams out of the detritus. By the time I had a small pile, I'd sliced my hands up enough that I had to wrap them with strips of torn shirt.

Almost worth being smothered in rats right now.

I shuddered.

"Eli?"

I kept my eyes on the aluminum as I bent and folded it together

"Yes?"

"I'm sorry I hit you and called you that name."

"What name was that?"

"You know what name."

"I can't remember, too many hits to the face. Please remind me."

When she didn't answer, I glanced over to find her smirking at me. "You just might be evil."

I shrugged and returned to my origami. While I folded, I considered the runes and incantations necessary for my other two new spells. I'd have given a lot for a lab, a library, and the leisure to perfect my work, but the sun was headed toward the horizon. I had to hurry.

"What is that thing?" Sunny asked.

I led the animated aluminum skeleton over to a pile of shattered tile. "Just a little backup. I'm a bit short on Colchis bulls."

I extended the trowel and invoked the thaumaturgic link between hose ends. Instant concrete oozed from the trowel into grooves in the framing. I pushed a tile into the concrete and reached for the next.

My bull leapt into the pile. Tile flew up around it in a whirlwind, snapping into place tile by overlapping tile until it even looked like a bull. Smaller tiles wrapped around the head and a long, slightly bent piece of rebar with concrete clinging to one end became its horns.

My origami bullock tossed its head, pawed the ground and snorted.

"Razcolm?" I asked.

The bull didn't answer.

"Who's Razcolm?" Sunny asked.

"No one." My new construct finished, I drew in all the magic I could eke out of the mananet.

Ready as I'm ever going to be.

"Stay here, Sunny." I watched her face for the imminent objection. It didn't come. "Let's go, Toro."

My animated bull stalked across the empty road. The factory's security didn't seem much better than the previous, but I figured Adam was too cheap to alarm anything but the gate. I sent my bull through the section of fence nearest my target and jogged up its wake.

If I hadn't sent the bull ahead, I might've ended up electrocuted. Sparks exploded as it plowed through chain-link. I thought for a moment it had caught the fence on its horns, but the chain-link wrapped around the tile frame, reinforcing the creature's strength.

Razcolm? Is that you?

The bull sat and cocked its head at me.

Strange.

Sneaking in took more time than I'd have liked. Every door I checked turned out to be locked, and I kept having to fight the all-too-eager bull back from breaking them down. I finally gave up the search and brought the hammer drill to bear.

The first kick threw me back into the bull's horns. Toro snorted at me with mocking joviality. My shoulder ached like I'd yanked it from its socket, but it moved when I tried. I set the drill bit against where I thought the door's lock resided, braced it with my body and turned it on.

The drill slammed the door and my chest in equal measure. The door broke. I couldn't be sure about my ribs. Breaking in the door probably triggered any alarms the factory had, limiting my time inside but also calling the police. The hostages had to be present—despite my growing doubts—if for no other reason than to distract the summoned police.

A small office area spread out in front of the door. Fluorescents flickered to life in response to movement. A hall stretched ahead, turning out of sight and offering a view of the factory ceiling above and beyond the wall where a roof should've capped the hall.

I rushed forward with the bull on my heels, turning with the hall in search of a way into the factory floor beyond. I threw open a door and charged onto a metal catwalk overlooking the assembly plant. A pungent chemical scent I didn't know clogged my nostrils.

Golems worked the assembly line just like I'd seen before. Not one eye socket glowed. Plastic beads tumbled from feed vats, into machines that melted and pressed the beads into transparent nodule bases and caps. The molded containers slid down rattling conveyors, beneath a spray of sterilizing steam and into another shower of no doubt cold water.

Nothing seemed out of order.

Shit. What now?

The obvious answer was to flee before the cops arrived, but I just knew that my cowled visitor intended something horrible before the night was over. Tunoh had no reason to lead me to the wrong place.

The blood came here.

I looked at the bull. "Razcolm, if that's you. Search this place for some kind of basement."

The bull looked at me.

I cursed again and rushed down the nearest stairs, each footfall ringing on the metal. I thrust a fist into the plastic beads. I turned over cooled nodules. I found nothing suspicious. None of the golems even batted a figurative eyelash.

"Crap," I snarled. "What am I missing?"

I had to hurry. Even if the area was lightly patrolled most of the time, my incursion into the other factory had units circling nearby enough to catch me. I raced into the warehouse and tore open crates. The magical stink hit me, fouler than before but less pervasive. I yanked out a handful of nodules precisely the same as the ones I'd checked on the line.

Except they hadn't reeked of infernal magic.

The puzzle fell into place and knocked me in the head.

Shit! How could I be so stupid?

I closed my eyes, taking a deep, slow breath. The blood taint left me choking. I caught my breath and tried to calm myself enough to focus on feeling for magic. The crates drew me immediately, but less so than something behind me. I turned toward the more substantial source as a golem parted a curtain of thick plastic strips and marched into the warehouse carrying a pallet of crates.

I raced past him toward the curtain. I barely caught the sudden green flicker in my peripheral vision. The bull slammed its head into my back. I fell headlong, sliding on the smooth concrete. A crash proceeded the bull's bellow.

Whipping around gave me barely enough time to throw myself out of the path of a careening nodule crate. I scrambled to my feet. Rapid booms of golem footfalls sounded the stone automaton's charge. I ducked a fist only to get clipped by a kick I hadn't expected. The blow drove me into the nearest wall. Thunderous footfalls allowed me to mostly pretend at being dazed.

Golem fist smashed concrete where my head had been only moments before. The bull slammed into the thing's back. I took cover between several small crates and the wall. The bull's assault bought me time to shift several containers from a bottom shelf onto my pile of cover.

Thank God for backup.

The sound of bending metal drew my attention from my hasty construction attempts. The golem smashed my helper into a tile and aluminum medicine ball. He hurled the ball at me.

I ducked.

The projectile clipped my uppermost cover, deluging me in tile shards, broken nodules and shattered concrete. I threw off the debris and stood back up. A massive stone fist sped toward my face.

Sunny's prediction of that exact moment had inspired the new spell. I'd kept the incantation at the tip of my tongue from the moment the golem's eyes lit green, but I wasn't ready for the terror.

Adrenaline coursed through every suddenly gooseflesh-covered inch. All warmth washed out of my body. My life might've been parading by, but I couldn't look away from the impending fist.

"Eli!" Tunoh hit my calves with all the fairy dust propelled speed she had. I'd prepared my escape through the shelves, but she knocked my feet completely out from under me.

The fist slammed into the already dented wall, showering me with more shards. Several cut my face, but I hurled the trowel at its fist and spoke the first incantation.

Wet concrete budded out of the trowel, over its arm and hooked tentacles into the damaged wall like living mud.

I spoke the second.

The concrete hardened, robbed of moisture returned to the cement mixer where it had originated. Moving water and concrete across the street drained the magic from me in a rush that blinded me and left me feeling altogether starved. I hit the ground, my head cracking against the floor.

"Eli? Are you all right? How bad are you hurt?"

"Help me up." The moment I said it, I felt stupid. The rhet didn't even come up to my knee, and I wanted her to help me stand. "Never—"

Magic washed through the room like a tidal wave. Tunoh reached down with one hand and lifted me off the floor until we were eye to eye. She blushed and looked down, her nose only a small distance lower than my own. I opened my mouth to ask how such a thing was possible, but the golem struggling to break free of the wall took precedence.

I seized the drill and shifted my weight to turn. Tunoh caught me before I hit the ground again.

"What do we need to do?" she asked.

"Help me brace it against its knee."

Even with two of us, the drill's kick forced us to try three times. By the third, the golem kicked at us before we could get close. I summoned more concrete, anchoring his feet.

The world went dark a moment.

Tunoh bent over me. "Eli?"

"Shit, need to work out better energy efficiency on that one." I hurt everywhere. "Help me up. We have to disable the golem before he escapes."

"I used your drill to take its knees and elbows. That was the goal, yes?"

"Got it in one."

She helped me back to my feet, and I directed her toward the curtain. "The goblin blood's that way. We have to help the hostages."

"There are no hostages here," Tunoh said.

"They have to be somewhere."

Tunoh pointed. "How about there?"

I followed her gesture out through a rear window. A glowing dome of milky white power silhouetted the hydroelectric plant's ruins.

"Shit. That's a big damn circle."

"Freez—what the hell?" The cop stared dumbfounded at us.

A soap bubble snapped into place around us, filling quickly with fairy dust. Tunoh sped us to the nearest door, out into the night and across the street. She stopped next to Sunny gasping. The bubble popped taking with it the cinnamon-honey aroma.

Sunny started. "Sh-sugar on a f-fudge-covered cracker."

Hysteric giggles broke the night around us. It took a moment to realize they were mine and several more to stop.

"Tunoh?" Sunny asked.

"Yes," Tunoh answered.

"Don't take this the wrong way, but have you gained weight?"

"Eli's hurt," Tunoh said.

"That's an understatement." I groused. "Unless you've got a rhet swarm handy, we don't have time to coddle me."

"Did you find the hostages?" Sunny asked.

I pointed.

Sunny's gaze rose toward the far-off ruins. "Oh."

Tunoh's voice sounded strained. "I need you to take him."

"Why can't y—"

Tunoh popped back to her original size and collapsed.

I scrambled on hands and knees to her, unsure how to check a pulse on someone so small. Luckily the cold offered me a few reassuring little clouds as a compromise. I tried to scoop her up, but my shaking arms refused to lift her.

Sunny took over, cupping Tunoh against her chest with one hand and helping me up with the other. She helped me into the car first before laying Tunoh in the back seat. Car seats shouldn't be so comfortable, but Sunny's passenger seat stole what little will kept my eyelids at bay.

·21·

OVERDOSE

"Eli, wake up," Sunny said.

The groan came all the way up from my toes. Pain met my return to consciousness, encouraging a return to blissful oblivion.

"Here, this should help." Sunny shoved a Styrofoam cup into my hands, a straw ready for my lips.

I gave the drink an experimental suck. It fought me, but the straw eventually surrendered an icy explosion of sweet and tart fruit. The always pervasive taste of banana hit me first. Tangy mango took over next, overshadowing honey and strawberry. I groaned.

"Good?" Sunny asked.

I set the cup down in a holder. "I hate mango."

"Well, drink it anyway." She shoved it back into my hands. "It's good for you. I had them triple up on the vitamin and protein powders."

I cringed but lifted the smoothie back to my lips. Pushing past the mango, the drink's gritty nature registered on my tongue almost thick enough to require chewing. I hated the flavor. I hated that she'd forced charity on me, but truth be told, I felt wrecked. I needed the energy and the powdered additives probably wouldn't hurt either. I swallowed another gulp of medicine. "Thank you."

"You're welcome. The hydro plant is just ahead. That dome is huge."

Sure enough, ahead of us the swirling, milky sphere visible through the trees filled the horizon as she approached from the

228

eastern access road on the Oregon side. Magic prickled my skin beneath hair rising in protest to its touch. I checked the backseat. Tunoh remained unconscious from her efforts to save me.

"Did you get Tunoh anything?"

"I wasn't sure what a rat might—"

"Rhet." I corrected.

"Either way, I wasn't sure what she could eat."

"Probably anything we can."

"What about fruit allergies?" Sunny asked.

"What if I had food allergies?"

Shark lingered behind Sunny's smile. "If you had an allergic reaction I'd probably be able to take you to the hospital and coerce you into letting SMLE handle things."

Another swallow of medicine helped avoid answering.

The sprayer had been left far behind in the cavern along with the ley line that powered it. I wasn't sure whether it was even possible to maintain a third rez link over so extreme a distance. The trowel was equally lost, clogged with the concrete probably harder than my head.

Razcolm hadn't reappeared. Kenrith didn't know where we were, and Tunoh remained unconscious. I had no support beyond Sunny, and I just didn't think perky, preachy sunshine could make any difference to what lay ahead. Truth be told, I was one man without the background or preparations to tackle the job.

Nothing stopped me from driving away. Society branded me a criminal for helping others then turned its back on me.

I should be wise, not get involved. That was the plan...until that asshat tried to kill me.

I pushed my cup into Sunny's hand. "Stay here and hold my smoothie. I've got a score to settle."

Sunny stared at me. "A score to settle? Not a city to save? People to protect?"

I shrugged. "That should happen too."

Rather than march up the overgrown road to the waiting sphere, I cut through the woods. The large full moon in the sky and the glowing light from the sphere made seeing easier, but I needed to see about crafting something to help in situations like this—or buy a flashlight. My childhood hadn't included a lot of camping. The only scouts where I grew up had been those fiendish creatures with the cookies—Zahda among them.

Most of the Wasteland had been, obviously, a wasteland, but enough wilderness remained that I'd been forced to learn forest survival. Even being in the Wasteland, the woods I'd learned in hadn't been dotted with rusting hulks from fifty-year-old cars. One hillock caved in under my weight, swallowing me in grass-edged metal. I dropped inside an old car, rotten bench seat attacking me with vicious springs.

I'm going to need a tetanus shot if I survive all this.

A shadow moved through the branches overhead.

I held very still, not even daring to breathe. Weeds, vines, and sod blocked the broken windows. I eyed the new sunroof without moving my head.

Moonlight vanished.

It returned.

It vanished once more.

Something's stalking the woods.

A beam of light shot across the canopy above me. Two more chased it in rapid succession.

A familiar voice whispered so close to me I nearly jumped. "Approaching the magical sphere, no sign of the suspect."

"Keep your eyes peeled, Flowers. We've got GPS on the missing golems just ahead of you, and a traffic eye has him headed this way."

"Sure thing, Sarge," Flowers said.

Another familiar harsh whisper came from just beyond Flowers. "Jesus, Flowers, lower your voice. He'll hear—"

Someone screamed.

"Winslow!" Flowers yelled.

Gunfire barked above me. A bullet pierced the ceiling to my left and further shattered the driver side window.

"Sergeant Donaldson, something's got Wins—" Flowers's scream wasn't anywhere near as manly. "They've got me, Sarge! Help, we're under attack!"

Sargent Donaldson's shouts reached me. "Flowers? Winslow? Report. What's got you?"

Whatever had the two officers crashed through the overhead branches. I raised my head high enough to peek from within the car. Two stone gargoyles with glowing, acid-green eyes carried each of the fighting officers toward the circle.

My first instinct was to leap to their defense. I'd made my first fortune focused on helping first responders. Animated gargoyles were just as out of my league as golems. Love it or hate it, I had to be stealthy until I knew a way I could help without being captured.

Magic grew as I crept slow and quiet tree to tree. Silent stalking required patience, careful foot placement, and luck. All three accompanied me to the edge of the woods—though some of the luck might've been thanks to the two captured officers. Old bones of time-worn chain-link bent beneath cars knocked through it by the plant's destruction. The still young moon loomed huge and heavy just above the horizon and right of the fifth rez sphere.

The gargoyles fought the officers into smaller circles just outside the central sphere, one gargoyle losing an arm when a fifth rez cylinder sprang up to cage the cop. At least a dozen of the smaller cylinders contained law enforcement officers.

Runes and lines glowed thick as my arm in the center of the old parking lot. Glow sticks lit smaller circles around silver bowls the same size as industrial kitchen woks. A handful of golems paced around the sphere, dumping components by the crate into the woks.

Inside the main sphere, people had been crammed too tightly for them to split into individual groups. Business types and street punks were forced side by side. Most sat, some with someone on their lap to share space.

They've been in there a long time. Almost no fight left in them.

I scanned the parking lot until I found the boss golem. I'd expected to see the cloaked figure beside him but couldn't find the bastard anywhere. Boss Golem stood at the northernmost side of the circles facing the moon. The runes intricately carved into his body glowed only slightly less intensely than the eyes fixed on her. Beside him, I recognized the vat of goblin blood from the cavern.

Oh, shit. I totally underestimated the number of demi-goblins he's planning to unleash on Seufert Fells.

Outmanned, probably outclassed and definitely under-equipped, I should've turned tail and called SMLE. A sardonic chuckle escaped my lips.

A lot of good that'd do. Half of SMLE's already here, and the other half couldn't get out here in time to stop Glamour-pocalypse

Transforming the hundreds imprisoned would've blacked out any mananet in Seufert Fells, but they'd chosen their location for the same reason PGE had tried to make the hydroelectric dam generate magical electricity too.

Are they using the tap rooms too? Are they going to level the city again?

I looked out at the circle and the people, the golems and their plan. My mind went blank. No ideas offered me a way to stop the impending creation of a demi-goblin invasion.

Back to basics, Eli.

In the Wasteland, there were only a few rules for survival. Always have a secondary escape route. When facing a stronger enemy, run. When you can't run, outsmart them. Guile trumps honor, and when it comes right down to it, nothing is below the belt.

A circle flared to life over a component pile near me. The golem feeding it moved to help the next nearest. I crept forward, staying low and quiet as I tried to keep the bright energy sphere as cover. Up close, it became apparent the runes and circles had been painstakingly carved into the old concrete lot. Runes around the circle lit in oscillating sequence between a mag three fifth circle and a mag three third.

Shit, now that it's energized, I can't even remove the components to foul the spell.

My gaze shifted to the blood vat guarded by Boss Golem.

If I can somehow get rid of that, everyone inside receives a free beauty makeover. Can't just spill it though.

Another component circle flared to life.

I'm running out of time. Think!

I scanned the ruins around me. Concrete chunks and twisted metal ringed the spell area, relocated by the golems to prepare enough room to perform their spell. A huge hole gaped in the main generator building's side, displaying the twisted remains of generators, shattered crystal, and collapsed roof. A turbine the size of a semi-truck lay in the broken remains of a smaller building. Gouges between buildings traced the path of destruction which ended with the turbine atop the gutted ruin.

Between terrain and golems, encircling the site with another circle was impossible. I'd never gotten the chance to see if cutting the possessed golems off from magic would free them from possession.

There aren't any mananet pylons.

My eyes sought the crystals. I'd thought their soft illumination a trick of the light, but as I watched they brightened and dimmed in slow pulses like a heartbeat.

Of course, they were designed to collect energy from the ley....

My attention shot to the nearby component pile enclosed in magic. I reached fingers out to the glowing sphere. The fifth rez kept me from breaking the circle. Touching it gave me the answer I expected.

Energy from ley lines and other naturally motive magic sources flowed in one direction like a river or direct current. The power ebbed and flowed like the tide, much to the chagrin of any mage trying to accomplish a long working. The pylon network had been designed to store and weave multiple magical sources at varying resonant frequencies into a mostly stable flow of power. Without the arcanology equivalent of voltage regulators, magical energy could vary from calm to bucking bronco.

Giving birth to that living magic nonsense.

The power beneath my fingers didn't feel smooth and civilized. It was wild, raw ley energy—the exact same energy Kenrith had

234 | MICHAEL J. ALLEN

warned me against touching. My gaze shifted to an old pickup on one side just outside the spell area then back to the ruined generator room.

I smiled.

Iron and fey magic are antagonistic.

I drew a fifth-first rez circle around the component circle nearest me. I hurried to a nearby unenergized circle and curved another circle around it with the switchback lines I'd used in the cavern. I raced the next nearest unfinished component wok, slapped my pink sidewalk chalk down sideways and dragged a thick pink line across lines and runes carefully carved into the parking lot.

A combination squawk-roar deafened me a moment before gargoyle talons ripped me away from the circle. I struggled against them but didn't even have the benefit of a gun like the officers.

"Bring him to me." The voice belonged beneath a cowl but came from the ancient golem.

I jerked my belt out of my pants and wrapped it around the gargoyle's torso. Using the canvas length as a circuit, a fifth rez circle sliced wings, arms and one foot from the gargoyle. We hit the ground.

He shattered.

I landed awkwardly but regained my feet ready to at least limp a hasty retreat. A backhand knocked me off my feet. Pain enveloped my left side. A few sharper novae of agony evidenced broken bones in my arm, shoulder and possibly my ribs.

My attacker glowered down, eyes burning a swirling reddish gold flame. Before I could say anything, Boss Golem interposed himself. "I offered you a way out, Magus."

"Are you referring to your offer or your attempt to kill me?"

Boss Golem turned back toward the blood vat. "Seal him in."

My previous attacker grabbed me by my broken shoulder and carried me around the sphere until I was on the side nearest the river. Pain eclipsed everything until he dumped me inside a fifth-third rez circle—the walls snapping over me before I recovered.

The golem knelt close and leered through the wall circling me like I was prey. He couldn't smile without an articulated mouth, but I could almost feel the menace in his expression. His face dipped toward the ground. One eye winked out just before the golem turned his back on me.

It could have been another imp and not Razcolm until my eye caught a third line scratched around my fifth-third cage.

My smile blossomed, but I thought before I acted. There'd been empty lesser circles on the side where I'd been captured.

Why bring me to this side?

My search hit pay dirt almost at once. Huge, thick cables snaked out of the water and into the nearest destroyed generator building.

I couldn't see what was happening on the side with Boss Golem and the goblin blood, but the screaming inside the central sphere proclaimed they'd begun the ritual.

Before they could connect the smaller circles—particularly the one holding me—I invoked a first rez circle in the outermost ring.

A blue white glow sprang from the golem-drawn circle scratched into the concreted and blocked off the outside magic feeding my cage. It vanished.

I leapt to my feet and sprinted around the sphere toward the truck, thankful the golem hadn't injured my legs. I grabbed the hood. Pain nearly dropped me.

One arm, genius.

Wrestling the rusted hood from the truck's stubborn housings one-handed was a feat for Greek demigods, not a homeless ex-con without a gym membership. Two golems closed before I could get the hood to tear free. I abandoned the truck, tossed a handful of pocketed bullets at the first golem and reached into all the magic around me.

The effective shotgun blast of nine-millimeter rounds shattered the first automaton, leaving behind a ghostly green afterimage that vanished before I could get a good look.

Off to one side, the light flickered on and off as the circles I'd marred struggled to life. I reached out to the ley line I knew passed

236 | MICHAEL J. ALLEN

through the nearby tap room at the other end of the cables. Power flooded me—raw, wild, thrice and thrice again as intoxicating.

Agony left my body to go on holiday. I smiled at the second golem, raised both fists and waved the automaton in close for a tussle.

I ducked one blow. I sidestepped another, leading the second golem back to my squiggly circuit. Prisoners screamed, but it didn't matter if Boss Golem changed them all and unleashed them against me.

I am invincible!

So much power ran through my veins I could've slammed my fist through the concrete construct. I could destroy all of them with a thought. I was a magus. They were merely a child's plaything.

I barely noticed the third golem in time to duck his blow and spin past another fist from the second. My grin widened. I took three quick steps back and threw enough power into the circle beneath the second's feet to conjure it at magnitude five.

The massive outrush of energy staggered me. I managed to keep my feet and dropped the circle. Sliced golem chunks tumbled to my feet. I drew on the ley line again, physically shaking with elation.

I hurried back to the truck, seized the hood in both hands and tore it free. A pinch in my shoulder accompanied the sound of breaking celery, but the irrelevant noise had nothing to do with my victory. I tacoed the hood, slamming the bent metal through the third golem, showering the parking lot with shattered asphalt.

I sprinted across the lot, lowering the hood edge to carve a jagged circle around the blood vat. The boss golem charged in, but not before I triggered the first rez circle that killed the third rez and stole the blood from the spell.

I laughed at him and pummeled him with my weapon. His block gouged a chunk out of the old hood. I hit him with it, ducking left under a blow. Boss tried to hit me again, but I caught the strike on the hood. I dumped the bent and broken truck part into the vat of goblin blood and smiled at Boss Golem.

"You're beaten."

"Eli!"

I turned to find Tunoh blurring across the parking lot toward us.

Just in time to help me celebrate my—

Tunoh expanded to my size with an explosion of fairy dust, arms outstretched to embrace me. I like to be wrapped in female body parts as much as the next guy, but she hugged me so hard she drove me back against the blood vat.

Boss Golem's blow missed me, but he grabbed her tail, yanked Tunoh off of me, swung her through the air and slammed her into the concrete with a truncated scream. He swung Tunoh off the ground by her tail, trying to forcibly merge Tunoh with the concrete several more times before releasing her.

I rushed to her side. Her long tongue lolled out of her mouth, and blood trickled down her fine coat from one ear. My temper rose. Before it could rise to a true fury, a bloody truck hood slammed into me.

I pushed off the ground, sucking in more ley energy to deal with the golem.

Only wish I had the sprayer and a tap circle.

Boss Golem thrust a fist into the goblin blood and fished out broken pieces of the iron hood. He stood within the fifth-third rez he'd prepared for the spell. Nothing about his third rez circle and accompanying runes differed from those poor Tunoh had helped me draw on the sprayer.

Mananet pylons used third resonance circles to network magical energy throughout Seufert Fells. There were other resonances involved and other functions in their design, but essentially they moved power from one location to another.

Like from one particular cavern to the circle beneath Boss Golem.

I reached out with my boundless will, empowering my desire with more power from the nearby ley line. My will leapt from the closest mananet pylon to the next, riding the already-connected third rez circles I'd designed into them until I finally reached the closest to the cavern. Ley power forced the connection across the vast swath of Edison blocks.

I opened the tap beneath the raw ley line, shunt through one mananet pylon after another. In the distant industrial zone, explosion after explosion lit Seufert Fells's night sky. Pillars of ley closed on us one by one, throwing tiny black disks skyward.

The wave of power reached the river. The next pylon had been close enough for my will, but not enough to transfer the ley energy. I tried to force it. I was desperate to complete the transfer, roast the golem that had hurt Tunoh.

I failed.

Darkness engulfed me like quicksand. I struggled against a narrowing iris of reality. If I lost consciousness, I lost everything, but I couldn't drag the power from the distant ley tap.

<Pity there isn't a closer tap>

Like in the tap room!

I felt for the twin circles in a tap room identical to the one the Ottiren had shown me. I activated the closest tap circle. Pure ley line geysered up through the circle beneath Boss Golem.

Every rune on the intricate golem lit with swirling rainbows of light. Boss Golem seemed to suck in the energy I threw at him. His eyes glowed brighter and brighter, energy flaring from his sockets like living flame.

Spots in my vision started to distract from the sight of my conquest. I kept my focus, rubbing my nose to keep the stench of burning feathers from causing a sneeze that might interrupt my concentration. I willed the second tap open.

Boss Golem's face started to melt. Clay ran down his body like an ice cream cone in summer, coating and clogging the runes drawn into his body.

A fist wrapped around my chest, squeezing my lungs until I couldn't draw breath. I reached for the fingers to pry them away, but there were none. My broken arm suddenly really hurt.

My knees buckled.

My sight blurred and doubled.

A phantasmal acid green elf, more beautiful than Tunoh or any of Thoth's advertisements, stood within the golem's melting clay body. He sneered down at me. "This isn't over. I will not allow you to devour our world, Magus. I'll destroy both sides of the Silver first."

I think he vanished before I died.

It was too close to tell for sure.

·22·

ESCAPING SUSPICION

The steady beeps and chemical scent told me I was in the hospital before I managed to open my eyes. I felt weak, empty and as if I hadn't drunk anything for at least a month. I reached out to draw in energy from the mananet every hospital maintained for backup power.

Nothing.

My pulse accelerated. I reached out harder, a sudden panic knotting my gut. Flashes of the battle came back in a rush.

God, what happened? Did I burn out my ability to use magic? I can't have. I have to have magic. I need it.

My eyes sprang open, darting left and right in search of a pylon. I was trussed up much as Darrin had been. Two SMLE officers bracketed a wide window beside my door. The younger ducked his head out. "Detective Brooke?"

The aging, well-dressed detective stepped into the room, separated from me by a thin wall of blue-white magic. He stopped outside the wall and glanced at the floor. Leaning let me see the tiled circle radiating magic from the floor.

First rez. Looks like someone added runes for fifth and second too.

"I need to ask—"

"Lawyer," I rasped. "I want my...Sunny, I mean Marisol Terrell."

Brooke's lips pressed together beneath hard eyes. He inclined his head and poked his head out the door. "Miss Terrell. He's requested your presence."

Sunny entered wearing the same jeans, t-shirt, and flannel she'd worn that first day in the Manger, though her smile seemed a little less bright. A picnic basket hung from the crook of her arm. "Good boy."

I rasped a soft bark.

She brightened.

"May I begin my questions?" Brooke asked.

"Are you feeling up to it, Eli?" Sunny asked.

I tried to minimize how hard my hands shook, nodded and licked my lips. "Sure."

Brooke read his questions off a notepad, jotting down my answers using a cheap pen with a hotel logo. The first questions covered the basic parole violations even though I wasn't on parole. He asked about illegal drugs several different ways until Sunny shut down the line of questioning. At long last, he came to the question he wanted me to answer most. "What happened at the hydroelectric plant?"

My gaze shifted to Sunny. She pressed her lips into a thin line, nodding silently. With her consent, I told him about Darrin enlisting my help to investigate problems with a spell.

"What were you supposed to investigate?"

I opened my mouth, but Sunny cut across me. "That's a matter of confidence between my client and Mister Silus. Eli was only explaining why he found himself at the hydro plant."

"And in violation of a restraining order?" Brooke asked.

"My client will admit to violating the court restraining order in his attempt to save the people kidnapped by Thoth Corp golems."

Brooke grunted and made a note.

The longer my story went, the more dubious Brooke's expression grew, and the more I ached for the feel of magic. I didn't mention the rhet. I wasn't sure if any of the prisoners had been changed or if my intervention had aborted the spell. I carefully sidestepped the subject of demi-goblins without actually lying. I told him about the goblins in case any goblin blood survived direct contact with a ley line.

When I was finished, Brooke leaned forward. "Are you sure that's all you have to say?"

"That is all I," *choose to,* "recall."

"Can you explain witness testimonies of a gigantic rat tackling you after shouting your name?" Brooke asked.

I smirked at Sunny. "Rats of unusual size? Didn't see any."

She rolled her eyes.

Brooke glared, apparently not a fan.

"Sunny?" I licked my lips once more. "When can I check out of here?"

"Mister Graham, you are in no shape to leave, but even if you were, I cannot let you leave our custody until we've finished questioning witnesses."

"Sunny?"

"You need medical care, Eli."

"I have alternate care in mind."

"You'll only leave this hospital in SMLE custody," Brooke said.

"I'm sorry, Detective, are you placing my client under arrest?"

Brooke smiled. "Protective custody."

"Which I refuse." I pulled a broken arm from its sling. "Well, I can't afford to stay here, so let's get going."

Sunny rushed forward and pushed me back down, breaking the first rez. Magic washed over me, sweet as birdsong or cool water to a man dying of thirst. I closed my eyes, inhaling the wondrous power in a long, deep breath

"You don't have to worry about money, Eli," Sunny said. "Your father's covering the bill."

My high crashed hard, elation vanished. "What? You called him? I didn't give you—"

"Calm down, Eli. The hospital called him. He was apparently your emergency contact. He granted me power of attorney over you until he can arrive."

I yanked myself up, pain shooting down my side. "I'm leaving."

Sunny struggled to shove me down. "A little help, Detective?"

Brooke joined her in restraining me, summoning the other two SMLE officers to strap down my limbs. Nurses, doctors, orderlies— I have no idea, but they joined the pile until I wasn't able to move.

"Thank you for your help, Detective," Sunny said. "But I think my client needs some time to collect himself."

Good, I can get out of here as soon as they're clear.

Brooke left without complaint, leaving his subordinates in place. Sunny gave them a hard look. "I need a *private* moment."

The older of the two stepped forward, eyes on the floor. Magic vanished, and I felt as if my heart had suddenly been ripped from my chest. "Wave to us when you're done, ma'am, so we can release you."

Before she could answer, a wall of swirling milky white sprang up around us cutting off my escape. Her frown wrinkled furrows in her upper lip. She sighed, brought her basket up onto her lap and turned toward me with a bright smile.

I gave the basket a dubious look.

She laughed. "Dinner and fellowship. You didn't think a little thing like being hospitalized was going to get you out of our deal, did you?"

My hard glare only made her laugh harder. She dug a handkerchief-wrapped bundle from the basket and handed it to me. "Open it."

A sunflower was embroidered in the white silk. I slid the contents onto my chest. Green and silver sparkled at me. I picked up a triangular-cut emerald framed in an elaborate silver filigree that fit within my palm. Clay clung on in some of the recesses and wrapped one whole side of the frame. A subtle, throbbing glow lit the emerald's heart.

I raised my brows at her.

"Found it near you stuck in some clay before SMLE arrived."

The Boss Golem? Is this how the elf possessed the automaton? I passed it back to her. "Hold onto this for me?"

"Sure." Her smile warmed. "So, what would you like to discuss?"

Dinner had been fantastic and the conversation God-free. If I wanted a friend, Sunny would've been a good choice, but I didn't want a friend. I wanted out before I had to face Dad. SMLE watched from outside the room, the first resonance circle kept me from magic, but nothing held the temporarily broken man strapped into the bed from getting up and walking out.

"Kenrith?"

"He isn't here, human." Thinly veiled rage undercut the mature female rhet's tone. "You've displeased a lot of people."

You among them I guess.

I sucked in a breath and asked the question that desperately needed answering. "Is Tunoh? Is she..."

THE END

Thank you for reading *Discarded.*
I hope you enjoyed it as much as I did!

If you did, please help other readers find it by leaving a review.

Keep reading for the excerpt from

DUMPSTERMANCER 2:
DUPLICITY

BLOOD DEBT

Adam Mathias stormed out of SMLE headquarters, bulling through the two security goons waiting by the door. "Can you believe that?"

Neither goon answered.

Adam turned back, yelling at the doors. "He violated the restraining order! He's a criminal! How could you *idiots* let him go free?"

"Sir?" Terry, the smaller and darker haired of his bodyguards gestured to a reporter badgering her cameraman to hastily set up on his tirade.

"Thanks," Adam mumbled. He straightened his suit and marched straight over to the woman.

She adjusted an evergreen skirt suit and slapped her cameraman. He managed to get the camera pointed at Adam as the two bodyguards stepped to either side, clearing the shot.

Adam addressed her with an eagerness often reserved by children awaiting Santa Claus. "If it isn't Megan French."

She raised a fine brown brow and tilted her head at the camera. Adam straightened his lapels and nodded. Megan stepped up beside him, smiling into the camera. "Good afternoon. I'm here with Adam Mathias, CEO of Thoth Corp, outside SMLE headquarters. Mister Mathias, it looked as if you were displeased with your visit with Seufert Fells's magical law enforcement."

Adam shifted his expression to one of disappointment. "I'm afraid so. As my fellow citizens are doubtless aware, a horrible crime was committed against our city and once more my former partner Elias Graham seems at its center."

"Mister Mathias, witness testimony claims Mister Graham stopped the attack on over a hundred Seufert Fells citizens almost single-handedly. Are you suggesting he was behind the attack to begin with?"

"I'm loathe to speculate without all the facts, but I do know a powerful wizard took over Thoth's assembly golems and forced them to commit heinous crimes. Elias was seen near them—in violation of an active restraining order—on numerous occasions."

"Is Thoth's former CAO a wizard in addition to being a talented spell architect?"

"I think his conviction proves out what Elias is capable of."

"Are you suggesting Mister Graham took control of those golems and his rescue of Seufert Fells citizenry was meant to cover his tracks?" Megan asked.

"SMLE investigators would be more qualified to comment on that, and I'm sure they'll release a statement once they take Elias back into custody and question him thoroughly."

"Wait," Megan beamed at the camera. "Are you saying Mister Graham escaped and is at large?"

"He's at large, Megan, but with the full consent of SMLE."

Megan's expression turned to one of shock. "Mister Graham violated a restraining order in front of law enforcement, may have been behind the abduction and assault on citizens including law enforcement and they let him free?"

Adam looked down, shaking his head. "I can't imagine why they'd jeopardize our friends and neighbors, but yes. A convicted and highly capable criminal is back on the streets."

"We can only hope SMLE knows what they are doing and that Mister Graham doesn't return to his old, illicit ways." Megan made a cutting motion and extended her hand. "Thank you, Mister Mathias.

"Thank you, Megan, and please call me Adam."

Megan pushed a brown lock back to expose more of her face. Her posture shifted her chest into greater prominence. "You're very welcome, Adam."

Adam smiled at the reporter, noting a modest frame hidden in her professional attire as she flirted. He undressed her in his mind, weighing his options and resisting the urge to lick his lips. "Good citizens should stick together."

She nodded. "We need to take care of one another."

"I couldn't agree more." Adam's grin widened as he handed her his private business card. "Feel free to get in touch if I can do anything else for you."

"I will." She exchanged his card for hers, her voice growing husky. "I'm at your service day or night if you have anything newsworthy to share."

"Front page, Megan. Now, if you'll excuse me."

She inclined her head as Adam strode toward his limousine. Terry and Dennis stepped in on either side. A drone rose into sight from behind the limo as they approached. Terry set a restraining hand on Adam's shoulder.

The drone stopped, cameras projecting a hologram of an attractive man in a more expensive suit than Adam wore. "Mister Mathias, I need to speak to you regarding your former partner."

"Who are you?" Adam asked.

"Lucian Fayer and I'm a gardener of sorts. I can offer you help removing persistent thorns."

Adam shot a look over his shoulder, cataloging Megan's cameraman and SMLE cameras and wizard eyes. He shook his head. "I don't know what you're talking about, and I wouldn't discuss it with you out here in the open if I did."

"No matter." Lucian gestured toward a box truck. "Allow me to offer my card in case you change your mind."

Terry and Dennis stepped between Adam and the truck.

"I believe you lost these," Lucian said.

The back rolled up, and three golems with glowing, acid green eyes tromped out onto the concrete.

Nearby pedestrians still wary after the recent abductions by similar automatons screamed, ran, and pulled up phones or illusionary comm panels. SMLE officers disgorged from the building behind Adam in rushed response to the screams.

By the time they arrived, the golems stood passively awaiting instructions—their eyes empty. Adam turned back to Lucian to find drone and hologram gone.

A SMLE officer walked an envelope over. "Mister Mathias?"

Adam looked at the envelope with his name handwritten in elaborate calligraphy. He inclined his head at it. Terry took it, ripped it open and frowned. He dumped a business card into his large palm and extended it.

Adam took the card, flipping it over. A simple handwritten note read: Someone really should do something about the homeless. Nod if you agree.

Adam glanced around. He nodded.

Wayne limped away from a corner next to the recently constructed high rise lab. He'd done better than usual.

Shouldn't tell Duval how well I really did.

The late afternoon sun beat down on him, soaking his artfully tattered clothes. A half-dozen blocks away he did away with the limp and turned into a storage facility.

His stomach grumbled.

He smiled to himself. His wife, in her role as the assigned runner for all of Duval's workers north of the Columbia River, should've delivered his lunch shortly before, stowing the piping hot Firehouse meatball sub in his insulated cooler to keep it warm.

He rounded the multilevel facility to a first-floor garage, scanned for observers and worked the combination lock that opened the doors. They rolled up easily, granting him access to his silver Mercedes.

A man that looked exactly like him yanked Wayne inside and hurled him at the car. Wayne scrambled to his feet and dug for the small shiv in need of sharpening that he kept in case of trouble. His copy closed the door, eyes glowing a soft silver.

Wayne brandished the little knife. "I don't know what this is about, but you'll leave if you know what's best for you. Attacking one of us will bring Duval's wrath down on your head."

The doppelganger marched across the dim storage garage. Wayne slammed the shiv all the way into his copy's chest. None of the blood that should've gushed out appeared. Wayne's attacker seized the knife hand, broke Wayne's wrist, yanked out the knife and sliced Wayne open from belt to chin.

Wayne watched his own blood deluge the copy of him but not soil, stain or otherwise alter the doppelganger's clothes. Darkness closed in. He glanced forlornly at the dent his body had left in the car as his legs collapsed. Wayne lay in pooling blood, gazing at his wife's sightless eyes.

A crumpled Firehouse wrapper lay on an island between two oceans of blood.

LOVE SCIENCE FICTION?

ADVENTURE INTO THE FARTHEST REACHES OF A WHOLE NEW VERSE

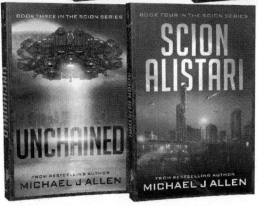

WANT MORE FANTASY?

FILL YOUR LIFE WITH A LITTLE MAGIC AND MURDER

OR BRAVE GUNSLINGERS AND FAIRIES IN A WILDER WEST

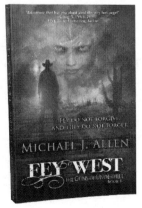

KEEP CONNECTED:

Keep up to date with book news, giveaways and expanded lore on my website:

- www.deliriousscribbles.com

Follow along on social media:

- http://www.twitter.com/TheDScribbler
- http://www.instagram.com/TheDScribbler
- http://www.facebook.com/DeliriousScribbler

GET INVOLVED:

While you're waiting for my next novel, get involved with helping your other favorite authors by being part of the little rectangular miracles called books. Here's how you help <u>ANY</u> author:

- Read our books and <u>enjoy</u> them. That's why we wrote them.
- Tell your friends about the book so they can enjoy it too.
- Follow an author on social media. Say hello. Writing is a lonely profession.
- Share links to reviews, posts, etc. on social media. The more, the merrier!
- Post a review to help others find the book you enjoyed so much. This REALLY helps.
- Click "Like" on their Book and Author pages on Amazon
- "Share" links to their Book and Author Pages on social media
- .

ACKNOWLEDGMENTS:

So, we've come to the end of our first journey into a whole new series. I hope you've enjoyed this first foray into Eli's world and my first foray into urban fantasy. Thank you for being there on the other side of the page and giving this world like so many others meaning. I hope this new world has delighted—and delightfully frustrated—you through many enjoyable reading hours.

Among all the other people that helped bring this story to life, I want to acknowledge Stefanie for hanging with me through the creation of my first fully custom professional cover art. Ever patient and talented, she brought Discarded's cover to life for us in epic strokes.

No B, B or J were tortured during the creation of this novel, but my love and thanks go out to them anyway.

This novel's helpful crew that answered the trumpets and put in the hours to help with this project all deserve thanks: Jennifer and Jason, Scott and Simeon, Tina, Rebecca, and Frank. Thanks for all your hard work finding so very many of my mistakes.

There are still so many pros that deserve thanks for lending me guidance and wisdom as my journey continues. They've helped me shed my green and beat most of the star-struck gazes away with hearty back slaps and barbed jibes.

To Eli, Sunny, Razcolm, Kenrith, Tunoh and the rest, thanks for the adventure. We're looking forward to what you bring us next. See you very soon in Duplicity.

ABOUT THE SCRIBBLER

(Photo credit: Jim Cawthorne)

Michael J. Allen is a bestselling author of multi-layer science fiction and fantasy novels. Born in Oregon and an avid storm fan, he lives in far too hot & humid rural Georgia with his two black Labradors: Myth and Magesty. On those rare occasions he tears himself away from reading, writing, and conventions he can be found enjoying bad sci-fi movies, playing D&D or the occasional video game, getting hit with sticks in the SCA or hanging out with the crew of Starfleet International's U.S.S. DaVinci.

To learn more about Michael, check out his website at www.deliriousscribbles.com

99963649R00157

Made in the USA
Columbia, SC
17 July 2018